Presented to:

FROM

OCCASION

DATE

FOCUS ON THE FAMILY®
presents

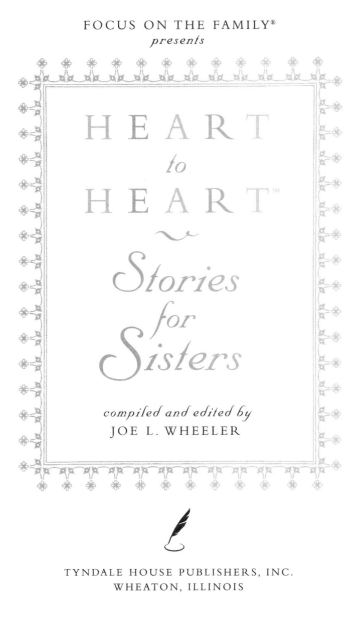

HEART
to
HEART™

Stories
for
Sisters

compiled and edited by
JOE L. WHEELER

TYNDALE HOUSE PUBLISHERS, INC.
WHEATON, ILLINOIS

Visit Tyndale's exciting Web site at www.tyndale.com

Copyright © 2002 by Joe L. Wheeler. All rights reserved.

A Focus on the Family book published by Tyndale House Publishers, Inc.

The text or portions thereof are not to be reproduced without written consent of the editor/compiler.

Author photo by Joel D. Springer. All rights reserved.

Focus on the Family is a registered trademark of Focus on the Family, Colorado Springs, Colorado.

Heart to Heart is a trademark of Tyndale House Publishers, Inc.

Designed by Jenny Swanson

Woodcut illustrations are from the library of Joe L. Wheeler.

Published in association with the literary agency of Alive Communications, 7680 Goddard Street, Suite 200, Colorado Springs, CO 80920

Scripture quotations are taken from the *Holy Bible,* King James Version.

Library of Congress Cataloging-in-Publication Data

Heart to heart : stories for sisters / compiled and edited by Joe L. Wheeler.
   p. cm.
   ISBN 0-8423-5378-X (hardcover)
   1. Sisters—Fiction. 2. Domestic fiction, American. 3. Christian fiction, American.
I. Wheeler, Joe L., date.

   PS648.S54 H43 2001
   813'.01083252045—dc21   2001005283

Printed in the United States of America

08 07 06 05 04 03 02
7   6   5   4   3   2   1

A long time ago, I considered her to be little more than a pestiferous
sibling. But as the years have flown by, she has become ever more
cherished, ever more appreciated, ever more loved.

Along the way she has known Trouble with a capital *T* firsthand.
Disappointment, disillusion, and heartbreak—she's had considerably
more than her fair share. Yet even in her darkest nights she
sings her joy, her gratitude to God.

Late in life, against all odds, she has become an award-winning artist,
astonishing us all by this long unexpressed talent
for revealing beauty wherever she finds it.

She is not only a loyal sister, she is an equally loyal daughter—
the rock upon which our mother's life is built.

Thus, it gives me great pleasure and joy to dedicate this book
of sister stories to my own beloved sister:

MARJORIE WHEELER RAYMOND

of
RED BLUFF, CALIFORNIA

CONTENTS

ACKNOWLEDGMENTS

"Mary and Martha," by Joseph Leininger Wheeler. Copyright © 2001. Printed by permission of the author.

"Too Many of We," by Marie Barton. Originally published in *The Christian Herald*, date not known. Text published in *The Youth's Instructor*, August 27, 1929. Reprinted by permission of Joe L. Wheeler (P.O. Box 1246, Conifer, CO 80433) and Review and Herald Publishing Association, Hagerstown, Maryland.

"The Greatest," by Harriet Lummis Smith. Published in *The Youth's Instructor*, December 24, 1912. Text reprinted by permission of Joe L. Wheeler (P.O. Box 1246, Conifer, CO 80433) and Review and Herald Publishing Association, Hagerstown, Maryland.

"Aunt Jerusha Makes a Test," by Ida Alexander. Published in *The Youth's Instructor*, July 30, 1929. Reprinted by permission of Joe L. Wheeler (P.O. Box 1246, Conifer, CO 80433) and Review and Herald Publishing Association, Hagerstown, Maryland.

"By Candlelight," by Grace Margaret Gallagher. If anyone can provide knowledge of the earliest publication and date of this old story, please send this information to Joe L. Wheeler (P.O. Box 1246, Conifer, CO 80433).

"Mother, Why Don't You?," by Virginia McCarty-Bare. Published in *The Youth's Instructor,* September 28, 1926. Reprinted by permission of Joe L. Wheeler (P.O. Box 1246, Conifer, CO 80433) and Review and Herald Publishing Association, Hagerstown, Maryland.

"The Lone Stallion," by Gil Close. Published in *The Young People's Weekly,* January 2, 1938. Reprinted by permission of Joe L. Wheeler (P.O. Box 1246, Conifer, CO 80433) and David C. Cook Ministries, Colorado Springs, Colorado.

"The Secret," by Arthur Gordon. Published in *A Touch of Wonder,* Fleming H. Revell, Old Tappan, N.J., 1974. Reprinted by permission of the author.

"Meddlesome Mattie," by Lillian G. Copp. Published in *The Youth's Instructor,* April 20, 1920. Text reprinted by permission of Joe L. Wheeler (P.O. Box 1246, Conifer, CO 80433) and Review and Herald Publishing Association, Hagerstown, Maryland.

"The Gingerbread Men," by Mabel McKee. Published in *The Youth's Instructor,* November 20, 1923. Text used by permission of Review and Herald Publishing Association.

Story reprinted by permission of Fleming H. Revell, a division of Baker Book House Company.

"Just One Thing Beautiful," by Catherine R. Britton. Published in *The Girls' Companion,* February 19, 1939. Reprinted by permission of Joe L. Wheeler (P.O. Box 1246, Conifer, CO 80433) and David C. Cook Ministries, Colorado Springs, Colorado.

"Ruth and Rebecca," by Mary R. Platt Hatch. Published in *The People's Home Journal,* February 1901.

"The Miller's Third Son," by Helen Ward Banks. Published originally in *The Youth's Evangelist,* date not known. Text published in *The Youth's Instructor,* November 27, 1917. Text reprinted by permission of Joe L. Wheeler (P.O. Box 1246, Conifer, CO 80433) and Review and Herald Publishing Association, Hagerstown, Maryland.

"The Perfect Background," by Leota Hulse Black. Text published by the Wetmore Declamation Bureau, Sioux City, Iowa, 1933. If anyone can provide knowledge of the earliest publication and date of this old story, please send this information to Joe L. Wheeler (P.O. Box 1246, Conifer, CO 80433).

"Brother Tom's Room," by Winifred Arnold. Published originally in *Young People,* date not known. Text published in *The Youth's Instructor,* February 13, 1923. Reprinted by permission of Joe L. Wheeler (P.O. Box 1246, Conifer, CO 80433) and Review and Herald Publishing Association, Hagerstown, Maryland.

"Tony's Turn," author unknown. If anyone can provide knowledge of the author, publisher, and earliest publication date of this old story, please send this information to Joe L. Wheeler (P.O. Box 1246, Conifer, CO 80433).

"The Family Hinge," by Alice L. Whitson. Published originally in *Young People,* date not known. Text published in *The Youth's Instructor,* December 22, 1922. Text reprinted by permission of Joe L. Wheeler (P.O. Box 1246, Conifer, CO 80433) and Review and Herald Publishing Association, Hagerstown, Maryland.

"Merry 'Little Christmas,' " by Agnes Sligh Turnbull. Published in *Farm Journal,* December 1947. Reprinted with permission of *Farm Journal.*

"Vacation Days," by Dee Dunsing. Published in *The Girls' Companion,* August 30, 1936. Reprinted by permission of Joe L. Wheeler (P.O. Box 1246, Conifer, CO 80433) and David C. Cook Ministries, Colorado Springs, Colorado.

"The Inseparables," by Harriet Lummis Smith. Published in *The Girls' Companion,* November 29, 1936. Reprinted by permission of Joe L. Wheeler (P.O. Box 1246, Conifer, CO 80433) and David C. Cook Ministries, Colorado Springs, Colorado.

MARY AND
MARTHA

Joseph Leininger Wheeler

When our Lord was on this earth and walked the dusty roads of Galilee, there was one home we know He loved to visit: that of Lazarus and his two sisters, Mary and Martha, in Bethany. In this peaceful household, away from the continued harassment of the scribes and Pharisees, He could experience peace. Here, we can imagine, He could speak naturally and not have to weigh each word before it was spoken. Here not only were His creature needs met, but His every word was treasured. With such cherished friends, perhaps parables were not needed—with them He could speak from the heart.

The older of the two sisters, Martha, was a typical older sister—a rock of responsibility, the one who kept the household attractive and running smoothly. Mary, on the other hand, was a typical younger sister, more concerned about personal interests than work. While Martha scurried around preparing the food (a *big* job in those pre-refrigeration and pre-microwave days), Mary much preferred to sit at the feet of the Master, eagerly drinking in His every word.

Martha suffered in silence for a time, but she finally lost her cool. In front of all her guests, she publicly embarrassed her sister by saying, "Lord, haven't You noticed that my sister just loafs around instead of helping with all my work? Since she won't listen to me, won't You tell her to get to work?" Jesus, looking down at the attentive and deeply hurt younger sister and then up at the angry older sister, spoke words that have rung down through two thousand years: "Martha, Martha, you are concerned about your many responsibilities, but your sister has chosen what can never be taken away from her." In the long years that followed, Martha must have often thought back to those prophetic words when Jesus, that magnetic Presence endowed with all the wisdom of the ages, was no longer with them.

Yet, after reading hundreds of sister stories, I cannot help putting in a good word for Martha. Had it not been for her, no one would have had any food to eat! So perhaps there is a golden mean here that the Gospel writers failed to comment on. But since they didn't, we are left for all time with two extreme prototypes: Martha, the conscientious workaholic, and Mary, the devoted slacker. Keep Martha and Mary in the back of your mind as you read the stories in this collection, and see if they don't endow each story with unexpected insights.

⋆⇒◉⇐⋆

WHAT IT MEANS TO BE A SISTER

When I asked a dear friend, Sheree Parris Nudd, to define sisterhood for me, this was her heartfelt response:

> There is no other woman–to–woman relationship comparable to that of sisters.
>
> Sisters often go through cycles of being companions, competitors, or co-conspirators, or regarding one another as friends, enemies, or with indifference. Depending on the age and the players, these cycles can happen in the course of a day or in the course of a lifetime. But like other family connections, "once your sister, always your sister."
>
> In girlhood, sisters who frazzle their parents' nerves with the incessant sounds of sibling rivalry will often be the first to stand up for and protect each other if an outsider threatens.
>
> Sisters know things about each other that no one else knows. (This can be good or bad!)
>
> Fortunate are the sisters who grow up as friends. Fortunate are the sisters who become friends after years of being unable to tolerate one another in childhood and adolescence, or even into adulthood. When this happens, the parental relief is palpable.
>
> While many sisterly "patterns" are developed or more or less fallen into during the growing up years, there is power in each individual to choose to change. And thus sisters who wish it can choose to journey toward a friendship and closeness they never thought possible. Whether they sense it

now or not, there is a reservoir of compassion for one's
sister buried in the center of the soul.

Those who make a "life decision" to cherish sisters (and
all family members) with love, esteem, support,
encouragement, and an occasional reality check have the
chance to experience the depth of the sister relationship that
those without sisters will never have.

It used to be a lot easier to define what it meant to be a sister,
just as it used to be a lot easier to define what it meant to be a
woman, a wife, a mother. For a hundred years ago, a woman's
primary roles were limited to two: wife and mother.

But today's woman lives and interacts in an unbelievably complex world, significantly more complex than a man's. It's socially
acceptable for her to marry or remain single. If she marries, she
will carry all the burdens of the world on her shoulders. In her
daily scripts she will in all likelihood choreograph such diverse
subject matter as meeting her husband's needs, being a good
daughter and daughter-in-law, running a household (complete
with food preparation, meals, and clean-up; shopping; garden
upkeep; paying the bills; shuttling the children to school, sports
activities, music lessons, dentists, doctors, friends' houses, and
church). In all likelihood she will also have a full-time career outside the home, requiring so much energy and commitment that it
leaves precious little for anything else. Besides all this she is
expected to lead church activities and to become involved in
civic organizations and causes. Furthermore, she is expected to
remain current educationally and professionally as well as staying
well-informed in her general reading. Meanwhile, of course, she
will do her level best to remain youthful and attractive!

Because of death and divorce, many women will raise their

children alone, take care of parents alone, and grow old alone. Statistics show that even those who remain married will significantly outlive their husbands. At the end of their lives, sisters may be living again with their sisters, life coming full circle.

Is it any surprise, given all these variables, that sisterhood is not a luxury today? It is a necessity!

The definition of "sister" is broadening. In these days of world travel and complex family roles, a biological sister may live two thousand miles away or may be too busy with job and family to be a companion and lifeline. The one who really knows us and supports us may be a friend, an aunt, a cousin, a mentor—and she becomes a "surrogate sister," or a "soul sister."

Being a soul sister is hard work. It is not merely a shift or a change of pace; it means being there for the other—for life. Being there in good times and bad, in joy and sorrow. It means being vulnerable by opening up the heart to the other, for the only way to avoid being hurt or misunderstood is to wall out the world and seal yourself into a living death.

It means being compassionate and empathetic rather than harsh and judgmental, encouraging rather than critical, choosing to live by the spirit of the law rather than the letter.

It means loving the good qualities of the other rather than dwelling on the weaknesses. It means caring enough for the other to be a lifelong vault for the other's secrets—and that can be mighty difficult. It means loving the other so much that you're willing to lose the friendship itself rather than permit that "sister" to self-destruct or lose the respect of family, friends, and society. And, most important of all, it means bringing into the relationship the greatest friend of all, our Lord. Without Him, there can be no "soul" in "soul sister."

ABOUT THIS COLLECTION

I had a tough time finding the stories for this collection, primarily because great sister stories don't surface very often. And when they do, they are rarely contemporary ones. The best ones tend to be at least sixty to one hundred years old. Because stories about biological sisters are so rare, many of the stories in this collection focus more on sisters of the heart, or surrogate sisters.

The next problem I had was trying to find a wide variety of genres to be represented in my story finalists. The most moving stories tended to have a Mary/Martha emphasis. Clearly, writers of sister stories are convinced that the most significant problem in relationships between sisters is that resulting from Marys and Marthas living in the same household.

Paradoxically, the more Mary/Martha stories I've read, the murkier my conclusions have become. Is beauty less significant than drudgery? Are the arts less important than household efficiency? I don't know which is worse: slacking in one's responsibilities or developing an insufferable sanctimonious martyr complex.

Christ weighs in on the side of the Marys. In the parable of the Prodigal Son, for instance, the self-righteous elder son is clearly a Martha prototype. Christ's main concern evidently has to do with the correlation many of us attempt to make between mere obedience and good works with salvation. Again and again He drives home the point that salvation is not something we earn; it is a divine gift.

Some of the greatest names in inspirational literature are represented in this collection: Agnes Sligh Turnbull, Harriet Lummis Smith, Helen Ward Banks, Leota Hulse Black, Mabel McKee, and Arthur Gordon, as well as others who were once well known to readers of family magazines.

CODA

I invite you to search out other stories of equal power, stories that move you deeply and that illustrate the values upon which this nation was founded. Many of these stories will be old, but others may be new. If you send me copies of the ones that have meant the most to you and your family, please include the author, publisher, and date of first publication if at all possible. With your help we will be able to put together additional collections (centered on other topics) for home, church, and school. You may reach me by writing to:

Joe L. Wheeler, Ph.D.
c/o Tyndale House Publishers
Editorial Department
PO Box 80
Wheaton, Illinois 60189-0080

May the Lord bless and guide the ministry of these stories in your home.

TOO MANY
OF WE

Marie Barton

Martha was tired, dispirited, and angry at the whole world. There she was, eager and ready to go to college, and suddenly the lion's share of the burden for taking care of five brothers and sisters fell on her. It just wasn't fair! And she said so, not caring who would overhear her.

Two little pairs of ears did.

*O*h, these big families!" exploded Martha, in the privacy of her own room. "No wonder we're poor—so many of us." She changed her one good dress for just any old house frock. It didn't matter which. Nothing mattered any more. Nothing. "Why couldn't I have been an only child?"

All through the academy she had dreamed of college. "I'm going with Eloise," she told her father in June, "if I have to work my way! Mother'll surely be well by fall." And under her breath she added, *Then no more farm drudgery for Martha Holmes!*

Mr. Holmes sighed heavily and passed a tired, calloused palm across his sun-browned forehead. "I wish you might, daughter."

In July her mother went from them, like a frail white rose, leaving the home burden on the capable young shoulders of her eldest. Martha hated that word, "capable." But the hate for it was only part time. Most of the time she did her level best to live up to it.

September came. Martha managed a courageous smile when she kissed Eloise good-by at the station. There had been three of them in the graduating class, till March. Then Marguerite died—Marguerite, who loved Martha and Eloise with a loyal heart. And Mr. and Mrs. Wray, who had moved to the country for Marguerite's health, returned to their home in Austin. Yes, three had planned for college together, and now only one was going!

Martha gulped hard and waved a long, brave farewell as the train pulled out. Then the bravery went from her and the girl's lips tightened to a rebellious tenseness as the shabby old car covered the seven miles home, the road cutting a sultry gray swath through the green and white cotton fields, where the afternoon's blinding heat hovered low.

At the rambling old farmhouse two long-armed pecan trees

gathered her momentarily into their shade. She put away the car and came in. She walked softly past her mother's silent door and bolted up the creaky stairs to her own pathetically plain, low-raftered room.

Here the storm within her broke. Even repeating Bible verses couldn't hold it off any longer. Five young brothers and sisters were five too many. There was no getting around the fact. They just were. Her whole rebellious self cried out against the injustice of it. "It isn't fair," she ended with a burst of pent-up tears. "It isn't! Eloise has everything; and I, nothing. *Nothing!*"

"Sister!" shrilled from below. *"S-i-s-t-e-r!"*

Martha stuffed her fingers in both ears. Wouldn't they even let her have a cry to herself?

The floor shook. Rob was bounding up the stairs. Martha slipped into the closet and pulled the door nearly to.

Rob, shedding cotton lint from overalls and shirt sleeves, stuck his head into the room, glanced about, and went down the stairs, at three bounds, again jarring the house.

"No'm, she ain't here." (Rob persisted in saying "ain't"!)

"She went to town right after dinner," piped Goldie's plaintive little voice. "I spec she ain't—*isn't* comin' for a orful long time."

Martha was puzzled. She had not heard a car come in. "Wonder who it can be?" She stole to the window and looked down on the youthful lines of a smart blue hat shot with silver. Her beautiful new Sunday school teacher! An angel sent from heaven in her hour of need!

"O Mrs. Dearborn!" she called. "Come right in. I'll be down in a second."

Her glance whipped to the driveway. "If there isn't old Bobbins and the 'one-hoss shay'!"

"Yes," smiled Mrs. Dearborn, after greetings had been

exchanged. "I requisitioned old Bobbins. John had to have the car. And Father Dearborn had rubbed up the buggy and harness this morning, to be ready for a muddy spell. As though these sun-baked roads could ever mire to the hubs!"

The laughter of her words rippled across Martha's consciousness like silver moonlight on dark, troubled waters.

"Bobbins fits into the landscape out here," she went merrily on. "But I couldn't think of driving him to town. Did Eloise get off all right?" she asked.

Then Martha poured out her heart to her teacher friend. She, too, wanted a higher education. Suitable clothes. The chance to make something of herself. Eloise had all these things. So many girls had.

In the sweet blue eyes Martha read a swift response: and in the compression of the firm-lined mouth, a desire to do something about it.

"Yes, I know," Mrs. Dearborn's voice held understanding. "It isn't things, though, that make or mar us. It's our attitude toward them. An educated heart is what counts, after all, even more than an educated intellect. But then, you need not give up college. Merely postpone it. Let's see, Ted will start to school—?"

"In two years," supplied Martha.

"And your sister will finish the academy by that time. Then she can take her turn at a delayed education and let you have your chance first. In the meanwhile, you can take up your college studies one at a time, by correspondence."

Martha had not thought of that.

"You are more than welcome to my books," the silver voice rang true. "Let me help you map it all out. And I'll explain the lessons, too, whenever there's something you can't dig out for yourself. Why, Martha girl, you can make every day count toward your degree while you are waiting."

"Too slow," was Martha's honest confession. "I could never stick it out."

"I did."

"What? *You?* Why, I supposed you had always had things—like Eloise."

"No. I was tied down like you. A houseful of youngsters kept me on the job day and night, and I did not get my diploma till this last June—exactly one month before I married John and came here. It took me ten years. But—" a spark leaped into her eyes and voice—*"I got it!"*

For one wavering moment Martha felt an urge to follow the shining example. The next instant, though, the old rebellious feeling choked it down. She shook her head sadly.

"It isn't that I don't appreciate your wanting to help me, Mrs. Dearborn. But it's no use—with me feeling the way I do." Martha heard her refusal thud like lead against the silver of her teacher's words, yet hurried on in the same despairing tone. "No piecemeal education for me. I must have the whole cake or none. I feel like an old hen with a brood of chickens wished onto me. I can't shake them, so I have to scratch for them, whether I want to or not. There are just too many of us—that's all!"

The small patter of bare feet outside on the porch startled Martha. She hoped the kiddies hadn't heard. Bless their hearts! They couldn't help being too many!

Mrs. Dearborn did not reproach the girl. "Oh, but your chicks are so precious!" was all she said.

She rose to go. Martha followed her into the pecan shade, where the antiquated horse was idly rubbing noses with the fence post.

"Mine meant everything to me," Mrs. Dearborn could not resist adding. "Just at first I called them my 'stumbling-blocks.' But I soon discovered they were precious stones instead."

Martha smiled wryly. "That's what mine are—stumbling blocks."

"Or rubies and gold!" flashed the other.

Martha went around the house, got an armful of stove wood, and pushed her unwilling feet into the kitchen. The sky was clouding over, greenishly. It matched the girl's mood. How dark it was getting! And it was still an hour before sundown. Dully she rekindled a fire and made biscuits for supper. "I'm all wrong inside," she had the grace to admit. "But I can't want to be any other way." She peered anxiously out at the thickening south- west. Her uneasy glance swept the cotton field, flecked with white harvest, far as the eye could see. There they were, the cotton pickers, hurrying in, dragging full sacks. Her father in the lead, watching the storm clouds as he plodded ahead down the long, long row.

Ruby Jim kept only a stride behind him. How tall and lanky she had grown this summer! She was quite old enough, too, to share Martha's burdens. But Ruby Jim threw responsibility to the winds whenever she could escape to the fields.

Why, where were Goldie and Ted? Hiding in the barn, most likely. Mechanically she lighted a lamp and went after the morn- ing paper, which came by afternoon rural delivery. A letter lay under it—*to her!* Curiously she tore open the envelope and looked at the signature. It was from Mrs. Wray, Marguerite's mother!

She read the letter through, gasped for joy, and read it a second time.

"Oh! oh!" She pinched herself to see if she was awake. She whirled out to tell her father. "Daddy! Listen—"

But he thrust the full milk pail into her hand. "Can't you see it's going to rain pitchforks! Close the windows! Run! And all the doors!" he called back as he put his shoulder to the cotton-heaped wagon which Ruby Jim and the boys were pushing into the barn.

Not a breath of air was stirring. But the sky was angry— biliously angry. Martha ran back to the house.

Bursting with her new-found happiness, she flew from room to room, repeating to herself: " 'We want to send you to the university in Marguerite's place.' 'Travel with us summers.' 'Be a daughter to us for four years.' 'Don't bother about a trunk. We'll see to your clothes after you get here.' "

Go? Of course she would go! Ruby Jim could take her turn at housekeeping, whether or not she wanted to. That tomboy couldn't make a decent biscuit. But she could learn. Rob and Andy could shift for themselves fairly well. It was Goldie and Ted that most needed mothering. Well, Daddy'd just have to look after them himself. Poor, lonely, overburdened Daddy—it would be hardest on him. But this was the chance of a lifetime. She would wire in the morning. Wouldn't Eloise be sur—

What was that? A swish! A roar! Martha ran to the kitchen window. A funnel-shaped cloud, greenish yellow in a back-ground of inky blackness, was charging to earth. Louder and louder it roared. Fiercer and fiercer!

Martha threw herself on the floor, face down, and pressed the flattened length of her against the bare boards, arms outstretched, palms clutching one table leg and one sink brace. The twister wrenched the kitchen loose from the rest of the house, twirled it swiftly around and set it down, then zoomed on. A deluge of rain poured in through the broken wall and slapped out the blaze from the disrupted stove.

Martha, shivering between terror and relief, got to her feet in profound thankfulness. It might have been a thousand times worse. But the children! and Daddy! Where were they? Frantically she dashed off the floor ledge and stumbled out into the blinding rain.

A streak of lightning showed the path of the tornado through the cotton field, a hundred feet wide, swept clean as a road. One of the pecan trees was ripped open. The others were partly wrecked. It must have been they that saved the kitchen from being demolished. But the barn—where was it? She ran past the corner of the turned-around room, past the stampeding mules and the dead cow, and came upon a heap of shattered lumber where the front half of the barn had been. She groped in, screaming, "Daddy! Ruby Jim! Rob! Andy! Goldie! Ted!" at the top of her voice. The rain drowned her words. No words. No answer. What if she had been left an only child, after all? Could anything—anybody—even the Wrays, ever take the place of her own precious family?

Spent at last, she stopped out of breath, and lifting her head from the debris, searched the rain-filled night. A light glimmered faintly. It was moving. A lantern—in her father's hand!

"Daddy!"

She flung herself into his arms.

They closed strongly about her in the beating downpour. "Daughter, are you all right? We've hunted the house over for you."

" 'We!' Then the others are safe, too?"

"Not a splinter touched us! You see we were behind the barn.

But you had us mighty near scared to death about you and the kiddies."

"The *kiddies?* Aren't Goldie and Ted with you?"

"No." His voice shook with alarm. "I let them go to the house when you came home."

Martha went cold. *"Then where are they?"*

Father and daughter clutched each other in wordless terror and ran to the house.

Instantly the search started. Martha and Mr. Holmes with the two lanterns, and the other three, empty-handed, combed the rain-lashed farm in five watery directions. Though it seemed hours, in reality it was just twenty minutes till Martha heard Zip's muffled bark.

The barking issued from a cave which Bob and Andy had dug for the children in the high bank of the old creek bed. And the cave was in the path of the tornado!

Martha's heart lost a long beat. Torn between hope and fear, she climbed the steep, slippery bank to the cave entrance, and held up her lantern. The opening was blocked with a tangled clump of uprooted blackberry bushes.

"Goldie!" she wailed. "Ted, darling!"

"Sister!" sang out two scared, wee voices, in glad relief. *"Sister!"*

Three minutes of super effort, and Martha's determined pole had cleared an entrance. "Coming!" she shouted. "Just a minute more! Here we are!"

The kiddies were safe as two peas in a dry brown pod. She gathered them both to her, a lump of joy in her throat, a song of thanksgiving in her heart.

"But what were you doing here? Why didn't you come home?"

"We runned away," Ted told her.

He lifted a questioning, tear-smeared face in the weird lantern light. "Is there still too many of we?" he wanted to know.

"No, Ted, *no!* Why, Ted, sister wouldn't take a million dollars apiece for you and Goldie!" She gave them the first real, honest-to-goodness bear hug they had known since their mother's death. "Not six million for the bunch! Sister's going to stay with you, too, as long as you need her!" And to herself, *I'll study hard and make myself worthy of my precious chicks, mind and heart, fifty-fifty!* And aloud, "Come, let's hurry home. The biscuits'll be all burned up!"

Marie Barton

Marie Barton wrote for Christian family magazines early in the twentieth century.

THE GREATEST

Harriet Lummis Smith

Jealousy. It has been with us ever since Lucifer, and it shows no sign of going away. In the Graham household, Celia was jealous of Bernard and Bernard was jealous of Celia. And then—how humiliating to discover that an unsung member of the family was more important than either of them!

*W*ell, anyway, Bernard said I could go."

"Oh, if Bernard said so, of course that settles it!"

Celia tossed her head, her drooping lids concealing an angry flash of the eyes. But there was no like concealment for the color that rose in waves to the roots of her hair.

Her younger brother, Wallace, looked after her thoughtfully as she left the room. "Celia's as mad as anything, but anyway Bernard did tell me I could go skating this afternoon, and I guess he's got as much say about it as Celia."

A gentle tapping sounded in the next room, a soft little sound full of pathos when one understood its meaning. The face of the listening boy changed. His look of mingled perplexity and resentment was lost in a rush of transforming tenderness.

The tapping sounded nearer, and in the doorway of the room appeared a little figure supported by crutches. Long suffering had robbed Iris Graham of the beauty which is the birthright of healthy girlhood, though her sweetness of expression did much to take its place. A wealth of yellow hair fell over the shoulders, and the blue eyes, though sad with the sorrowful wisdom that comes through pain, shone starlike in the wan face.

Iris was nearly two years younger than Wallace, yet the boy appealed to her eagerly. "Listen, Iris! Bernard said this morning that I could go skating, and when I told Celia so, she began to act as cross as anything."

"That's because you weren't well the first of the week," Iris said, wisely. "Bernard has so much to think about in his business that he can't remember little things about our health."

"But I want to go." Wallace's look of deep dissatisfaction deepened by degrees to a frown. "I haven't had a good skate this winter."

"If you've waited as long as that, you shouldn't mind waiting a little longer," coaxed Iris. "A skate wouldn't pay for making Celia feel bad, and it's only on your account that she cares."

Wallace answered only with a little shrug, and Iris went on softly: "Poor Celia! She's been tired all week. It was Monday, wasn't it, when your throat was so sore, and you had such a high fever?"

"Yes, Monday." Wallace had the grace to look ashamed of himself. A sudden cold had developed into a sharp, feverish attack which had kept his older sister up nearly all night caring for him. With the recollection of what he had suffered, Wallace recalled Celia's face as she had bent over him, and the touch of her fingers on his hot forehead. And now, less than a week later, he was ready to be sulky because she was not willing to have him go skating.

"Come to think of it—" Wallace's tone was elaborately careless—"I believe Tom Gifford and I were going to the library after school to look up something for our debate. So the skating will have to wait." Like many boys of his age, Wallace was given to apologizing for his good resolutions. But Iris, who had a wonderful faculty for knowing what was going on in other people's minds, smiled upon him brightly, and remained quite satisfied with her victory.

The Graham household was often referred to in the neighborhood as an extraordinary example of family life proceeding smoothly and satisfactorily without either father or mother. When Mr. and Mrs. Graham died within a short time of each other, Bernard assumed the responsibilities of the head of the house, while Celia, the oldest daughter, had taken on herself the duties which had belonged to her mother. There were four younger children, ranging from Wallace, who was fourteen and had recently entered the high school, down to little Grace, who had just turned four. Mr. Graham's sister, Aunt Jane, was also a member of the household; but partly because of ill health, and partly because of a natural lack of initiative, she counted very little in the family life.

Outwardly, affairs in the Graham house moved with wonderful smoothness and harmony; but as a matter of fact there was between the brother and sister who had taken as far as possible the place of father and mother, a lack of cooperation, which seriously threatened the peace of the household. Bernard turned the greater part of his salary in to supplement the income of the property his father had left, and, as the wage-earner, was inclined to plume himself on his importance. Celia, who had given up her dreams of college to take upon her shoulders her mother's work, resented Bernard's assumption of importance, and looked upon herself as the indispensable factor in the family life. Gradually, between the two, so closely allied in aim and effort, a spirit of resentment had grown up. Bernard thought Celia exaggerated the importance of her part of the work. Celia was sure Bernard made too much of what he was doing. And so the two whose cordial cooperation was so essential to success were gradually drifting apart, looking on each other with suspicion, each jealous of the other's share in making the home life what it was, and each inclined to under-estimate the other's value.

Conflicts of authority were not infrequent. Wallace was inclined to appeal to Bernard from Celia's decisions, and Celia made no secret of her belief that Bernard was foolishly indulgent where Grace and Ethel were concerned. Yet, so far, the growing resentment between the two had not seriously affected the outward serenity of things. In some mysterious fashion the discordant notes were blended into harmony. And neither of these two young persons, who stood in the eyes of the neighborhood as heads of the house, guessed that it was little Iris who contributed most to the making of the home.

They made the discovery in a rather roundabout fashion. One afternoon Uncle John came unexpectedly for one of his twelve-hour visits. Nominally the guardian of the younger children, Uncle John was too occupied with business to spend more than twenty-four hours a year in the society of his charges. With Bernard he discussed the family finances, questioned Celia in regard to the children's standing in school, and then reached the real point of his visit.

"I'm going to take Iris back with me. I've found a physician who I think will be able to help her."

It was late when he made the announcement. The younger children were in bed. Bernard and Celia looked at each other with a mingling of joy and dismay. It was wonderful to think that Iris might be helped, but both shrank from the thought of sparing her even for such a purpose.

"It wouldn't be for long, would it, Uncle John?" Celia asked.

"Why, in a year he ought to be able to tell what he can do. And that would be quite a relief to you, Celia. The care of a delicate girl like Iris must be a great responsibility!"

Celia straightened, her cheeks flushing. At that moment she caught Bernard's eye, and felt a closeness of sympathy, new of late.

"It may be a responsibility, Uncle John, but it's a great pleasure when done for Iris."

"Very likely, very likely," returned Uncle John, who always was impatient of sentiment. "The point is that if anything can be done for her, it must be done right away. And so it will be best for me to take her with me tomorrow."

The parting was a sad one. Grace and Ethel wept without

restraint, and the older ones held back their tears only for the sake of the others. When the carriage containing Uncle John and Iris had disappeared, there was a sudden scattering. What went on behind the locked doors of the bedrooms, none of the Grahams ever told, but it was a sober circle of faces that gathered about the dinner-table that evening.

"Queer thing," remarked Wallace, who was nothing if not outspoken, "the house is here, and everything the same as ever, and yet this place doesn't seem a bit like home any more with Iris not here."

As time went on, others in the household began to share Wallace's opinion. There was no longer a gentle influence at work to harmonize what was discordant, to take the sting out of sharp speeches, to smooth away the little unpleasantnesses which threatened the peace of the home. Altercations grew common. Wallace was hard to control. Grace was becoming spoiled. Bernard and Celia no longer had reason to resent the other's assumption of being the chief factor in the harmony of the family life, since it was becoming only too apparent that their combined efforts were not meeting with success.

One day there came a letter from Uncle John bringing the news that Iris was very ill, too ill for comfort. "It may be," wrote Uncle John, "that the illness is a turning-point toward such health as Iris has never known. But all of you ought to know that it's very possible that there may be a final rest for the one who has suffered long, and so patiently."

All day after receiving the letter Celia went about like one in a dream. She did not seem to hear the talk that went on around her. It was necessary to speak to her several times before her attention could be attracted. A strange quiet rested over the household.

That night Celia and Bernard sat up late, each dreading to be alone. For more than an hour there had been silence between them. At last Celia rose, and walking to the window, looked long toward the east, the direction of the great city where their little sister was fighting the battle between life and death.

Bernard arose and stood by her, then said, "If she were worse, Uncle John would telegraph."

"I know." Then Celia turned and began to pace back and forth across the room.

"Bernard," she exclaimed suddenly, stopping short, "it's strange how blind I've been. I thought I was so important here in the house, yet the work I've done could be done by a well-trained servant. It is Iris who makes this a home, just as Wallace said the day she went away. I've been merely the house-keeper——it's Iris who is the home-maker."

Bernard looked at Celia, his face paling. "It's the same with me," he exclaimed. "I've turned my salary in toward the house-hold expenses, all of it I could spare; and I've so believed in myself that I assumed I was the mainspring of the home, and all the time Iris was giving something worth a hundred times as much as I gave." He hesitated, then went on quickly in a tortured voice: "There's no use pretending now, Celia. I've been jealous of you. I wanted to feel that the house couldn't be run without me, and it made me angry to think that you felt you were just as important as I was."

Celia looked at her brother with an expression of dry-eyed misery.

"I know, Bernard, I've felt just the same—proud of my own importance, and anxious to be first. And all the time it was Iris, who never thought of herself, who was doing what was worth doing."

The door-bell rang. Bernard hurried to the door, Celia close behind him.

After Bernard had signed for the telegram and closed the door, he stood looking dumbly at the yellow envelope which brought the message of life or death, no one could say which. It was Celia's hand that broke the seal at last.

> *Iris's condition much improved; doctor hopeful; wire again in the morning.*
> *John H. Kent*

Celia read the words aloud, then murmured them over for the second time, the tears raining down her cheeks. Bernard put his arms around her.

"Celia, we won't worry any more about who's doing the most. We'll just let Iris teach us how to help by forgetting all about ourselves."

Harriet Lummis Smith

Harriet Lummis Smith, born in Auburndale, Massachusetts, was a prolific writer of inspirational and value-based stories early in the twentieth century. The author of *Other People's Business,* she also wrote three books in the Peggy Raymond series and the four later books in the Pollyanna series (1924–1929). Smith died in 1947.

AUNT JERUSHA
MAKES A TEST

Ida Alexander

One sister knew how to push all the right buttons. As a result, success and favors came to her often. The other sister was quiet and unassuming, and thus she was almost invariably passed by.

Then came Aunt Jerusha's visit.

he news that Aunt Jerusha was to visit them before she went to Europe caused much excitement in the Varney household. Mr. Varney, who had not seen his only sister for years, could think of nothing but the meeting. Mrs. Varney, who had known and loved her before her marriage, was much the same. It remained for the younger generation to think of housing the guest-to-be, for the house was small. There was no question about that. Each had a room; even Edwin had a small cubby-hole to call his own. But there was no extra room. Every Varney made a wry face, remembering that.

"She can have my room and welcome," spoke up Harriet. "I'd just as soon. And I'll bunk with Sis."

"No," interposed Edwina's soft voice, "you mustn't think of giving up your room, sister dear. Aunt Jerusha must have mine. I'd rather."

"But you won't like it," protested Harriet, "while I don't mind a bit in the world. It'll do me good to move out for a while. You get in a rut, living in one room all the time. Let me, Wina. It'll be fun for me. And I won't mind the muss as you will."

"It isn't likely that Auntie'll upset things."

"She's liable to move them about. And how would you like that? And I don't mind a bit."

"Why should you? Your room is always upset, isn't it?"

"Always," agreed Harriet cheerfully. "Things get that way, somehow. But I can get it in apple-pie order before she comes. Then she can do as she pleases."

Edwina's golden head moved with gentle obstinacy. Her serene blue eyes dwelt on her sister. There was nothing that would have told an outsider that Edwina's mind was made up, that she could no more be moved than a mountain. But Harriet knew. She sighed.

"Have it your own way," she conceded. "But my plan was best."

"I couldn't let you put yourself out, Harriet," said Edwina gently. "I couldn't, dear."

"But why should *you* always be the one?" demanded Harriet a little hotly. "I can't see why you should. I'd like to give something once in a while myself."

Edwina patted Harriet's hand.

"It's all right," she said. "I'm more than willing to be put out for Auntie."

"But I shouldn't have been put out," said Harriet. "That's the difference."

"There, there, girls," said Mrs. Varney before Edwina could answer, "let it rest as it is. Edwina's is really the nicest room, if it comes to that. The sun lies there almost the whole day long. And the furnishings are prettier, too. I suppose it's really wisest. Though why the dear child should always be the one to give up, I don't know."

"I'd like to, now and then," Harriet said quickly, "but she won't let me. Well, never mind, Sis! We'll have just as good talks in my room as we would in yours. And if there's anything out of place, you won't be able to see it in the darkness."

The cloud had quite passed from Harriet's bright face. At Edwina's next words it came back.

"But I'm not going to share your room, sister mine. I'm going to sleep on the couch in the dining room."

"Oh, I wouldn't!" cried Harriet. "I wouldn't do that, Sis, if I were you. It'll make Auntie feel bad if she thinks she has made anyone so uncomfortable."

"She doesn't need to know it. I can go to bed later and get up earlier than she. It will be quite all right."

"In some way she'll find out," warned Harriet, "and imagine that she's in the way. I know just how that would make a person feel."

"She need never know, dear. I'm more than willing to stand the discomfort for her. I hope to prove that while she's here."

"No need to prove it, my child," chimed in her mother. "No need at all. Everyone knows that you're willing to sacrifice yourself for anybody. Harriet would be glad to do anything, too, of course."

"I'd love to," said Harriet. "I'd be willing to do anything that would make her stay more pleasant. I hope you all know that."

"Me, too," put in Edwin ungrammatically and a little sulkily. "I'd give up my room, all right, but no one would want it. So would good old Harry. But Wina thinks no one but herself has a right to give up. It's a flimflam game, too, if anyone could see—"

"That'll be all from you, son, for the present," said his father a little sternly. "If you can't find anything better to do than quarrel with your twin sister, you'd better go outside."

Edwin shot a quick glance at Edwina, but she was not looking his way.

"Of course I didn't mean—"

Edwina hushed his apology with a gesture.

"It doesn't matter," she told him. "Nothing matters now but Auntie."

The sullen look fell over Edwin's face again as he left the room.

It was a grief to Mr. and Mrs. Varney that the twins no longer "got along." For sixteen years they had shown the deep affection usual between twins. But in the seventeenth year something had seemed to come between them. Edwin's fault, of course. Edwina showed nothing but goodness to him, as she did to everybody.

But there appeared to be some irritation in her very perfection. Every now and then Edwin flamed out with some bitter speech that hurt the mother as much as the one it was directed against.

"He'll outgrow it," Edwina always said, in her sweet, low voice. "Don't mind, Mother. Edwin will understand some day."

The preparations for Aunt Jerusha's visit went on. However, there was little to do in the room she was to occupy. Edwina left even her favorite books on the table.

"It will make her feel more at home," she said.

"But why don't you leave a variety?" asked Harriet. "She may not like your kind of books. Frankly, I don't. I like tales of travel and adventure."

"I guess she's had enough of travel not to care to read about it," said Edwina.

Aunt Jerusha, of course, *was* a much-traveled lady. She had never married. She had taken care of her father and mother until they died. Then she had hied herself to the lands about which she had loved to read. For years she had flitted from place to place, sending letters and presents to the Varney family from the very ends of the earth. They wondered how she would like their quiet, simple living.

They went to the station to meet her in the little runabout of which they were so proud. There was room for three, with a squeeze. Mrs. Varney wished to stay at home to be ready for the coming guest. One of the girls, she said, could take her place.

"I can't get away very well," objected Harriet, when Edwina suggested that she go. "I want to finish the salad. Do go, Wina. I'd really rather not."

"But I want you to have that time with her. You've been in the house all day. And it will be nice to see Auntie first."

"But the salad—"

"Oh, the salad!" scoffed Edwina. "Get on your hat and coat, and don't think about that."

"Thank you, dear," said Harriet. "It's good of you. I've kind of a headache that the fresh air may brush away."

How sweet of her! she thought as the runabout started on its way. *She's always doing things for other people. I'm glad to get out for a minute. The work has been pretty strenuous today.*

But when they returned with the stranger aunt, the salad was still to be made. Harriet sighed over that. There were many little last-minute duties to attend to. Mother was occupied with the guest. Edwina had donned a dress that made the idea of kitchen service out of the question, thus all the responsibilities landed on Harriet. There was a little red spot on her cheeks as she hurried over to the belated task.

I'd much rather have stayed, she thought. *But there! My headache's gone. And I shouldn't complain.*

When her mother and aunt came from the guest room, everything was in readiness. Aunt Jerusha praised everything, especially the artistic centerpiece of flowers.

"Edwina arranged them," Mrs. Varney explained eagerly. "I think she has quite a touch, sister, don't you?"

"Why, yes," replied the guest. "They show an artist's fingers."

"Harry raised them," spoke up Edwin from the other side of the table.

"Dear me," said Aunt Jerusha; "that's better still. Do you like to garden, Harriet? And have you a garden?"

Harriet looked up, blushing.

"You couldn't dignify it by the name of a garden, it's such a small place. But I love to work among flowers."

"Is that what you like to do more than anything else?" asked her aunt, plainly interested in the glowing face turned toward her.

"No. I like to paint best of all. So does Edwina. And she paints better than I do."

She has more time. The words trembled on Edwin's lips, trembled and died away unsaid.

Aunt Jerusha turned to Edwina, who sat beside her.

"I might have known it," she said. "I said an artist's fingers arranged these flowers. Tell me about how far you've progressed, my dear. And what are your hopes and ambitions?"

"I want to work hard, Auntie," said Edwina's soft voice, "and make a success. I want the world to be better because I have lived. Harriet and I both go to a teacher here. He is an able artist, and takes a great deal of pains with us. I love to work. I often paint far into the night."

And sleep late while Harry gets the breakfast, Edwin thought to himself.

"And you, Harriet, do you work late at night?"

"Not often," Harriet confessed. "I'm such a sleepyhead. But—"

"Young folks require a great deal of sleep," said her aunt. "But the true artist disregards such things.

> 'He who would climb Fame's giddy steep
> Must watch and work while others sleep.'

"There! That isn't a lecture, you know. I just happened to think of the words."

She smiled at Harriet as she spoke. But her real interest was in Edwina from that moment on. Every one at the table saw it, Harriet included. But she didn't mind. It was Edwin whom it hurt the most. He frowned over his favorite dessert, and had nothing to say. But his thoughts tumbled over one another, like boys in a football game: *Harry's worth a dozen—Why, if Harry didn't help mother so much—And Wina always makes every one think—I'd like to tell—Oh, they're all blind as bats.*

That night both Harriet and Edwina were called to see a girl-friend who was ill. Edwin had intended to go out but decided to finish a book instead. And so he happened to hear words not intended for his ears.

"You know," said Aunt Jerusha as she sat with the Varney parents by the fire, "I had a special purpose in stopping by this time. I want, if you'll allow it, to take one of the girls abroad with me."

"That would be wonderful," said Mrs. Varney after a second's pause. "Which one did you say you wanted to take?"

"I didn't say. I don't know yet myself. Edwina seems to be the one. But I'd feel very selfish taking such a blessing from your house. Harriet is dear, too, of course, so frank and unspoiled. But there's something about the other—"

"I know. Never thinking of herself, always considering others first. A beautiful life Edwina's promises to be."

"No more so than Harriet's," the father interposed. "Some-times I think—"

"They're both wonderful girls," said Aunt Jerusha. "And now not a word to them or their brother, either, until my choice is made. I'm old enough to move cautiously."

Edwin came from the window seat, reddening to the ears.

"I couldn't help hearing," he said. "I was finishing a book, and didn't know I was to hear any private conversations."

Aunt Jerusha looked vexed for a moment, but soon recovered herself.

"It's all right, Edwin," she assured him. "We have your promise, of course, not to mention this to either of the girls?"

It was with reluctance that Edwin gave his word. He would have liked to explain the case to Harriet and give her at least a chance of the wonderful trip.

It's always Wina, he thought, *who gets everything of any account. She acts the martyr all the time. Then when there's anything really big, she's in line for it. While dear old honest Harry—*

He was ashamed of the choke in his throat.

Edwina moved steadily forward in her aunt's good graces. Whether by accident or design, Aunt Jerusha found out that she had given up her room, and was touched to the heart about it.

The dear, generous child! she said to herself. *Harriet keeping, she giving. Well, I'll make it up to her. I've half a mind to tell her now.*

But something seemed to hold the words back. Her New England caution was not to be thrown away within a day.

Time enough, she thought, and let it go at that.

Edwina talked a great deal to her aunt about her ambitions as the days went on. She spoke about the old masters with a reverence Aunt Jerusha liked to hear.

"How wonderful it is, Auntie, that you have seen all those treasures, that you will see them soon again!" she said. "A person could ask no more than that from life, I think."

Aunt Jerusha and Mrs. Varney looked at each other. Edwin groaned, catching that congratulatory glance. Harriet did not see. Nor Edwina, either, apparently. But Edwin saw her white teeth click together in a way he knew.

He would have given a good deal to recall his promise, to have "put old Harry wise," as he said to himself. For Harriet did not "take on" as Edwina did over "art" and "art treasures." She was thoughtful and preoccupied much of the time. Edwin knew why.

But try as he would, he could not bring the subject into the conversation, could not let Aunt Jerusha know that Harriet was having a time helping with all the household duties, working with the sick Harris family (poverty-stricken and helpless), and trying to sandwich in a little painting in odd moments.

Might as well give it up, he thought. *Wina is slated for that trip, just like the one to Yosemite. One thing for sure: Harry's a good loser. She won't whine. She'll be helping Wina off, giving her all her clothes, never thinking of herself. I wish there was some way to put the two of them to a test.*

Strangely enough, Aunt Jerusha was thinking something very like that herself. She was a shrewd old woman, moving slowly, weighing well before deciding. She had not been unmindful of several little things which Edwin had endeavored to bring to her notice. She did not want to reject a diamond and choose paste. She pondered long over a way to find the straw which would show the way the wind was blowing.

She had noticed the steady progress Edwina's painting showed. She had observed the talent apparent in some of Harriet's unfinished canvasses. She was not at all sure that Edwina's careful work showed as much. And she had found out the reason why Harriet's progress was slow. She had also seen, after Edwin had been at pains to call it to her attention, that Harriet, who said little, did more than Edwina, who talked much. She gave herself a little shake, like one who tries to throw off a previously formed conclusion.

I'll set them each a task, she thought to herself at last. *The personal shouldn't enter into this, as it seems bound to do. The girl best fitted for advantages should have them. The head should rule in this, and not the heart. However—*

She proposed it that night at the dinner table, speaking casually.

"I wonder," she said, "if each of you girls wouldn't make me a little picture to take away with me. I'll be going soon now. And nothing could be as sweet a remembrance of this happy time as some work done by you for me."

Edwina's soft voice answered first, as usual.

"I'd love to, Auntie," she said.

"And you, Harriet?"

"I'll—try," promised Harriet.

It sounded ungracious after Edwina's smooth speech. But Aunt Jerusha took no notice of that.

"Then I'll depend on you both," she said. "The pictures don't need to be more than a foot long. You ought to easily finish them by Tuesday night. I want to be able to look them over then. I'm going to be a hard master, you see. Your best work in a given time. The subjects left to you."

"But," pleaded Edwina, "can't you tell us what you'd like best? Our one desire is to please you."

But Aunt Jerusha would not say.

Edwin caught Harriet as she left the room. He put a hand on her arm. His eye gleamed with the knowledge of the secret that he could not tell.

"Oh Harry, do try!" he pleaded. "You can if you will. Do put something over on Wina for once."

"I'll do my best," she assured him. "I do want to please Aunt Jerusha. I'm going to try a snow scene, or a storm at sea. We've only two days."

"I'll take up a load of your chores," he promised. "But don't you fool me. You take the prize."

"What prize?"

"The prize of praise for the best work. Isn't that a whole lot? Won't you try, Harry?"

"Sure, I'll try. I'll do my best. I'll work on it tonight and tomorrow night. I can't spare the days."

"Well, I'll get up and do your work. You can sleep late. Do get in for once, Harry."

"I will."

But that night old Mr. Harris took a turn for the worse. His wife was distracted. And Harriet could not leave. Before morning she had a widow to comfort. And when she crept home and to bed, she was too heartsick to work, though the canvas she had prepared stared her in the face.

Tuesday night she was not at home when Aunt Jerusha asked for the finished work. Edwina went up, and came down with the two canvases in her hands. She passed them to her aunt.

"Dear sister hasn't finished hers yet," she said. "But no doubt she will."

The hardly touched work looked like a deliberate affront. Aunt Jerusha frowned, then turned smilingly to Edwina.

"This test meant more than either of you knew, my dear," she said. "I must tell you I'm going to take—"

She paused as the door opened to admit Edwin. He held a red-eyed girl by the hand.

"Tell her," he said gently.

"My pa's—daid," said the child. "Miss Harriet's been down with Ma. She allus helps us—"

Her voice broke down in sobs.

Aunt Jerusha went with them to the little house. She carried her well-filled pocketbook. And she fixed it so that the need of money did not intrude upon the widow's grief. Then, alone with Harriet for a few moments, she took the girl in her arms.

"My dear," she said, "come home and rest. You're worn out. You'll love the trip across the ocean. For you're coming with me, child! I thought it was talent I wanted to discover, that the head, not the heart, should influence my decision, while all the time I was just a lonely old woman, seeking for someone to love."

Ida Alexander

Ida Alexander wrote for Christian and family magazines during the first third of the twentieth century.

BY

CANDLELIGHT

Grace Margaret Gallagher

They were happy as they were. Why in the world should they invite that flighty little freshman, Nora, to room with them? Let someone else be a big sister to her!

But all that was before the ice cracked beneath Nora's feet.

*T*he three girls had worked hard that day at school, and they were tired. The fire in the quiet corner of the room had burned down to red embers. Three tall candles in a branched candlestick on the table shed a dim, mellow light. Their pale rays touched Martha's yellow head as she sat on the hearth, showed Eleanor's long slim hands in her lap as she nestled in the "sleepy-hollow" chair, and suggested Sally's shadowy lines on the couch. Outside, a great round moon climbed slowly up over Pine Top, flooded the snow-covered world with white magic, and thrust a narrow sword of silver through the unshuttered window.

As the moonbeam stole across the floor, Sally started awake.

"Look at that moon!" she cried.

Martha raised her head and turned to look out of the window. "Must be full tonight."

Even lazy Eleanor, Sally's roommate, leaned out from her pillows and exclaimed, "Magnificent! What a night to coast!"

"Let's go!"

"The ice isn't thick enough yet," said Eleanor. "We've had only two cold nights."

"And what counts a heap more," said Martha, "the faculty won't let us coast or skate on the lake till they give the word."

"Should I be expelled if I took just one little coast?" asked Sally.

"Don't you dare try, child," warned Eleanor. "Doctor Thorsen forbade us to go today in chapel, in his do-and-you-die voice."

"All the same I'll wager my new slippers that some of the freshmen will creep out tonight to try the hill."

"And if they do, Martha's little friend, Nora Lovett, will be among them."

"She isn't my friend at all!" Martha exclaimed. "I just knew her elder sister at camp last summer and promised to look out for her here at school. Do you really think she'll go? The faculty won't stand much more from her; they're tired out with her antics."

"Do you think that child has two grains of character?" Eleanor asked.

"Loads. But she's going downhill faster than coasting. I wish you girls would help me try to make something of her. Someone must help her, and she adores you both."

"Nonsense, Martha!" said Eleanor. "We never did one blessed thing for her in our whole lives."

"But she has for you—sent you candy at Halloween, and flowers at Thanksgiving, and run your errands—why, she'd be your slave if you'd let her."

"I suppose, on that account, we ought to like her," said Sally.

"Not at all. You don't like people because they do things for you, but because you do things for them."

"Cart before the horse!" Sally cried. "You do things for them because you love them."

"The other is just as true," insisted Martha doggedly. "Father says so, and he's a professor of philosophy. He hated a fellow in college; then he made a tremendous sacrifice to pull him out of trouble, and he cared about him always after that."

"There are our fathers and mothers," began Eleanor in her slow way. "They certainly make sacrifices for us all the time, and—"

Martha cut in ruthlessly, for she knew how easily Eleanor and Sally could lure each other off on the trail of abstract discussion.

"Well, some one must get hold of Nora. She's at the end of her rope, I do believe. She's tried every silly freshman trick—and some of her own. She won't work, she hands in her essays and things days late, and she's just flunked fearfully in the mid-year's. I tell you, the faculty won't stand it much longer."

"What could we do even if we tried?" asked Eleanor. "She's the kind of child that won't stand lecturing."

"No, she won't. What she needs is to get away from the silly crowd of freshmen and sophomores she lives among and to get in with some girls like you two. There's one thing that you two could do that would change her completely. Take her in with you to live."

"In our rooms!" cried Eleanor and Sally together, in surprised, protesting voices.

"Exactly. Mrs. Willow told me that seniors like you with a bedroom apiece and a study have got to take in a third girl next semester and make room for more from the cottage. Come now, Nelly, take in Nora. You'll just be the making of her, and I honestly believe you'll like her!"

"I can't, Martha," Eleanor said firmly. "I particularly dislike Nora Lovett. She's hard-hearted and shallow-minded."

"She doesn't like me," Martha went on. "I've scolded her too hard; but she worships both you girls. There's a great deal more in her mind and her heart than you think. I lived next door to her the first of the year, before she was shifted around. Her roommate was homesick every night, and Nora was sweet to her; and she stood by that queer Joanna Coman when everyone else turned against her, and she's as bright as steel when she really works. I tell you, you know her only in a certain way; if you could see her in another light I just know you would think differently. You remember the verses:

"Yes, I answered you last night,
No, this morn I say,

Colors seen by candlelight
Do not look the same by day."

"May I come in?" broke in a high voice outside the door.

"It's Nora!" whispered Sally.

The door was flung open and a girl in gauzy white ran into the dim light. Her dress was like wings for her to float on; the too brief skirt swirled about her knees; her hair was soft and fluffy.

"Eleanor," the newcomer said at once, "I heard you found my purse by the lake today."

"No," said Eleanor gravely. "It's May Sterrett's; her name is inside."

"Same thing. I was desperate for money this morning, so I raked round in her desk till I found a purse with the great sum of two dollars and nine cents in it. Then I went and lost it."

"You freshmen are abominable the way you borrow," cried Sally, "and May, I know, hasn't any money to spare!"

"We're all paupers on our corridor," Nora said, laughing.

Eleanor held out the purse. "Here it is, whoever owns it. And I certainly wouldn't go on the lake, since Doctor Thorsen has expressly forbidden it."

"Thank you." With a shrug of her shoulders, Nora was gone.

A moment later the dinner bell rang, and Martha hurried away, unhappily conscious that her protégée had deepened the bad opinion Eleanor and Sally already had of her.

After worship Eleanor wandered about her room, picking up books and flinging them down and fussing aimlessly at her desk. At last she seized a notebook and put on her hat and coat. "I'm going over to the library," she said to her roommate.

"Wait a minute and I'll go, too. I've got to do some work on my report."

As they crossed the campus Eleanor said, "Let's have a look at Pine Top even if we can't coast."

Pine Top stretched above them—a long slope of glittering white across which the pine trees flung bluish shadows. Below the slope, the smooth ice of the lake gleamed in the cold moonlight. The night was still.

"Isn't it beautiful!" Eleanor whispered in an awed tone.

"It's a dream, but we'll freeze here," answered matter-of-fact Sally. "Trot along."

As they turned, Eleanor stopped short.

"Sally, do you think we ought to take that Lovett child to live with us?"

"Do you want her?"

"Horrors! No!"

"Then don't. It's one of Martha's crazy notions, that's all."

In the library the girls worked steadily until time to close.

The two went out again into the snow-white world, and tramped arm in arm across the lower slope of Pine Top.

"Well, I could swear those shadows over there on the side of the hill are human beings," Sally remarked.

"They are," said Eleanor quietly. "Two girls with a sled."

The friends walked to the foot of the hill and waited. They watched the figures mount the hill to the crest, where they stood out clear against the sky.

"It's Nora Lovett," whispered Sally, "and I'm sure the other is Elizabeth Redgate."

The sled got under way. Slowly it went at first, then faster, until singing like the wind, it whizzed by the waiting girls. "My," Sally cried, "I wish I were on it!"

The sled struck the lake without a jolt, shot out on its smooth surface and turned in a wide arc toward the shore. It went smoothly until it was within a hundred yards of the bank and had almost lost its headway; then, so suddenly that Eleanor and Sally could only gasp, it swung around, toppled on its side, and disappeared into a gaping hole that opened in the ice.

"The water's twenty feet deep!" Sally cried, as she ran behind Eleanor along the edge of the lake.

When they were nearly opposite the place where the sled had gone down, Eleanor stopped and caught Sally's arm.

They could see a great gap in the glittering ice and two dark objects floating in the water. The accident had happened at a place where several springs poured into the lake. Eleanor knew that the springs kept a current always moving there, and that therefore the ice that stretched from the yawning hole to the shore was thin and unsafe. To reach the girls, they must make a wide circuit on the stronger ice that covered the rest of the lake.

"Sally," Eleanor cried, "if we go out round we can get to them! The ice will hold."

Moving cautiously, but as swiftly as possible, the girls made a wide swing on the stronger ice, and at last reached the back edge of the water. The ice cracked on the surface and sagged a little under their weight, but did not break beneath them.

"Lie down, Sally," Eleanor said.

They stretched themselves flat and reached out into the freezing water to grasp the struggling girls.

"Nora." Eleanor said it quietly, as if there were nothing to be excited about.

Hands clutched her shoulders, groped round her neck, and dragged her face to the water.

"Oh! Oh! Oh!" The voice was muffled to a thin wail by cold and fear.

Another voice, broken but controlled, said, "That's Elizabeth. Pull her—out."

"I can tread—water."

"Swing her, Sally. Easy!" Elizabeth was a little slip of a girl: Eleanor and Sally each took one of her arms and swung her through the water to the edge of the ice.

"Now! Jump!"

There was a mighty heave and a fearful thrashing struggle; the ice cracked and bent until the water flowed over it, but Elizabeth lay safe beside the girls.

"Run—for—your—life—to school!" cried Eleanor.

"Scream loud for help!" gasped Sally.

They heard her stumbling and slipping as she climbed up the bank; she was trying to shout, but her voice was a mere croak.

"Nora!" Eleanor called again.

"Here!" Her arm came round Eleanor's neck; her hand clung to Sally's hand.

But that minute's struggle to pull Nora's companion from the water had changed the situation. The girls now lay half-covered by freezing water; their efforts had drained their strength, and as they now tried to support Nora's dead weight, their arms trembled with exertion.

"Keep treading water, Nora," Eleanor said. "That helps."

"I can't; my foot's caught in the sled rope."

Even as she spoke she sank lower into the water. Eleanor set her teeth.

"Put both arms round Sally. Nearer, Sally. This ice is strong."

Nora reached up to Sally, who grasped her under the arms with both hands. Eleanor reached into the water until she could twist her fingers into the belt of Nora's Mackinaw coat.

"Kick loose."

With all the forces of her numbed body, Nora strove to draw her knees up. Eleanor shut her eyes, ground her teeth together, and pulled until her arms strained in their sockets. She felt Sally's breath coming in great sobs. The sled was inexorably drawing Nora down.

The water flowed up round them. For all her tremendous exertions, Eleanor felt chilled to the bone. A piece of the solid ice on which she lay broke off and left a raw, splintered groove about the size and shape of her arm. Instinctively she fitted her right arm into this, and pulled back. The brace gave her a new leverage. She summoned all her strength for a desperate effort.

"Once more!"

Nora leaped, Sally pulled; the weight of both bodies came over against Eleanor's arm—Nora from the front, Sally from the side. The crushing pressure forced the arm against the edge of the groove; the ragged ice socket held unflinchingly, and the bone snapped.

Moon, stars, and earth whirled round Eleanor in a black dance; then, by a tremendous exertion of her will, she steadied her spinning senses. "Steady, Nora," she said. "Hold her tight, Sally."

Nora spoke now in a tiny voice like the scratching of a pin. "You can't—pull—me—out. You'll—freeze—or drown. Let go!"

"Never! Sally, how long—can you—hold out?"

"Long as—you."

Eleanor knew it for the truth. Sally was small, but she was strong. She needed only a stout-hearted mate to screw up her courage.

Eleanor could feel something warm running down her sleeve; her body ached as if it had been trampled upon; her arm throbbed with pain. She tried to pray, but instead found herself whispering "one, two three, four, five, five, four, three, two one" over and over and over. Then even that stopped, and a voice that seemed a thousand miles away groaned:

"I've got—to—give—up!"

Another, seemingly yet farther away, pleaded, "Please—just let me go!"

"Hold on!" Eleanor muttered. "Help's coming!"

With their eyes shut tight, with their teeth clenched, with their breath coming in great racking gasps, the two girls clung doggedly to their burden.

After what seemed to be years upon years of agony a new sensation pricked Eleanor's brain. Hands were drawing her backward, a strange voice was saying:

"Pry her hands open, Jim. Her grip's froze to the other one."

With a mighty burst of strength, she shouted—although by the time the shout reached her lips it was just a whisper:

"Get Nora."

The other voice answered, "We got you all."

<hr/>

A bright beam of sunshine flitting across her eyes woke Eleanor. She lay in a white bed in a long room; in another white bed beside her she saw Sally's black hair loose on the pillow; and in a bed by the window a small, pinched face showed against the light. Eleanor was stiff, and sore, and incredibly weak, and her arm seemed to be a part of the iron bedstead. She pulled at the tangled threads of memory until she had woven a pattern of the night's adventure. "Sally!" she whispered.

"Hurrah!" Sally sat up in bed with a bounce. "I thought you'd never come round. It's tomorrow afternoon, you know."

"What?"

"Yes, sir, we slept all day, and they gave you something so that they could set your arm."

"How did we get here into the infirmary?"

"Elizabeth ran into the watchman and his son on the campus, and they did the rest."

"Nora?"

"All right. Just asleep now."

Both girls looked over at the small figure in the bed by the window. Nora's fluffy hair was brushed tightly back, her cheeks were colorless, her features were pinched. Remembering the airy, rosy little creature who had flitted into their room the night before, Eleanor stared in wonder.

Sally read her amazement. "Colors seen by candlelight," she quoted, with amusement.

"Martha was right," Eleanor said. "Things are all different—when I look at them in another light. Sally, should you mind so awfully much if we asked that child to live with us?"

"No, I shouldn't mind. Do you want her?"

"You see—it—it—well, you know what terrible work it was keeping her up in that freezing water. I can't bear to waste all that on a girl that isn't ever going to amount to anything, and I held her in my arms so long—and—tight, and truly, Sally, I did almost die of pain out there, so—so—I don't feel I can let her go on the way she's going and be turned out of school—and there's something splendid in her. You remember she begged us to save ourselves, and when we've done so much already—Oh, I can't say what I mean, but I just have to help her now."

Sally smiled broadly. "All right, Eleanor. I guess I feel that way myself."

Grace Margaret Gallagher

Grace Margaret Gallagher wrote for family magazines during the first half of the twentieth century.

MOTHER, WHY DON'T YOU?

Virginia McCarty-Bare

*A*nn *felt she knew better than Mother how to run the house and get the other children to behave.*

So Mother gave her the opportunity to put her theories into practice.

*M*other, I think you ought to make him!" Ann burst resentfully through the door, waving something in her hand, and from the tone of her voice, Mrs. Tennant thought she might have represented the girls of all ages who have cried out in protest against younger brothers.

"Make him do what, Ann?" she asked, looking up from the lemon she was slicing, and trying not to smile.

"Make him wash his hands clean in the first place, instead of wiping off the dirt on the towel; and make him leave my guest towels alone, whatever he does! I had just put out fresh ones for Barbara and Prudy, and look at this!"

"It's a shame, dear," said Mother, looking sympathetically at the poor towel, whose beautiful cross-stitch had been overlaid with prints of the "black hand," "but you know boys just don't think about such things. A towel is only a wiper to them, where it's a thing of beauty and a treasured possession to you. Who did it—Bobby?"

"No, that's just it!" Ann's indignation burst out afresh. "Harvey did it. I wouldn't mind so much if a baby like Bobby did such a thing, but I think a great big eleven-year-old boy ought to know better."

"Yes, dear, he really ought to," soothed Mrs. Tennant. "I'll speak to him about it."

"But, Mother, speaking to him won't do any good. You've spoken to him hundreds of times, and he still goes on. I think you ought to *do* something about it."

"What would you do, Ann? What punishment do you think would really fit the crime?"

"Take his bicycle away," suggested Ann stoutly; and then, as if assailed by doubts, "or something like that. Of course he couldn't go for the milk if he didn't have the bicycle. But you could think up something. I know I could if I were his mother." And Ann departed on a note of triumph.

If you only were his mother once in a while! Mrs. Tennant mused, as she washed the lemon from her hands. And so the idea was born!

Barbara and Prudy McDonald came over to supper according to plan, for this was "free night," when there were no algebra problems or school lessons to be studied, and joy might be unconfined. After a very special meal there was ball rolling on the floor between Prudy and the two "youngest" Tennants, Bobby and Jim, four and six respectively; puzzle constructing by Ann and Chris—Chris was eight and studious like Ann, so they were great chums; and a hilarious game of Parcheesi, indulged in by Mr. and Mrs. Tennant, Harvey, and Barbara. Finally, the two young ones had to be dispatched to bed. Mr. Tennant sank into his evening paper, and Mrs. Tennant introduced her plan.

"How would you three girls like to look after the boys while I go to town tomorrow? Mrs. Murphy will be here doing the ironing, so you could refer any very difficult matters to her, but otherwise you would have to play mother to all four of the boys, and you'd have to be on the job every minute, I can tell you. It's a chance to work out some of your theories," she finished demurely.

"Balloon juice!" snorted Harvey, that being his newest and choicest bit of slang.

"And to the person who breaks Harvey of saying 'balloon juice,' " went on Mrs. Tennant, "I'll give a bonus of—say, a new middy tie!"

"Oh, I think it would be fun," said Prudy. "I'd like to do it, Mrs. Tennant. And I get along so well with Jim and Bobby, I'd like to have special charge of them."

"I don't believe Harvey would mind us, Mother," was Ann's rather dubious conclusion. "You know how he acted last time when I was here alone."

"That's all arranged," said his mother, giving Harvey a quiet smile. "You see, I'm going to town with father to see about a radio, among other things, and Harvey has promised to sacrifice his dignity for just this one day on behalf of the radio."

Harvey made an indeterminate sound, and urgent business suddenly called him upstairs.

"I think I could manage Harvey," Barbara said quietly. "I think I know how he feels, and why he does things the way he does. Let me have Harvey."

"You're perfectly welcome to him," declared Ann. "And if you girls have the other three, I'm sure I can get along with Chris—I always can. Of course we'll do it!"

"All right," said Mrs. Tennant, "it's a bargain, signed, sealed, and delivered. I give you my four precious but irresponsible boys, and you give me a day's freedom in the city. Now you will try to make things easy for the boys, won't you, girls?" Then, more seriously, she advised, "Don't stir up antagonisms if you don't have to; it only makes them fractious, and they're gentle as lambs if you manage them right."

The girls promised. "But make them promise, too, Mother, the older ones, anyway," insisted Ann, and Mrs. Tennant gave her word.

"Now, Ann, dear," she added, "please don't bury your head in a book and forget everything around you. Don't let her, girls; she'll sit right beside an open window with the rain blowing in if you don't watch out!"

"We'll watch her," grinned Prudy, "and I think it'll be lots of fun. We'll play outside all day long."

"I'm going to stay on the porch and knit and knit till I finish my sweater," declared Barbara.

"And I'm going to cross-stitch a new guest towel," said Ann, "and see that Harvey doesn't come within ten feet of it."

Little did they know!

Just before bedtime, Ann ran downstairs on one last errand, turned her foot on the step just before the last one, and sprained her ankle. Just as casually as that! They had to have Dr. Neal over to look at it, and he pronounced the sprain a severe one, bound it up, and gave directions that Ann was to stay off of it for several days.

Mrs. Tennant gave up her trip to the city at once, but the girls wouldn't hear of any such thing, and finally convinced her to go. Mr. Tennant gave the girls his vote of confidence, and so they eventually got to bed with their plans for the morrow unaltered.

The day dawned bright and warm.

Mrs. Murphy arrived at seven-forty-five, and began ironing in the basement. Everybody hustled around and helped get breakfast, so it was over and the dishes done by half-past eight. At a quarter of nine, Mr. and Mrs. Tennant took the train for the city, and the three young "mothers" assumed charge of their four very docile-looking boys. The girls settled in Ann's room with their fancy work, as even Prudy decided to wind yarn for Barbara, and the boys retired to their own devices in the back yard.

"Is somebody in Mrs. Tennant's room?" inquired Barbara, a few minutes later. They all strained listening ears. Somebody was.

"Hoo-oo," called Ann, and "Oo-oo," came back in Bobby's little treble.

"Your charge, Prudy," they declared. "You go see about him."

Prudy was off in no time, and ominous exclamations began to

drift from the other room. "Oh Bobby, my child, how did you do it? Look out, your sleeve! Oh Bobby, what a mess! Honey, what were you looking for? A–Ann, Barby, what'll I do?"

Barbara raced to her assistance.

Bobby was in his mother's room, standing with a very smitten look and gazing in awe at the overturned ink bottle, and the ruination it was dripping onto his mother's blotter and desk—a ruination which trickled off onto the floor and spattered itself there in indelible design.

"He spilled the ink!" Barbara called back to Ann.

"Bobby Tennant, you know you're not allowed to touch Mother's ink or desk!" declared Ann, sternly.

Bobby swallowed hard and said nothing.

"Why did you do it?" put in Barbara, and poor Bob swallowed again and burst into tears.

"Poor lamb," soothed Prudy, hugging him. "He didn't mean to, there was a pencil or something he wanted—but do let's clean this up. Ask Ann for a rag, Barb."

They salvaged things pretty well. Barbara was away before Prudy finished speaking, and back in a wink with a floor cloth. She mopped up the pool on the desk with extra blotters, and Prudy got most of the ink off of Bobby in the bathroom. But when they were all through and had done their best, there was still a *sizable* black spot on Mrs. Tennant's rag rug.

They conferred around Ann's bed.

"What is it that takes ink out?" asked Barbara, rubbing a knitting needle up and down behind her ear, and trying to think.

"Just plain milk, I think," suggested Prudy, leading the now clean Bobby back to the scene of the disaster.

"There's something about salt, too, I know," went on Barbara hopefully; "the chlorine in it, or something. I remember that from chemistry."

"I think we'd better ask Mrs. Murphy," decided Ann, and in great relief the other two clattered down to the basement.

Mrs. Murphy said, "Javelle water." There was a bottle in the laundry, and in about fifteen minutes the spot in the rag rug had faded out, as a result of vigorous applications of the remedy. True enough, a good deal of color had faded out with the ink, but the girls told each other that you'd hardly notice the change if you hadn't known of the accident. It seems Bobby had been looking for a big carpenter's pencil which Harvey had given him—the pride of his heart—and he just thought it might be in Mother's desk, so they couldn't be *too* cross with him.

They were all settled back around Ann's bed by a little before ten; they remembered afterward that the clock was just striking ten as Mrs. Murphy appeared in the door and announced, "There's a man at the back door; sez 'e wants to see the lady of the house. I sez to 'im that she ain't here, but 'e sez 'e's goin' to wait till 'e sees who's ever in charge."

Ann started up uncertainly.

"What do you think he wants, Mrs. Murphy?"

"That I couldn't say." She shrugged her shoulders. "But it's no sweet temper 'e's in—'e growled at me that mean I felt like throwing him a bone and sayin', 'Begone wid ye.' "

Ann shuddered in mock horror.

"I suppose I'll have to see him," she decided, and though they all protested, she got into her bedroom slippers, reached for Dad's cane, and started off hopping on one foot, with the other two girls and Mrs. Murphy trailing dubiously after her.

"Better be sweet to him, Ann," advised Barbara, on the way out.

"All right," said Ann, vaguely, and hopped ahead with resolution.

When they got to the back door and looked out, they found Bobby and Jim standing staring up at an old gray-haired man on a wagon. Harvey and Chris were just visible inside the woodshed door, peeking out through the crack where the door hinged.

Ann hobbled out to the wagon, while Prudy and Barbara and Mrs. Murphy remained clustered in the doorway.

They saw Ann and the old man exchange greetings somewhat stiffly, and then a good deal of talk followed which they were unable to hear. Ann was obviously "trying to be sweet," but it was a lead which her elderly friend refused to follow.

"He hasn't cracked one smile yet," whispered Prudy, hoarsely. "Looks as if he was terribly angry over something."

They caught phrases occasionally like, "Puffickly good windows, yes, ma'am," and, "Then two Tennantzes, them big ones," and, "Shuah thing I'm shuah!" and finally, "No, ma'am. Ah doan' leave tel—" something.

After that, Ann turned and came hopping in quickly with a strange mingling of expressions on her face, as if she were provoked and baffled, and yet a little amused, too.

"Do you know what's happened?" she demanded, as she stepped up into the doorway, and went on as they waited to hear.

"That's old 'Lija White who lives down in the red shack by the station, and he says that Harvey and Chris broke three panes out of his window yesterday, that it'll cost $2.50 to have them fixed up, and that he won't budge till he gets it!"

"A pest on him!" said Mrs. Murphy.

"Will you pay it, Ann?" and, "Have you got it?" asked Barbara and Prudy.

"No, I haven't got it. I don't know what we'll do if we have to pay it, but I'm going to see the boys first, and see if they really did it. They're hiding in the woodshed, so I'm pretty certain they did."

She hippity-hopped out to the shed, and as soon as she got in, the door closed suddenly behind her. Someone in the shed was apparently anxious not to be observed by Elijah White.

Elijah sat glumly and stared at his horse. Mrs. Murphy invoked the saints, washed her hands of boys in general, and went back to the basement. Barbara and Prudy waited.

"Harvey's my charge," Barbara mused doubtfully. "I wonder if I ought to go see him."

"Better let Ann settle this," advised Prudy, and they went on waiting.

"How much money have you got, Barb?" Prue asked a few minutes later, as if with sudden thought.

"Um—60 cents, I think." Barbara screwed up one eye and tried to calculate.

But just then Ann came back. "They *did* it all right!" she declared. "Harvey's full of excuses, and Chris is pretty vague. They were just 'havin' a little fun,' and they don't think they 'really broke more than one pane,' and they both say they didn't mean to do it. That doesn't excuse them a bit for their carelessness, all the same. How can boys be so awful! We'll just have to pay it, and how can we?"

Mrs. Murphy came lumbering back up the stairs. "Here's a dollar of the three-fifty your mother gave me for the day, Annie," she said. "That's all I can spare, for I have to pay a bill this evening and I don't dare risk her not coming back before I leave."

"Oh Mrs. Murphy!" declared Prudy in great relief, "you've saved us. Barbara's got sixty cents, and I've got fifteen—now if you can just get seventy-five, Ann."

"That's marvelous," said Ann, releasing a vast sigh. "Mother gave me eighty cents this morning, and said if nothing came up to use it for, we could all get ice cream this afternoon. But we'll just have to use it. Those awful boys!" she fumed, as she drew it reluctantly out of her pocket.

Prudy carried the money out to the wagon. Elijah took it almost grudgingly, slapped his reins on the horse's back, and departed.

Harvey and Chris scuttled out of the woodshed, and came stamping into the kitchen to get drinks. They were full of noisy repudiations—especially Harvey, with his scornful "balloon juice"—and the girls were full of reproaches. Oh, dear, what a morning!

"Of course, the boys should have paid for the window panes with their own money," Ann pointed out, as she prepared to return to her couch, "but they've been saving for a radio, and they emptied their banks to give the money to Mother this morning when she went to the city. You'll just have to save up though, and pay it back!" she warned the offenders.

Finally Harvey said he and Chris were tired of all this talk, they were going out to the woods to be by themselves, and started off. Prudy and Barbara reminded them that they had promised to help with the little boys, and Bobby and Jim were clamoring to go along. Eventually a promise was exacted that if they went they'd take the two small ones and be back at twelve for dinner.

Then the girls returned to Ann's room and spent five or ten minutes on their work.

"I really don't believe I'd better let Jim and Bobby go out to the woods," Prudy decided, uneasily, at the end of that time, and hurrying off after the cavalcade, which had just started, she retrieved the "littlest ones," and played ring toss with them until dinner.

Barbara started setting the table at about twenty minutes to twelve, and helped Mrs. Murphy get dinner, and they had it ready by the noon hour, about the time she finished setting the table. They carried Ann's meal up to her.

But Harvey and Chris didn't come, and didn't come, and didn't come, and by twenty minutes past twelve the others decided to eat. Just as they were sitting down, the recalcitrant two arrived—Harvey still belligerent.

He, it developed, was going to have his dinner in the back yard in the tent. Arguments from Prudy and Barbara that everything was already on the table proved of no avail. Neither did coaxing or urging or lofty reproach. Chris was quite content to eat at the table, and so was Bobby, but eventually Harvey interested Jim in his idea, and the two carried messy-looking plates, piled with heterogeneous helpings of everything, out to the hot, stuffy tent to "eat in peace," as Harvey put it. The two exasperated girls finally resigned themselves to the inevitable, and the meal was nearly concluded when Prudy, who faced a window, jumped up with a little cry.

"Look, what's that? Barby—the tent's on fire!"

They all dashed every which way. It was Mrs. Murphy who finally got the first bucket of water on the blaze, spilling a large amount of it on the disgruntled Harvey, and Prudy was close behind with a second bucket which extinguished the fire, and the boys' dinner at the same time.

Everybody teased Ann when she appeared hobbling along with an old hose after the fire was all out, and Chris came in for his share when he appeared a few minutes later with an antique fire extinguisher he had harbored for some time in his room against such an emergency.

And this time it was Jim who was in disgrace. He had carried the matches into the tent, and experimented with a small camp fire of his own, while Harvey was outside collecting flat rocks for a table from which they might eat their food. Now there was no food left, and Ann was reprimanding, saying, "You know, Jim, Mother doesn't allow you to use matches, or anybody to take them into the tent," and Harvey was scowling and saying, "Look at that big hole you burned!"

And Mrs. Murphy was wringing her hands, and finally it was so tragic that they all laughed, and felt better—they hadn't really laughed all morning.

A period of calm and respite followed. They adjourned to the front porch, where the girls took up their abandoned work, Ann lay down in the hammock, and the boys sprawled about on the floor, and they talked and played games like "I see something green and white and wavy"—games which the little fellows could enjoy, too.

About two o'clock Harvey suddenly disappeared around the corner of the house, hastily and without explanation. Chris soon thereafter found a book he wanted to finish, and lying flat on the porch floor quickly became absorbed in it. Jim and Bobby concluded this would be a good time to play catch with Chris and Harvey's baseball equipment, and adjourned to the back lot again.

After a time Barbara grew uneasy about Harvey.

"He's my charge. I'm going to look for him," she told the other two, and set off up into the woods. She found him before very long, coming home along the path, hot, tired, and dirty, and carrying one of his white rabbits. The rabbit looked hot, tired, and dirty, too, and somewhat bored in addition.

"Where have you been, Harvey?" demanded Barbara. Female relatives and girls in general are always getting at things like that, and throwing their erring men-folks on the defensive.

"Nowhere," he returned shortly.

"Well, it's all right," returned Barbara, with unexpected meekness.

Harvey was considerably mollified, and as they got near home, confessed that "Brer Rabbit" had run away because there was a board loose on his hutch that Harvey had forgotten to fix.

"But please don't tell Mother," he begged. "She reminded me of it this morning before she left, and I told her I'd fix it first thing."

"Why don't you want her to know?"

They had got nearly down to the Tennant lot, and Harvey stopped, fiddling with the rabbit's ears, apparently finding it hard to answer.

"Why, because I don't want her to think I'm so unreliable," he finally blurted out, and then began blustering at Brer Rabbit for his misdeeds. Barbara thought a little while.

"All right, I won't tell her, if you'll stop saying 'balloon juice,' " she finally announced. They had reached the hutch, put Brer Rabbit in it, and Harvey was blocking up the erstwhile exit. He straightened up and snorted, "And you'll get your prize middy tie—huh—not so easy, I guess."

"Look at me, Harvey!" called Bobby. Prudy had joined the

two little boys, and was pitching the baseball for them. Jim was at bat with Chris's big bat, and Bobby was attempting to catch with Harvey's enormous glove on his hand.

"Look at me, Harvey," he shrilled again. "I'm gonna catch this one. Watch!"

"Oh, balloon juice!" shouted Harvey, in derision and challenge. It was the last time he ever said it.

Jim made a mighty swing at the ball. Bobby pressed in close to be sure to catch it while Harvey's eyes were on him, and caught the end of the bat just over his right eye.

Those things always happen so quickly.

Bobby had screamed and dropped to the ground before anybody could take in what had happened. Jim just stared down at him, stiffened with terror, and held rigid in a sort of awful fascination.

Prudy got him up on her lap, and dabbed and dabbed at the blood with her handkerchief, but there was no stemming the rush of it. Barbara ran for Mrs. Murphy, and Ann came limping around the corner of the house, clutching the unfinished guest towel in her hand.

Harvey snatched it from her without a word, and made a determined effort to stanch Bobby's wound with it.

"Call up Dr. Neal, quick, Ann," he said to her in a funny, high, tight voice. Then, as the blood soaked the towel and continued to run, and Bobby's little groans grew fainter, "Here, Prue," he said, thrusting the towel into her hand, "I'll run for the doctor." And he was gone.

Ann's mind whirled. For a moment she hesitated in indecision. Go to help Bobby—telephone—which? Just then Mrs. Murphy burst out the back door, making for Bobby, and Ann decided to telephone. "I'm getting the doctor," she called, as she hopped off, and had the strange feeling that her voice made no sound.

She forgot about her foot, or remembered it only dimly, when it hurt. In the back door, up the familiar back stairs—how could things look so familiar and undisturbed when Bobby was hurt?—into the hall where the telephone was. Dr. Neal's number—how did you get a number when there was an accident?—the telephone book had the police headquarters' number, and directions for calling the fire department,—but could you just say 'Doctor!' to the exchange? No, you must have a number. She picked up the telephone book and started to fumble through the pages. Let's see, Mother might have it on the pad—Hunter, McDonald. Here it was: Dr. Neal—24—ring 3.

She took down the receiver.

"Dear God, please help me to get Exchange—dear God, please help me to get Exchange—dear God, please help me—" Ah, here she was—

"24—ring 3, please, Exchange—oh, quickly, please, there's been an accident!"

Then followed an interminable silence on the wire, and Ann filled up the awful blankness of waiting by praying. It was as if she stood blindly at bay fighting off her fears with—

"Dear God, please don't let Bobby die! Dear God, please don't let Bobby die!"

"Hello—hello, Mrs. Neal, Mrs. Neal!" Her words stumbled out and tripped each other. "Bobby's hurt, Mrs. Neal. Is the doctor there? We've got to have him quick—is—

"Oh, can you get him, Mrs. Neal—oh, please do—how soon? We *must* have him!

"All right—oh, quickly, please—goodbye."

Barbara appeared in the doorway with a white scared face.

"What did Dr. Neal say? Is he coming, Ann?"

Oh dear God, please help him to come! Dear God, please help to find him, was running on in the back of Ann's head.

"He's not there, Barby," she answered, swallowing a dry sob. "Mrs. Neal is trying to get him." Suddenly her teeth were chattering. "How's B-Bobby?" and they hurried out to the kitchen, where Mrs. Murphy had established him.

There lay the pathetic little figure on the kitchen table, Mrs. Murphy at his head with a basin of water, bathing, bathing, bathing the flow of blood which never stopped. And Bobby's right eye was closed. Blind!—Bobby might be going blind! Ann limped back to the telephone.

"24—ring 3." Again the wait, mercifully shorter this time.

"Mrs. Neal—isn't he—there yet? Can't you—Somebody else? All right—Dr. Warner? I will, but you'll still try, won't you? Thank you, Mrs. Neal. I'm afraid Bobby's—goodbye."

Dr. Warner—now she must try to find Dr. Warner's number. Oh, if Mother were only home! For Bobby might be dying.

The front doorbell rang, and the door was opened immediately. In stepped a strange man with a doctor's case, and behind him Harvey, red, panting, dirty, disheveled—Harvey had run to the nearest doctor's house and found him.

"Where is the boy?" Harvey's doctor was asking, and Ann led the way to the kitchen.

The doctor organized them at once. Mrs. Murphy was set to sterilizing instruments; Bobby wanted Ann and Prudy, one on either side of him, and the doctor allowed them to remain. He asked Barbara to take the other three boys out into the yard, and that cleared the atmosphere considerably, because Jim was weeping in great heartbroken sobs.

A few stitches and it was all over; the severed eyelid muscle rejoined, the skin drawn together, Bobby's eyes both functioning properly, and his head nicely bound up.

"They're nasty, these scalp wounds, for bleeding," said the doctor, replacing the needles in his case.

" 'Tis right ye are!" agreed Mrs. Murphy. "Why, when my Michael—" and she was off on a long tale of scalp wounds in her own family.

Suddenly Ann's mind snapped back into place—the world righted itself. Gladly she joined the procession that was carrying Bobby upstairs to bed. They rounded the turn into the front hall, and there was Mother coming up the front walk!

Ann surprised everybody—herself most of all—by hobbling down the path and bursting into tears on Mother's shoulder.

In about fifteen minutes the house was cleared and quiet. Mother had discussed things with the doctor, and he had taken his departure. Prudy and Barbara had left, too, with very evident relief. Chris had taken Jim out in the yard to play, and Harvey was sitting beside Bobby. Ann, now nicely tucked into bed, told Mother all the horrors of the day in one ten-minute burst.

In a little while Dad came home and went up to stay with Bobby, Mother came down and got supper, and they all ate in a kind of cheerful relief, Father carrying Ann down to be with them. The boys turned in early, and Bobby himself dropped off into a calm, quiet sleep.

Only Mother and Dad and Ann were left in the living-room, and Mother started setting things to rights for the night.

"I'm sorry, dear, that you had to go through with such a trying accident today when you were playing mother and were laid up yourself," she said, as she wound up her knitting.

"Oh," Ann made an indeterminate gesture, "there never was such a horrible day!"

"You mean—?"

"Why, the fire in the tent, and 'Lija's coming after the boys, and—and Bobby's spilling the ink—"

"Oh, those things!" laughed Mother. "Why, those were just everyday occurrences."

"Everyday occurrences!" echoed Ann in horror.

Father looked up over his paper with a grin.

"Why, yes, daughter," he said, "the tent's been on fire twice before, you know. That's why we made the rule about the matches."

"And don't you remember that Harvey was nearly arrested last year for killing Mrs. Hastings's pet rooster with his air rifle?"

"And even taking Bobby's accident into consideration," went on Dad, with just the trace of a twinkle, "it wasn't such an unusual day. You know, Chris has broken both collar bones on different occasions, Harvey has thrown his knee out of joint, and he and Jim have both broken their arms!"

"How about your theories, dear; did you get to work any of them out?" Mother inquired demurely. "How about Harvey and the guest towels, for instance?"

Ann grinned ruefully. "Now I know you're both making fun of me," she accused. And meanwhile she was thinking of her new guest towel, of how it had looked with the crimson stain from Bobby's head soaking it through and through, and she shuddered. She also thought of Harvey: Harvey snatching the towel, and trying so hard to stanch the flow of blood with it; Harvey running for the doctor; Harvey returning with help just when they needed it most.

"I guess I'm not very sure of my theories any more," she said hastily. "But," with sudden conviction, "I'm sure of one thing: Being a mother is a harder job than being President."

Barbara received a package a few days later. In it was a new middy tie and a note. The note read:

"Dear Barbara:

"Here is the middy tie which I guess you deserved after all. I told Mother you ought to have it because I have quit saying—you know what. You are not so bad for a girl, Barbara.

"Yours truly,

"Harvey Reed Tennant, Esq."

Virginia McCarty-Bare

Virginia McCarty Bare wrote for inspirational magazines early in the twentieth century.

George Ford Morris

THE LONE
STALLION

Gil Close

*S*he couldn't believe her ears when her brother proposed
capturing the wild stallion that had come to trust them.

But what alternative had they?

*T*he first intimation that her brother had returned from his trip to Canyon City came to Merna Dunbar when she heard his pony, Paint, pawing at the gravel before the corral gate, waiting with growing impatience for its youthful master to finish his unsaddling.

At the time, Merna was preparing dinner in the spaciously cool kitchen of their adobe ranch house. Her blue eyes bright with hopeful expectancy, she lost no time in dropping her work and hurrying to the doorway to greet her brother.

Yet, despite her excitement, a premonition of fear gripped her. It was not like Larry to return from town like this. His usual arrival was punctuated by the thunder of galloping hoofs and a series of wild, ear-splitting yells. Today his sedate approach could mean but one thing—something had gone wrong. And how well Merna knew what that something must be!

Early that morning Larry had saddled Paint and ridden toward Canyon City. With him had gone Merna's prayers for the success of his mission, upon which hinged the future of their Bar Q ranch.

The entire forenoon had consisted of endless hours of anxious waiting. Now the waiting was over. But in Larry's attitude, as he walked toward the porch, Merna saw dejection that somehow chilled her heart.

"What did Dad Withers have to say?" she demanded, before Larry had even had time to reach the porch.

It took courage to ask that question. But during the long, drought-filled months that had made of the summer an ordeal of blasting heat, she had had to summon her courage so often that at last it had become a part of her daily life.

Larry paused on the steps and beat the dust from his chaps with his battered sombrero before answering. When he finally looked up, his gray eyes met and held his sister's anxious blue ones.

"Dad said it would cost us five hundred dollars to redrill that old well near the south water hole." His voice was calm, but he could not conceal the bitter disappointment that showed in his eyes.

Five hundred dollars! Why hadn't Dad said ten thousand? Either amount was equally impossible.

"Then that means we'll have to sell our cattle?"

Larry nodded. "Unless—"

He paused, and Merna wondered at the almost guilty expression that crossed his face. "Unless what?" she urged him.

"Unless we're willing to capture the Lone Stallion and sell him to Pete Morin, the rodeo manager. He's offered me a thousand dollars for him just to use as a show horse."

An unexpected whiplash could not have produced more astonishment than that which showed on Merna's face. For a moment she stood speechless with surprise, her eyes glued to Larry's face. When at last she spoke, words came in an angry torrent.

"Do you mean to tell me that you'd break the trust that wild horse has placed in us?"

The sudden look of pain that dulled Larry's gray eyes made Merna sorry for her hasty words. But before she could speak again, he had dropped into a chair and had begun to reason with her.

"Listen, Sis," he said, trying to speak in a matter-of-fact voice. "We've got to think of something besides ourselves and our feelings toward the Lone Stallion in this matter. We still owe Uncle Dave for the cattle he sold us to start the Bar Q. If we have to sell our herd in its present unmarketable condition, it won't even bring enough to pay off that loan. By fall they'll not only bring that much, but a tidy sum besides.

"For some time Pete has been after me to capture the Lone Stallion for him. He knows that my horse, Paint, is the only animal in this part of the country fast enough to overtake him. Pete approached me again this morning after my talk with old Dad Withers."

"And you accepted," Merna finished bitterly.

Larry shook his head. "Not at the time. But Pete told me that it was a standing offer."

⋆⇒━◎◎━⇐⋆

During the remainder of the afternoon, Merna worked in a daze. Somehow the whole idea seemed too cruel to even think about. Yet deep in her heart she knew that it was the only thing to do.

Two weeks more, Larry had said, would see the last hole of which the Bar Q could boast completely dry. After that, what would they do for water? The thousand dollars which Pete had offered for the capture of the Lone Stallion would enable them to redrill an old well that Dad Withers had sunk in former days, and which the old workman promised would still bring forth enough water for the entire herd.

Larry was right: there was no other way out. Bitterly Merna realized that her brother's decision had not been of his own volition, but had been forced upon him by dire necessity caused by the prolonged drought.

A vision of the Lone Stallion rose before her. She saw him again as she had on that day a week before, when she and Larry had ridden to the southern border of their ranch to repair the drift fence. It seemed as if the great white horse knew that the

"No Trespassing" signs, which Larry had purposely posted along the southern border of the Bar Q, were to protect him from the continual string of horse hunters who harassed his trail. He had become less and less cautious in venturing down from his hide-out in the wild mazes of Lost Mountains. He now grazed his fill on the sturdy *grama* grass that grew so abundantly on the plains.

As time passed, he even accustomed himself to the sight of Larry and Merna on their ponies. His trust seemed to increase with each meeting. Of late, instead of dashing headlong into the hills at their approach, he would merely gallop to some prominent knoll where he could watch their progress with wild, curious eyes.

Dinner that evening was a dreary meal. Twice Merna tried to stir up some conversation, but each time Larry failed to respond. Only once did he speak. Glancing up when nearly finished, he said suddenly, "Sis, I feel like a traitor. The way he has learned to trust us—and now this!"

This time, Merna did not reply. Despite her desire to assure Larry that she no longer blamed him for the decision which he was forced to make, she could not bring herself to talk about the capture of the Lone Stallion.

⊷≡◉⊜≡⊷

Early morning found them on the trail. There was no time to waste if the Lone Stallion was to be captured, delivered, and a new well drilled before the critical water shortage at the ranch became worse than it already was. The sun was spraying shafts of crimson across the prairie when they rode out from the ranch buildings and headed southward toward the Lost Mountains, still only purple blotches against the morning sky. They rode in silence. Words could not retract from the pain that each knew filled the other's heart.

The rugged tips of Lost Mountains had assumed a much clearer outline when Larry finally broke the silence. "I don't imagine he'll be down on the range this early. If not, we'll have to ride into the hills and haze him out to a place where I'll have a chance to run him down."

Merna nodded.

The Lost Mountains were a veritable fortress in their own right. Few people ventured far into their wild extremities. Dry wash, blind canyon, and rugged gullies choked with rank growths of scrub oak and chaparral crisscrossed in a way to deter even the most valiant explorer.

True to Larry's prediction, the Lone Stallion was nowhere to be seen along the southern border of the Bar Q. Brother and sister continued onward, riding into the hills.

It was high noon before they caught the first glimpse of their quarry. At the time they were riding along the bottom of a deep gully, that during wetter years formed the bed of a rushing mountain stream. Now only sun-baked sand muffled the footfalls of their horses.

Suddenly, while rounding a sharp bend, Larry reined quickly. Directly in their path, less than two hundred yards down the canyon, the Lone Stallion was ambling peacefully along in the same direction in which they were riding.

Larry withdrew quickly from sight, motioning Merna to follow. "Everything's in our favor," he whispered quickly. "The wind is blowing from him to us; so he won't scent us. If I'm not mistaken, this canyon opens onto the Bar Q near our southern water hole. He's probably headed for the range right now!"

Silently as shadows, their hands ready to suppress any revealing neighs if their own mounts should catch wind of the Lone Stallion, Larry and Merna followed, keeping just far enough behind their quarry to be out of sight and hearing.

A mile passed, two miles. Merna's excitement increased. She knew that they must be approaching very near to the southern boarder of the Bar Q.

"Wherever he's headed, he seems to know the way!" Larry whispered finally.

Hardly had the words left his lips when Merna, riding silently in advance, stopped suddenly and reined her pony back until it stood beside Larry's.

"He's stopped!" she whispered excitedly. "There's a large boulder blocking the canyon, with not enough room on either side to let him by!"

Larry was surprised. It was not like the Lone Stallion to blunder into such a trap as this. He sat silent for a moment, contemplating his chances. Then he outlined his quickly laid plans to Merna, shaking free the coils of his lariat as he spoke.

"You ride forward. I'll wait here behind this bend. As soon as the stallion sees you, he'll make a break past you, trying to run free. I'll rope him as he goes by."

Merna nodded dully. How she dreaded her part in this hateful task! For a moment she hesitated, feeling as one about to betray a friend. But with the same resolute courage that had carried her bravely through months of drought, she thrust the feeling aside. Their only opportunity was at hand. Now was the time to act. Without a backward glance she spoke to her pony and rode boldly around the bend.

Immediately a shrill squeal of mingled surprise and terror ranged through the canyon. Something in that wild challenge of despair gripped Larry's heart as he dismounted and waited behind the bend. His hands trembled as he shook free the remaining coils of his rope and dangled it ready at his side.

The stallion was coming nearer now, had passed Merna on his mad dash for freedom. Larry braced his feet as the magnificent snow-white beast bore down upon him. He steeled his nerves. Like Merna, he realized that the moment of crisis had now come. If he missed, the Lone Stallion, with his faith shattered in the only human beings he'd ever trusted, would be next to impossible to ever corner again.

At just the right instant he made his cast. With the blind speed of a striking snake, the loop hissed outward. Widespread, it settled directly in the path of the oncoming stallion. At the precise instant when the great horse's hoofs struck the ground in the center of the sprawling loop, Larry braced his feet and lay back. A bone-racking jerk seemed to tear him apart; but, setting his teeth grimly, he held on.

The Lone Stallion, caught entirely by surprise, fell heavily as his forefeet were jerked together by the closing loop. In one lithe bound Larry appeared from his shelter. A quick flick of his wrist sent more coils of rope to embrace the flailing rear feet of the fallen horse. Before the Lone Stallion was fully aware of what had happened, he lay trussed and helpless on the ground. But the fire had not gone from his heart. He struggled fiercely, squealing, biting, lunging against the ropes that bound him.

Panting, Larry straightened from his task. He glanced around for Merna. She was nowhere in sight. As if in answer to the question that sprang into his eyes, he heard her calling him from down the canyon. Something in Merna's voice made him forget the struggling stallion and hurry toward her.

She had dismounted from her saddle, and was kneeling on the

ground near the base of the great boulder that had blocked the Lone Stallion's progress. Now she stood up, smiling as Larry came forward. He noticed that she was pointing downward.

Then he saw it. Struck speechless, he could only stare. Bubbling from beneath the boulder was a goodly sized stream of sparkling spring water!

Still scarcely able to believe what he saw, Larry followed its liquid course on down the canyon to where, several hundred yards beyond, the last trace of it seeped into the thirsty sand. Then his gray eyes returned to meet Merna's happy blue ones. A smile wreathed his own face. He pointed upward to where, high above on the top of a sharp knoll, a lone tree stood outlined against the sky.

"That tree is less than a quarter of a mile from our south water hole. That means that a few hundred feet of pipe will lead this water on through the canyon to our ranch. We don't have to drill a well after all!"

Merna nodded happily. "And this water explains what the Lone Stallion was doing in a blind canyon." For several moments Merna stood contemplating the water that bubbled so merrily at her feet. Why hadn't they realized before that the Lone Stallion had to have had some place to drink in the wild fastness of these hills?

At last she raised her eyes to Larry's. A quizzical blue light glowed from their depths. "The thousand dollars Pete gives us for the Lone Stallion will be all profit now that we don't have to drill a well," she said.

Something in her voice made Larry laugh aloud. Grasping her hand, he started again up the canyon toward the Lone Stallion still struggling gamely against his bonds.

One lithe bound and Larry had secured the loose end of the

rope. A quick flick of his wrist was enough to free the struggling horse. Together, arm in arm, they watched the great beast lunge to his feet and race away up the canyon. The reverberating echo of his receding hoofbeats was the sweetest music that had reached their ears in a long, long time!

"His trust in us was tried, but I hope not broken," Merna said a bit wistfully, when the last echo had died away.

Gil Close

Gil Close wrote for family and inspiational magazines during the first half of the twentieth century.

THE SECRET

Arthur Gordon

She was lonely, she was awkward, she was homely, she was eight. Her sister, on the other hand, was everything she was not. Out there on the ice, skaters circled gracefully—while she . . .

She could have remained the proverbial ugly duckling all her life, for she'd never be beautiful in the sense that her sister was. She could have—had a seventeen-year-old boy not changed the course of her life in only minutes.

*T*here's a question that you ask them when they're obviously on their way to the absolute top of the tree, and so I asked it. "How'd you get started?" I said. "Who or what provided the necessary push?"

She gave me a quizzical look. She wasn't really pretty, but she had a merry sort of face. "That," she said, "is a stock question. But never mind: I can give you an answer. We'll have to go back about fifteen years, though."

"That's all right," I said. "Do we have time?"

"We have about five minutes," she said. "That'll do."

And, standing there in the chilly dampness, this is what she told me.

In those days, she lived in the twilight land between childhood and adolescence, and she didn't like it much. She was eight years old; she was awkward as a newborn colt, and when she looked in the mirror—which was as seldom as possible—all she could see was a pair of enormous eyes and a lot of complicated bands on her teeth. She was shy, she was lonely, she was convinced that she was hideous. Her name was Margaret, but everyone called her Maggie.

To make matters worse, she had a sister named Sybil who seemed to be everything she was not. Sybil was sixteen, blonde, and cunningly streamlined. She had decided opinions, and on this particular wintry afternoon she was voicing one of them—loudly. "Oh, Mother," she wailed, "do we have to take Maggie? She's only a *child*. And she can't even skate!"

"The Bancrofts asked her, dear," their mother said. "It won't do you any harm to have her along."

Sybil clutched her honey-colored ponytail. "But Larry is taking me! It's all arranged. He . . ."

"He can take you both," their mother said in tones that even Sybil recognized as final. "Heavens, it's only an afternoon skating party!"

Sybil gave her sister a baleful glance.

"You needn't worry," said Maggie in a small voice. "I'll sit in the backseat and not say a word."

He came at three o'clock, tall, lithe, the best athlete in the high school. He was seventeen, but he seemed older; there was a kind of quiet assurance about him. Sybil explained in tragic tones that they would have a passenger. Larry looked at Maggie and smiled a little. "That's all right," he said.

They went down the snowy path to the street, Sybil on Larry's arm, Maggie stumbling along behind like a lost puppy. Sybil opened the rear door for her sister. Larry raised one dark eyebrow, but said nothing.

They drove to the lake where the Bancrofts lived, a sheet of magnificent black ice under the gray December sky. Already twenty or thirty skaters were swooping and spinning, their cries thin and sweet in the frosty air. On the shore a bonfire blazed. There were hamburgers and gallons of hot chocolate.

Larry laced Sybil's skates for her. He offered to lace the pair that Maggie had been given for Christmas, but she refused. She would just sit on a blanket, she said, and watch. No, thanks; she wasn't hungry.

She sat there, small and alone, feeling her fingers and toes grow numb. Out on the ice the skaters circled like bright birds, their runners making rhythmic whirring sounds. Watching them, she felt a longing that was almost like physical pain, a longing to be as graceful as they were, as beautiful—as free.

Larry must have been watching her, for suddenly he left the ice and came over, walking on the tips of his skates. He looked down at her. "How about giving it a try?"

She shook her head, mute and miserable.

"Why not?" he persisted. "It's fun."

"I'm no good at it."

"So what?" he sounded genuinely surprised.

She stared at her mittened hands. "My father says that anything worth doing is worth doing well."

He did not say anything for a moment. Then he knelt, unlaced his skates, slipped on his moccasins. "Come on—let's go."

She looked up at him, startled. "Go? Go where?"

"Over there behind that point of trees. Bring your skates."

"Oh, no," she said. "I couldn't. Sybil . . ."

"Never mind Sybil." His hand was under her elbow, strong, insistent. Incredibly, she was on her feet, walking beside him through the silver dusk. She said, feebly, "Don't you like Sybil?"

"Sure," he said. "I like her fine. I like you, too."

Around the point was a little cove, frozen, secluded, quiet. "This will do," he said. "Put on your skates."

"But I . . ."

"Put them on. I'll lace them for you."

He laced hers, then his own. He stepped lightly onto the ice and held out his hand. "Come on, Maggie."

She shook her head, her eyes full of tears. "I can't. I'm afraid. . . ."

He said, gently, "I'll tell you why you're afraid. You're afraid because you're lonely. I know because I was lonely once, just like you. Afraid to try things. Afraid of not doing things well. Afraid of being laughed at. But finally I found out something."

He came back and stood beside her. She stared up at him,

puzzled, questioning. It was so quiet that she could hear her heart beating. Around them the sentinel pines stood black and motionless. Above the pines, now, the first star gleamed.

"It's funny," he said. "I couldn't tell this to Sybil. I didn't think I could tell it to anyone. But I can tell it to you. What I found out was very simple. It's that no one is ever really alone. Even when there's no other person around, there still must be—Someone. Someone who made you and therefore cares what happens to you. Someone who will help you if you do the best you can. So you're never alone. You *can't* be alone, no matter what you do. That's the secret of happiness, of doing things well, of everything." He held out his hand again. "Come on, Maggie."

She got to her feet and stood there, wavering. But now his right arm was around her waist, his left hand held hers. "All right, now; just relax. Slide your left foot forward and push with your right. That's it. Now slide the right and push with your left! Fine! Now once more . . . and again . . . and again. . . ."

⇥══○══⇤

That was the story she told me, in five minutes or less. Then the lights went out in the big arena, the music blared, the spotlight caught her as she left me standing in the runway and flashed across the ice on glittering skates to meet the members of the troupe who came spilling out of the other runway. The crowd roared as the rink became a whirling kaleidoscope of color and rhythm and movement. The Greatest Ice Show on Earth, they called it, and I guess it was.

A few yards away I saw her husband standing in the darkness, watching, as he did every night. I moved up and stood beside him. He gave me a quick smile, but all of his attention was out there on the ice. "She's wonderful, isn't she," he said, and it was a statement, not a question.

I looked at his face, so eager and proud. A reporter isn't supposed to feel much, but somewhere inside of me there was a little unaccustomed glow.

"Both of you are, Larry," I said.

But he wasn't even listening.

Arthur Gordon
(1912–)

Arthur Gordon still lives and writes from his natal seacoast of Savannah, Georgia. During his long and memorable career, he edited such magazines as *Cosmopolitan, Good Housekeeping,* and *Guideposts.* He is the author of a number of books, including *Reprisal* (1950), *Norman Vincent Peale: Minister to Millions* (1958), *A Touch of Wonder* (1983), and *Return to Wonder* (1996), as well as several hundred short stories.

MEDDLESOME
MATTIE

Lillian G. Copp

Miss Rachel was not pleased at having to take three girls instead of one. She was even less pleased that "Meddlesome Mattie" was to be one of her visitors. . . .

*M*iss Rachel pushed back her chair with a pronounced little gesture of disapproval, and impatiently arose. She walked to the kitchen and back with short, snappy steps, the letter crumpled tightly in one hand. Then she deliberately straightened out the creased pages, and reread the answer to her invitation that one of her cousin's three daughters spend the month of August with her.

Had she not known Cousin Ellen so well, she would have felt she was taking advantage of the intimate companionship of their girlhood days, in asking that the three girls be permitted to come for ten days, instead of one alone for a month. And even then it required all of Miss Rachel's self-control to keep her lip from curling as she scanned the closing words:

> It is hard to decide which one of the three will appeal to you most strongly, only I feel sure that you will love them all. Anna, the eldest, makes friends readily by her never-failing tact, and her affectionate manner. Ruth, the second one, is far too shy for people to understand at first sight, but under the shyness, she is pure gold. As for Mattie, the youngest—well, I won't try to describe Mattie. You will see her for yourself. It is only fair to tell you, however, that not only at home but throughout the village she is known as 'Meddlesome Mattie,' and the epithet bothers her not at all. I do hope that you'll find it possible to accede to my wishes, Ray, for I have set my heart on your meeting the three girls together.

"Accede?" Miss Rachel uttered the word explosively. "There is nothing else to do but to accede. I shall be heartily glad, though, when the ten days are over. The idea of Ellen's allowing a child to foster so abominable a trait! Meddling is just about the worst failing a person can possess." She wrinkled her straight, patrician nose in fine scorn, as she pulled down the lid of her desk, and penned the words which would bring charming Anna, shy Ruth, and meddlesome Mattie to her.

→═◉═←

It had been years since Miss Rachel had felt so much excitement over an expected guest as she did over the three girls who were to arrive within the next five minutes. For a whole week she had been preparing for them. *If it weren't for Mattie, the next ten days would be pleasant ones to anticipate,* she thought, hurrying from one room to another to satisfy herself that everything was in apple-pie order.

She tarried for a minute in the restful parlor, where fleecy draperies were fastened back with long, plumy sprays of feathery asparagus, and low glass bowls of late-blossoming roses filled the air with delicate perfume. Then the shrill whir of the bell announced the arrival of the guests, and she hurried out through the cool, shadowy hall to welcome them.

"Dear Cousin Ray." Anna's soft lips lightly touched Miss Rachel's firm, cool cheek. "It is so sweet of you to have us! When Mother read your letter saying that we were to have ten delightful, soul-satisfying days with you, it seemed too good to be true.

"This is Ruth!" Anna gracefully presented her sister, who despite her nineteen years was hanging back like an abashed child. But her painful shyness touched Miss Rachel nearly as much as had Anna's graceful charm, and she greeted her warmly.

"And this is Mattie, Meddlesome Mattie." Anna's tone was richly suggestive of exciting things to follow.

All undismayed, and with roguishly-dancing eyes, Mattie swept Miss Rachel into two impulsive arms, and planted a kiss squarely on the woman's lips.

"We're tickled to death to be here, Cousin Ray! I only hope that you are one millionth as glad to have us as we are to come. Anna gets all sorts of invitations, but Ruth and I are in the kindergarten stage so far as visiting is concerned. And to think that we are invited here for ten days!" Mattie gave an ecstatic little sigh, which proclaimed that life had little more to offer.

No wonder that Anna gets all the invitations, thought Miss Rachel. She closed her mouth tightly lest the words escape, as she led the way to the light, airy rooms prepared for the girls' occupancy. *Anna's manner is perfect,* her thoughts sped on. *But Ruth is altogether too shy, and Mattie's manner proclaims that she will be annoyingly meddlesome.*

And then as if in answer to Miss Rachel's unspoken thought, Mattie's gay, girlish voice called: "Do you keep a maid, Cousin Ray?"

Miss Rachel stopped short. Mattie's tone was neither curious nor impertinent, but the idea of her mentioning such a thing, almost the moment of her arrival! Struggling to keep all trace of resentment out of her voice, she explained that she had released Martha for war work earlier in the year.

"I wondered if you weren't alone, and that's why I asked." One of Mattie's arms encircled Miss Rachel's trim waist. "There isn't the slightest need of your making all this extra work for me. Just let me go in with Ruth. We share the same room at home, and we like it heaps, don't we, Ruthie?"

Ruth's confirmation was cordial if shy, and Miss Rachel

breathed easier as she went down to finish the preparations for dinner. Out in the kitchen her glance sought the clock anxiously. She had forgotten to make the butter balls. There would be plenty of time to get them hardened before dinner, she decided with a sigh of relief, when a sudden memory stung her. The butter had never been ordered. There was just one thing to do. She must ask one of the girls to go to the grocer's for her.

Anna and Ruth had just come down to the charming living-room when Miss Rachel hurried in to announce her predicament. Anna's smile was beautifully solacing as she listened.

"Why, Ruth will be delighted to do the errand for you. Don't give it another thought."

But Ruth's shyness made even going to a strange grocery a terrible ordeal, so she hung back in pitiful confusion. Then Mattie, who had tarried upstairs to hang her own and her sisters' dresses in the wardrobe Miss Rachel had placed at their disposal, breezed in.

"What is it, Cousin Ray? Some one to go to the store? Do let me go! I just love to do errands, and every one spoils me dreadfully." She gave Miss Rachel's arm an understanding little pat, and learning the direction of the store, she ran gayly on her way.

In a few minutes she was back, her face rosy, her hair wind-tossed, the light of discovery in her eyes.

"Will you mind if I run down the street a little way? I won't keep dinner waiting." Without staying to make explanations, Mattie was off again like a whirlwind.

A quarter of an hour later Miss Rachel passed the window just in time to see Mattie struggling along with the end of a pile of boards in one hand, the other dragging a shattered cart. Attached to the other end of the boards was a barefooted, beaming-faced boy. Miss Rachel drew her breath in sharply. It was easy to see what had happened. Why didn't Mattie tell her that she was going back to help that Wilkins boy, whose load had seemingly been too heavy for his frail, homemade cart?

Did the girl search out things like that to advertise her meddlesomeness? Miss Rachel closed her mouth grimly. She would wait until Mattie told of her wonderful goodness in going to the boy's assistance, then she would just tell her a few things that the girl didn't know. But when Mattie returned to the house, Miss Rachel listened in vain for the girl to refer to the incident. In no way did she respond to the cues Cousin Ray so adroitly put forth.

After dinner it was Mattie who asked for the privilege of being Miss Rachel's assistant, while Anna and Ruth sought the cool, inviting shade of the roomy veranda. With one of her cousin's enveloping aprons over her simple, girlish dress, Mattie attacked the pile of dishes as if she were experiencing the realization of a long-promised treat.

"Do you do these things at home?" Miss Rachel asked with an abruptness that caused Mattie nearly to drop the cherished tumbler she was polishing.

"My, yes! Mumsie calls me her right hand. She can't keep me out of the kitchen. I am not clever like the other girls, so I develop the only talent I possess—the art of meddling." Mattie's bright face and vivacious voice would never give one the impression that they belonged to a meddler, but Miss Rachel had hard work to control an audible sniff at the girl's announcement.

What a pity that Ellen had never taught her to restrain such abnormal curiosity! Evidently she was hoping to discover something of interest out here; that was the reason she was willing to become a maid of all work. Well, she wouldn't find out a single thing during the ten days of her visit, that Miss Rachel wasn't willing she should know.

As the days passed, Miss Rachel's pride in Anna increased hourly. The girl's charm never wavered. All of Cousin Ray's friends remarked on the girl's attractive personality. She was popular with young and old alike. Ruth's shyness had given way before Miss Rachel's persistent effort, and the young girl's sweetness was a never-failing delight to her hostess, who felt a sharp stab of envy whenever she remembered that Ellen was the mother of two such daughters.

Ruth was an extraordinary pianist, and with Anna's contralto voice, the old house rang with musical cheer. Miss Rachel, who was passionately fond of music, reveled in the wealth of entertainment the two girls furnished. It was cruel that Mattie should be so utterly different. She was certainly useful, Miss Rachel would tell herself with marked vehemence, in her effort to be fair to all three, but there was no escaping the girl's meddling.

That Mattie's meddling was never of the offensive kind seemed to count for little in Miss Rachel's estimation. There was something almost uncanny in the girl's always happening on the scene the exact moment her presence would prove most needed. If she hadn't been such a consummate meddler she would never have known that Anna's favorite waist needed a few stitches to be ready for evening, that Ruth's shoes were in need of polishing, or that Cousin Ray detested dishwashing with all her heart. And what always left a little rankling feeling deep down in Cousin Ray's soul, was the fear that in some way she was doing the girl an injustice.

Try as hard as she would, Miss Rachel could get no enthusiasm in her tone when she commented on Mattie. But her scrupulous sense of justice made her admit to herself that were it not for Mattie's meddling trait, she would have had far fewer hours to have listened to Ruth's polished polkas or to Anna's delightful rendering of popular patriotic airs. It was Mattie who would rush into the kitchen and coax Cousin Ray to go with the girls that she might be left undisturbed to rummage among the older woman's treasures. It was just that abominable habit, which made Mattie so seemingly unselfish, when all the time she was doing it for the sole purpose of what she could find out!

⋄⊷◉◉⊷⋄

The visit was nearly at an end, and Miss Rachel had a secret all unsuspected by any of the three girls. She had written Ellen asking that either Anna or Ruth be spared for the remainder of the month. Only that morning she had received Ellen's characteristic reply: "Select one of the three, Ray, arrange with her, and be sure that you'll have my good wishes added to my consent."

Miss Rachel sniffed ever so little at the phrase: "One of the three," then straightway dismissed the idea as preposterous. But she did wish that she were sure which one of the older ones to invite. She wanted to keep them both, but that would look strange if she sent Mattie home alone.

That afternoon the members of The Helping Hand Club were to meet with Miss Rachel, and somehow she felt sure that her decision would be influenced by the meeting. She watched Anna and Ruth flitting about the house, bestowing deft, artistic touches which only added to her longing for them both.

Out in the kitchen Mattie had turned her meddling to cake-making, and just for a minute, Miss Rachel's puritanical conscience gave her a terrible prod for not even considering including Mattie in that invitation for an extended visit. Oh, well, at seventeen Mattie was old enough to curb that desire to meddle instead of always gloating over it as she constantly did.

With the assembling of the club members Miss Rachel's pulses pounded joyously. Never had the girls shown to better advantage. Anna was Anna: sweet, gracious, charming. Ruth conquered her timidity and played delightfully. Mattie selected the work for which the members pronounced the least desire, and chatted with the guests as freely as if she had known them always.

"What are we going to do about raising the money to send that Wilkins girl away to school next month?" Miss Rachel asked unexpectedly, in an interval of silence, which made her tone audible to everyone in the room. "It seems a pity that she shouldn't be given the opportunity to cultivate her extraordinary talent for music."

The president of the club shook out the hospital pajamas on which she was sewing and looked over at Mattie. The young girl flushed hotly and bent her head lower over the button holes she was working with such infinite pains.

"O, Miss Rachel," cried impetuous Irma Blaisdell, "haven't you heard? Judge Hopkins is going to finance the scheme. And he's going to send Ramsdell Lawton to the hospital next week, too. We heard all about it last night at prayer meeting. But, of course, we were sure that Mattie had told you."

"Mattie?" echoed Miss Rachel dully. The work in her hands fell unheeded on her lap; then she rallied. "Mattie, have you been meddling in our affairs?" she asked the girl sharply.

"O, Cousin Ray." Mattie's face was a blaze of color. "I didn't mean to, honestly, I didn't, only it's just second nature for me to meddle. You know that day we came? I went to the grocer's for you." Mattie hung her head. She took two or three careful little stitches, then she reached for her spool of thread which rolled to the floor.

"We are waiting, Mattie." There was no evading Cousin Ray's question.

"Well, I got the butter and started for home, when I saw Danny Wilkins. Of course, I didn't know his name then—"

"For pity's sake, don't prolong the agony so." Cousin Ray's voice had a decided edge to its tone.

Everyone was listening avidly. Anna and Ruth leaned forward so that no word might be lost. Mattie's meddling was always worth hearing about.

"Well," she hurried on desperately, "Judge Hopkins' daughter was driving her father home in her car. She turned her head to speak to someone just behind them, when the car swerved and would have run down poor little Danny, if I hadn't happened along just then. It was nothing at all, but the poor little kid was nearly heartbroken over his ruined cart, and the judge wanted to do something to make up for it—the cart, you know." Mattie floundered for a minute, then catching herself, went on: "He decided to send Marion to school."

"How fortunate for the whole family that Danny got his cart broken," offered Miss Rachel dryly. "Now we want to know where Ramsdell Lawton comes in."

"Oh!" Mattie looked over to the president appealingly.

"Miss Mattie is far too modest," said the president. "The judge wanted to give her a diamond or something equally expensive, but she begged him to send Ramsdell to the hospital instead. But how in the world she knew about the boy's deformity is more than I can imagine. The judge knows that it was only Miss Mattie's risking her own life which saved Danny from Pearl Hopkins' criminal carelessness. No one saw the accident save the occupants of the car and one other, for the judge gave all the particulars at the meeting last night. And that is why you haven't heard it sooner, Rachel."

"Oh," cried Ruth, her eyes shining, her shyness forgotten in her admiration of Mattie, "I know now how she knew about the boy. He, Ramsdell, was the other, and Mattie coaxed him not to tell. Isn't that right, Mattie? And you persuaded the judge to send the boy to the hospital?" Ruth captured one of Mattie's industrious hands.

"Ramsdell will be a new boy when he comes out of the hospital," Mattie put in hurriedly, striving to turn the conversation away from her own exploit.

Cousin Ray deliberately arose, and crossing over to Mattie placed a resounding kiss on each rosy cheek.

"I've been a prejudiced ol' fool, Mattie. *You,* meddlesome? This town needs a heap of just such meddling! You stay with me until the opening of school, and we'll meddle until Help and Need become welded in the links of an indissoluble chain."

"Meddlesome?" Irma Blaisdell caught at the word. "And I always thought that meddlers were impossible people."

"Not the right kind," put in Anna, pride permeating her tone. "And our Meddlesome Mattie belongs to the right kind."

Lillian G. Copp

Lillian G. Copp wrote for Christian and family magazines during the first third of the twentieth century.

THE
GINGERBREAD
MEN

Mabel McKee

It was a day in which everything that could go wrong—did. What had started out as a happy day was rapidly turning into a disaster. And now Dorothea's sister Margaret had the nerve to leave the house wearing the new serge dress Dorothea had planned to wear herself!

It was just too much! But, bad as it was, that was but the beginning!

*I*t was a recreant sunbeam which came through the dormer window and fell across the pillow, wakening Dorothea. The first minute she gasped and sat up in her bed very straight. Late for work again!

Her first feeling of horror gave way to one of relief when she realized that it was Thursday. On Thursdays she didn't have to be at the library until eleven o'clock. The cadets on the library staff did reading-room duty on that day, and liked it best of all the days of the week. On the other days they arranged the books in the stacks, pasted labels, mended returned books, and did substitute work at the branches. Oh, yes, indeed, Thursday was the best day in the week for cadets of the Lindendale library. And Dorothea Burke was one of the cadets.

Quietly she sank back on her pillow once more. She was going to sleep until eight-thirty that morning, then toast some of her mother's fresh bread, and coax her to open some Sunshine strawberry preserves for her breakfast. After that luxury she would don her new serge dress, and saunter down to the library to enjoy to her heart's content the reading-room and the people who visited it.

Then she heard Bob thumping on the stairway. Before she could reach her door to lock it against his intrusion, he had it open. For one minute he surveyed his sister standing in her kimono with bare feet.

The next minute he said, "It's a good thing you're up now, 'cause I was going to tickle you with my cold hands to wake you. It's ironing day, and the Kiefners are all coming here to dinner. Mother wants you to hurry downstairs and make some gingerbread cookies before you go to the library."

Dorothea stood still and glared at Bob. But he, with all the stupidity of a nine-year-old brother, quite missed the severity of her glare. He gave her one more warning to hurry, was back in the hall again, and thumping his way down the stairs.

Dorothea reached for her clothes. Bother! She was furious at ironing day. If there were not so many younger children in the Burke family, ironing day would not be the bore for the older girls that it was. Why did Mother allow the Kiefner children to come to their house that day to dinner? She would have told them that Mother was too busy to entertain them that day.

Bother again! That was because making gingerbread cookies was such messy work. She would feel all stuffy and weary and out of humor by the time she reached the library. All the joy of being in the reading-room would be spoiled before it was begun. Even the wearing of the new dress lost some of its allure.

A few minutes later, clad in a big-sleeved apron, Dorothea entered the Burke kitchen. Quite omitting a good-morning greeting to her mother, though the latter looked up from her ironing to smile cheerfully at her daughter, Dorothea plunged instantly into a question. "Mother, did you remember to sew the hooks on my new serge dress? It wasn't on the hanger in my closet, and I was afraid you'd forgotten it."

Mother's brown head, streaked with gray, shook an answer, and then her soft, low voice gave an explanation. " 'Twas Margaret, darling, who sewed the hooks on," she answered, "and put a lovely bit of lace in the neck for a collar. And this morning, when she started for the teacher's institute to be on the program, your father and I both insisted that she wear the dress. She bought the twins' coats with her last month's salary, and didn't have any money left to buy herself even a dress, so—"

"She should have asked me for my new dress." Dorothea was half angry now. "I wouldn't have cared half so much on any other day. But today is Thursday, and we cadets are all in the reading-room, where everybody sees us. All the girls had planned to dress up, and now I can't."

Mother Burke was all contrition. She knew Margaret would be even more sorry than she was. She put the iron on the stove, and coming over to where her second daughter was kneading the cookie dough, gave her a motherly hug and kiss. "Just this once won't matter so much, will it, dear?" she asked. "You can dress up every Thursday afterward for the rest of the winter."

Dorothea couldn't be disagreeable after that. No one could resist Mother. Forcing a faint smile, she rolled the dough into a thin layer and went to get the cookie cutters. She would make rings, triangles, half-moons, and everything. And then once more disappointment lay before her. The cookie cutters were not to be found. Mrs. Kiefner, who was lending her children today, had borrowed the cutters last week and had not returned them.

"You'll have to use a can lid." Mother was frankly disappointed herself. Gingerbread cookies cut with a can lost half their attraction. The children liked them in many shapes and forms.

Dorothea did too, so she hesitated a minute. Hurrah! She remembered the little "gingerbread-man" cutter she had bought a few days before and had never used. She brought it from her room. When they were cut and baked, those threescore gingerbread men lay on the table ready for the hearty appetites the guests were sure to have.

"It will be a real party for them," Mother said in a happy tone of voice.

Now she would not have to cook a company dinner, but would feed the guests the simple lunch she had planned for her own family. That would give her a chance to get her ironing done. She patted Dorothea's shoulder. "Run upstairs and slip into your dress," she said, "while I spread a clean towel on the corner of the table and make you a bit of toast. I'm going to open the last can of Sunshine strawberry preserves for you. Surely, if any one deserves them, it's a girl who helps her mother as you do."

In spite of the crisp, buttery toast and luxurious preserves, Dorothea could not forget the pretty new serge dress her sister Margaret had worn to work. The thought took most of the joy out of the crisp November morning.

Arrived at the library, Dorothea, in her old dress, tried to look as trim as the other girls, but felt that she failed dismally.

She was sure she had when the head librarian walked into the reading-room. A supply of books was needed at the Thompson branch. Miss McCarty had been taken ill suddenly, and was obliged to leave for the day.

The Thompson was the worst branch in town. To begin with, the library was a dark little room and not always kept clean. Besides, Miss McCarty was cross most of the time, and the children disliked not only her, but all the members of her guild. They believed librarians were their avowed enemies. They couldn't often wreak vengeance on strict Miss McCarty, but they never missed an opportunity to do so to the substitutes who were sent to the branch when she was absent.

"Miss Dorothea," the head librarian said, "I'm going to send you to Thompson today."

Sighs of relief came from all the other cadets.

Dorothea shook part of her anger off into her coat as she put it on. Then she made a hurried rush for the telephone. No one was in the mending-room, and she wasn't going to miss the chance of telling her mother what a miserable day was before her and what had caused it.

"I won't be home to lunch." Tears were in her voice as she talked. "I have to go to that horrid old Thompson branch. The head sent me because I was the only cadet who wore old clothes today. She knew my clothes couldn't be hurt in that wretched little hole. Tell one of the girls to have the bed ready for me when I get home, for I know I shall be just ready to perish."

The telephone receiver went into its hook with a bang, and Dorothea was out of the mending-room, through the hall, and on the street. Here trouble still pursued her. The streetcars going east had been held up on account of a broken trolley, and she was more than half an hour getting out to the Thompson branch. Miss McCarty, already dressed in her heavy coat and scarf, was glaring. She snapped at Dorothea, much to the delight of several youngsters.

After they and Miss McCarty had gone, Dorothea dissolved into tears. Then, she happened to look out of the window, and instantly dashed the tears from her eyes. The six children who had been in the library had gone out after six more of their kind. The word that a substitute librarian was on duty was all the inducement needed to bring a crowd.

"Oh," Dorothea closed her eyes wearily, "what a day! First I had to get up early to make gingerbread men for those bother-some Kiefner children, because it was ironing day. Then I had to wear my old dress because Margaret chose to appropriate my new one. And since I was the shabbiest-looking assistant, I had this job wished on me for today."

She dashed the tears out of her eyes. "Gingerbread men," she scoffed, "and children, and branch libraries and—"

Then the telephone bell rang, and brought with it the worst news of the worst calamity of the day. It was Betty Bird, one of the most dressed-up cadets, talking. Roger Lewis had arrived at the main library, it seemed, right after she had left. He had walked in smiling, and introduced himself exactly as if he were just a citizen of their town, and not a famous New York writer.

"He's tall and thin and has sandy red hair." Betty was bubbling over with joy. "And he's asked us all out to dinner tonight. He said right at the start that he was looking for material and characters for his next book. We're all exerting ourselves to be interesting so he'll use us. It's a calamity you have to be at that Thompson branch instead of here. But the 'head' says for you not to miss the dinner, and—"

A crash from the reading table called Dorothea back to her own responsibilities. The dozen Thompson children, while her back had been turned, had staged a battle, using books as their weapons—and most effective ones they were!

Dorothea was across the room in a moment. Just as her grasp tightened on Benny Burris' shoulder, she heard a cheery whistle at the door, and turned. There was Tom, the oldest member of the Burke family, and in his hand a big basket covered by one of his mother's blue-and-white checked towels.

"Mother sent these to you and the kiddies," he murmured, when Dorothy reached him. "She thought they might help you keep them quiet. She said stuffed children, like stuffed bears, are always harmless."

The dozen children dropped their books and watched Tom when they heard his whistle. Now they stared at the big basket he handed the "library substitute." They continued to watch silently as she carried it across the room to her desk.

Curious herself, Dorothy lifted the towel. Under it were the threescore gingerbread men, brown, crispy, and alluring, the very ones she herself had made that morning. They looked so odd ranged in rows in the basket, that Dorothea herself had to giggle. That giggle brought the crowd of children to her side.

In the rush, Dorothea forgot that she was a dignified librarian who had to inspire awe in the hearts of the Thompson children if she would be a success after the ideal of Miss McCarty. She became, instead, a big sister, exactly as she was to the children at home when gingerbread cakes were being distributed. The old slogan her mother used at home sprang to her lips: "Gingerbread for just good children," she said.

Came an instant surge of promises, followed by definite examples. Several were picking up the books from the floor and placing them on the shelves, others arranging the chairs, and others skipping here and there, doing her bidding. More skipping, more sweeping, a little dusting, and the room was in apple-pie order.

"Oh teacher, put them all out on the table," begged one little Thompsonite with dancing blue eyes and a shock of sandy hair. "Let's put them out like a parade of soldiers, and tell stories about them."

Dorothea laughed. "All right," she agreed, the big-sister element still paramount. "Clean hands, everybody, and then we'll arrange the regiments."

Soon they were ready, and sixteen little youngsters—four new recruits had been added to the company—were ranged around the table while Dorothea told the story of the knights of the Round Table, adding the adventures of the followers of each knight. She had often wanted to explain chivalry to those children, but never before had she been able to do it. Now it was easy. They sat spellbound while she told of the virtues of each little gingerbread man in an armor of courage, a helmet of courtesy, and over all a mailed coat of goodness.

"Of course you'll all get a gingerbread knight and some of his followers for your own," she said. "I want you to choose which knights you want."

Their hands were clasped while they studied. Each was trying to remember the virtues of the knight he wanted for his own. The library was perfectly quiet until the door opened and the head librarian and the visiting author stepped into the room.

The tall, thin man, with blue eyes and thick red hair, Dorothea recognized instantly from Betty's description, and was rendered speechless. But not the children. Famous writers meant little to them. They were living the days of feudalism again, and as knights, they intended to show courtesy to the lady for whose graces they were all willing to struggle now.

So their childish choices went on, and Dorothea, called to attention by them, began to go on with her story. The visitors joined the group. While they stood motionless, the game and story went on and on and on.

At last the author spoke. "I must have this scene in my book in the chapter on community work," he said. "The children, the little librarian, and even the gingerbread men." He bowed to Dorothea. "I want to show the modern girl who has her own way of working out community problems."

Just before six o'clock Dorothea was sent home in a taxicab to get ready for the dinner. "The girl who is to be in a book must sit next to the guest of honor," the head librarian had told her, "and I imagine she wants to look very, very attractive."

"I want to see Mother most of all," Dorothea whispered back, exactly like a little girl.

It was Mother who met her at the front door. Dorothea's arrival home had been preceded by a telephone call. And Mother knew why she was coming. In her hand was Dorothea's one silk dress, which she had just pressed for the occasion. "I know all about it, dear," she said, "so you mustn't talk, but hurry."

It was Mother's way to laugh at big events. But her heart

thrilled with pride, and it thrilled even more when Dorothea insisted on telling her of how it had all happened because of the basket of gingerbread men she had sent to the library.

"I had a feeling that those gingerbread men were going to have a grand career when you cut them this morning," Mother said. "I felt they were going to help you win out at that troublesome Thompson branch. So I gave the Kiefners and Burkes bread and milk and doughnuts. And you're always to remember, my dear, that the biggest and best things are often started by the little things which seem unimportant at the time."

"Such as gingerbread men," Dorothea laughed back, her eyes shining.

"Yes," Mother nodded, "if you're sure to use as much love as sugar in the mixing, even gingerbread men can move a world of grown-ups from trouble to help, and from unhappiness to happiness."

Mabel McKee

Mabel McKee, who wrote early in the twentieth century, was responsible for some of the most memorable and beloved inspirational stories of her time.

JUST ONE THING
BEAUTIFUL

Catherine R. Britton

"*That's what my teacher said—" declared Dorrie—
"that everyone ought to have something outstandingly
beautiful in her life.*"

*So she set about to find that elusive something, only
to discover . . .*

*T*here is nothing I enjoy more than studying in Dorrie Potter's living room. With a family like hers something more exciting than Latin or European history is bound to happen.

I knew on this particular night that something was brewing because Dorrie simply couldn't keep her mind on solid geometry. She drew her fingers halfheartedly, forgot what she was doing several times, and finally she threw down her pencil.

"You know what, Jean Campbell? She was absolutely right," she said.

"Huh?" I asked, startled.

"Miss Williams," she explained. Miss Williams was our home-economics teacher, and I was beginning to see the light. She had given us a lecture that afternoon, and evidently something in it had impressed Dorrie more than was absolutely necessary. "I mean, what she said—that everyone ought to have something outstandingly beautiful in her life."

Dorrie's big brother, Lee, looked up with a grin. "It's sure lucky you've got me, Sis," he commented, and I chuckled. If there was anything less beautiful than Lee Potter! At the moment he was leaning both elbows on the table to puzzle over civil engineering problems in a library book. Lee worked after school, just as Dorrie did, to save money for college; and he spent his evenings studying things far in advance of his high-school work. So you could forgive him if he sometimes skipped a necktie and if his hair usually looked as if he had combed it by running the fingers of both hands through it.

Ten-year-old Vera, called the Vixen, was the next to add her bit. She was an adorable youngster who perpetually annoyed Dorrie by preferring anything to looking dressed-up and beautiful. "If you had a quarter—on account of I have a nickel—we could both have rainbow sundaes at Matthews', and they're utterly beautiful," she suggested. She was carefully applying red paint to a wobbly table of her own construction.

Dorrie ignored the two of them. "Look at this town, what's beautiful about it? Plain square houses and not even a hill to make a nice background," she said. "And what's beautiful about this house?"

"The Potters," I said.

She leaned back dreamily. "Here I am working night after night at the ugliest market in the world, just to save money for the future. What's the future, anyway, when you have only a barren present?"

Dorrie's father came out from behind his newspaper at that. He was mighty proud of his children, and dreadfully ambitious for them. "If you feel that way, Dorrie, why don't you spend your next salary check and get something for yourself? Dare say it'd be worth it to you."

A sparkle crept into Dorrie's eyes. "I won't take any out of the bank, but next time I'm paid I could spend it for just one thing that I want—for one thing that is beautiful."

"Honey," her mother reminded softly, "you should have new shoes next month."

"I'll have these fixed. What are shoes compared with beauty?"

Lee snorted. "Try going without them once. You'll see." The rest of us were silent, and Dorrie mulled over the idea in her active brain. When Dorrie thinks, it's like rubbing two pieces of flint together. You can fairly see the sparks fly.

"I'm going to do it," she decided suddenly, and she went back to solid geometry with a vengeance.

⋅–⟫═◉═⟪–⋅

That was the beginning of Dorrie Potter's search for something beautiful. Except in school I didn't see much of her for three days, and so in desperation I went to the Market one afternoon after school on the pretext of buying a loaf of bread just to get a chance for a chat with her.

As usual, she was fairly buzzing. Honestly, I've never seen anyone as capable of hard work as Dorrie. She went from one customer to another, making them all feel happy and friendly, wrapping up packages skillfully, and making change automatically.

Mr. Beemer spied me and grinned. "What's come over her?"

"What's the joke?" I demanded.

"She says we have to be beautiful," he chuckled. "Would you look at them Jonathans?" He pointed to the window where five baskets of Jonathan apples reposed. But at the top of the window hung a little fringe of green crepe paper, and streamers of the same stuff went back to each basket to tie in a bow at the handle. Frankly, I thought it was the silliest thing I had ever in my life seen but I didn't say so.

"And from now on our cans have to go in just so," he continued. I looked at the shelf decorated with crepe paper where the stacks of canned goods had been formed into graceful pyramids.

He shook his head once more. "She's good help, and if she says we got to be beautiful then we got to be."

It was almost closing time, so I hung around to walk home with Dorrie. She was full of chatter, but I got to the point where I thought I'd scream if she used the word beautiful once more.

But of course she did.

"Jeannie," she said wistfully. "I've always saved my money

carefully, and this isn't asking too much, is it? To want just one thing beautiful in all my drab life?"

The Vixen saved me from exploding and saying that there was certainly nothing drab about her life. The Vixen, it seemed, had been helping the neighborhood gang dig a cave after school, and she was filthy dirty when she loped up to walk with us. But there was something in her eyes that made up for all the dirt.

"Have you picked out what you're going to buy, Dorrie?" she demanded.

Dorrie smiled at her and nodded. "Yep. But it's a secret. It's something perfectly, utterly beautiful."

The Vixen sighed. "Isn't she funny, Jean? Wanting something just on account of it's pretty. A box of tools would be a lot more useful."

Small towns have a habit of catching on to a joke and developing it. And thus the joke of Dorrie Potter's beautifying the Market was all over town. "Wonder when she'll start puttin' bows on the tin cans," someone might ask; and a guffawing comrade would retort, "Yeah, or stick posies out of the potato sacks." But they all liked Dorrie so it didn't matter much if they wanted to laugh at her. They would also add, "She's a fine girl, Dorrie Potter."

And they were right. Disgusted as I was at this latest idea of hers, I had to admit that friends didn't come any finer than Dorrie. I had to sympathize, too. There had never been any extra money in the Potter family, none left over to buy the little things that I took for granted. Dorrie's clothes were made over more than once before she handed them down to the Vixen. Dorrie's room was shared with the Vixen, and the small sister did have a dismaying habit of stuffing the room with her homemade cabinets that wobbled, doll tables that were tipsy, and boxes that wouldn't close. But I would have given my nice room with all its beautiful trimmings any day in the year in exchange for one of the worshiping glances that the Vixen freely bestowed upon Dorrie, or for a big brother to tease me as Lee teased Dorrie.

I really thought all along that this mood of Dorrie's would wear off. But as the days went on, her zeal for beauty increased, much to the disgust of Lee and the Vixen. Her mother and father remained sympathetic to the end.

After all, Dorrie wasn't asking for so much, I told myself. She wasn't asking for a life of ease. In fact, she loved the hard work that her job gave her.

⊷⊶

"People are so funny," she laughed one night when I was studying with her. "Honestly, Mrs. Weeks picks out every string bean separately, and the kids get all wrought up over how to spend their pennies. You never really know your neighbors until you've quoted the price of everything in the store to them, and then sent them out with one five-cent bag of salt."

"Don't tell me you like them!" Lee grinned.

Off guard, Dorrie responded enthusiastically, "I love them."

And that, of course, left an opening for Lee's teasing retort, "Oh but they aren't beautiful!"

The nicest thing about studying with Dorrie is that the minute the last lesson is done, the whole family sits around to talk chummily for a while before bedtime. Then Dorrie's father tells about work. Her mother gets in a few worried bits of advice about getting our feet wet or eating too many cookies. The Vixen tells in detail about the latest thing she has made with her prized possession—a hammer rescued from the junk heap—and Lee tells about the things that he plans to do with the long life that lies ahead of him.

"Think maybe I'll squander five dollars," he said once. But he wasn't going to squander it for ice skates or new clothes. "I saw a set of civil engineering books in the second-hand store. Mighty good books."

There was never a nicer family than the Potters, nor one that had so much fun, nor one whose individual members cared more for what happened to all the other members.

But I didn't try to explain that to Dorrie during those days.

"Just two more weeks," she said once. And suddenly it was one more week, and then only a few more days until her month of work was up and she could buy her heart's desire.

"If I work all day Saturday Mr. Beemer's going to let me off half an hour early on payday because I told him I had some shopping to do. Will you go with me, Jean?"

Dear Dorrie! Her eyes were shining brighter than diamonds, and for the life of me I couldn't have refused her plea. "I wouldn't miss it," I told her.

⇥≡◉◖≡⇤

When the great day came I was at the store about half an hour before closing time. I saw Mr. Beemer count out her month's pay—fifteen dollars. Twinkling all over he cautioned her, "Now don't forget to put some by for a rainy day."

Dorrie choked a little bit and looked at the precious money.

"Good night, Mr. Beemer," she said.

Outside the door she grabbed my hand. "Hurry, Jean. We have to get to the art store before it closes."

We fairly ran, and when we reached our destination she

slowed to a dignified walk. "We have to look like patrons of the arts," she grinned as we stepped into the town's one really first-class store. She led me straight to the spot where her treasure lay.

It was a picture. Oh, a nice enough picture, but I must admit it was a little disappointing. Imagine being so excited over a landscape with a few trees and a little blurb of water.

A clerk came up, and Dorrie said softly, "How much is it?"

"That oil? Isn't it a lovely thing?" purred the woman. "One hundred and fifty dollars."

I gasped, thinking of how lonesome Dorrie's poor fifteen dollars must feel in such an atmosphere. But Dorrie looked stricken with paralysis. Without a word she turned and walked from the store.

"Dorrie, honey, don't mind it so much," I cried, wondering what I could possibly say to comfort her. The doors swung into place behind us, and we walked along the street silently. I watched her face, and I knew that she was close to tears. After all, a person like Dorrie Potter does nothing by halves, and when she had made up her mind that she wanted that picture she had made it up completely.

We were passing the hardware store when she paused, looking in at a beautiful set of tools just right for a ten-year-old.

"Jean," she said unhappily, "if you had a sister who liked hammers better than dolls, what would you do?"

I could answer that all right. "I'd simply love her to death," I said.

Dorrie nodded and walked into the store. "Someone might as well be happy," she said. She bought the tools for two dollars. While she was there she invested five dollars in a toaster.

"Mother always has to use an old one on the stove," she explained.

Then we hurried on, but not toward home. She was going to do this right.

We reached the second-hand store and went in. "There was a set of second-hand books here that Lee Potter was looking at," she began, and in a minute it was all settled. I was staggering under the tool chest and the toaster while Dorrie carried the four huge books. It was a good thing that we had only a few blocks to go, or we never would have made it.

The entire Potter family was gathered at the door to see what it was that Dorrie had planned to get—her one thing that was beautiful. You can just imagine the excitement that followed, but you can't possibly imagine the look in the Vixen's eyes as she reverently handled each piece of her tool kit, or the energy with which Lee plunged into his books, or the fun they all had hooking up their parents' new toaster.

"But how about you, Daughter?" Dorrie's father wanted to know, looking for another package. "You were going to get yourself something beautiful."

She was watching the family, and a strange something was dawning in her eyes. "Maybe I did, Pop," she said slowly—looking at Lee buried behind a book, at the Vixen already mending a crippled chair.

I was to stay with Dorrie that night and just as we were ready to hop into bed the door was pushed silently open. A small Vixen crept in with both hands behind her back.

"Dorrie," she whispered, "on account of I love you so much, I got something perfectly beautiful for you."

And she produced it from behind her back—a picture cut from a magazine and all framed in the Vixen's best style of carpentry.

The edges didn't fit, and the frame was painted a most hideous purple. But I could tell that Dorrie, looking from the funny picture to the adorable Vixen, was viewing perfect beauty at last. She hugged her small sister and then went gravely to the wall to hang the picture on a nail that was there.

"Know what, Vix?" she asked chummily. "I put that nail there just yesterday. I thought that sometime I might have the most beautiful picture in the world to hang there. And now I have it."

Catherine R. Britton

Catherine R. Britton wrote for family and inspirational magazines during the first half of the twentieth century.

RUTH AND REBECCA

Mary R. Platt Hatch

This is the oldest story in the collection, not only in its setting but also in terms of when it was written (late 1800s). It takes us back to the early world of America's Quakers, when a father's decisions were absolute, when an engaged couple was required to declare their intentions three times in the meeting house, when people were referred to as "thee" and "thou," when men were referred to as "Friend" and married women as "Dame."

Ruth and Rebecca (cousins raised as sisters) and Jacob (who loves the one who doesn't love him and is loved by the one whom he doesn't love) represent the triangle upon which this old story is based. And Anson is the wild card.

The author intrusion, use of "I," pontification, and overt moralizing are all typical of nineteenth-century writers.

Nestled cosily among the hills of New Jersey, there stood an old farmhouse, browned and discolored by the winds and tempests which had beaten against it for half a century. The low roof and small windows added to its homely appearance; but the eye seeking to find some beautiful features upon which to rest, would not be disappointed in the general surroundings.

Nowhere did the sun shine more brightly than around that old farm house, and, as if trying to make amends for its ugliness, lighted it up with its rays, just as happiness with its vivifying power lights up the most rugged countenance. Sturdy elms and "saplings tall" encircled, where sang and twittered the birds amid the foliage, and undisturbed built their nests and reared their young. At a little distance a brook wound along its silver course where the fish sported in its limpid water.

Nature, not Friend Hazlett, had made the scene beautiful. "Everything for use, nothing for show," could plainly be seen was the idea carried out by the worthy owner of the farm house. The neat fences and substantial barns betokened thriftiness; while pervading all was a Quaker-like simplicity, very different from the noise and bustle of the city not far distant. The cows browsing in a pasture hard by had a quiet and subdued look, never indulging in any of those antics which even the *cows* of the world's people occasionally display, but placidly chewed their cuds, evidently in profound meditation. The old gray mare that had carried Friend Hazlett and his good wife to meeting for almost twenty years, moved about with a slow and stately step, as though feeling her great responsibility. Even the hens clucked less and laid oftener than those of the world's people; and the lusty chanticleer, scorning to deceive, crowed only at daybreak.

As his surroundings indicated, Friend Hazlett was a good, substantial farmer, with none of the foolish sentimentality that would prompt him to spend his time in externals which were of no value; but he had acquired a competence by quiet, persistent efforts, aided by his wife, who was a helpmeet, indeed.

Friend Hazlett, with his broad brimmed hat shading a shrewd, good humored face, was the facsimile of one's idea of a Quaker, as was the rather more subdued wife upon whose countenance mildness and humility had left their impress.

Growing in dark places and among the marshes and swamps, one often finds the choicest flowers; and there, in that old farmhouse, sheltered by a father's care, fostered by a mother's love, lived and grew to womanhood two fair maidens, both beautiful, but as unlike in disposition as in features.

Rebecca was tall and queenly, with hair which would rival the raven's wing for blackness, and eyes that should rather have belonged to some Egyptian princess than a simple Quaker maiden. Somewhat willful was Rebecca, and she sometimes grew restless at the restraint placed upon her by her parents, and she often wondered why it was wrong to wear anything but drab. Nature was gorgeous in coloring, with its brilliant flowers and its beautiful green. The blue sky was often filled with clouds of many hues, while the rainbow spanning the heavens was a delight to the Quaker, though he refused to adopt any of its colors.

Affectionate and loving was Rebecca, and all these little fancies she kept to herself, knowing, if told, they would worry her mother without benefiting herself; so every day she donned her humble garb and went about her work, though she would wish to herself it were pink instead of drab, for it would be so much more becoming.

Ruth was not the daughter of Friend Hazlett. His brother had married the only sister of Dame Hazlett; and when little Ruth was bereft of both her parents, too young to feel her loss, they were replaced by the uncle and aunt who were ready to take her to their hearts and rear her with their own daughter, scarcely more beloved.

Ruth was the image of what her aunt must have been at her age. The same dove-like eyes, the same sweet placidity of manner marked them both; but while many silver threads streaked the brown hair of Dame Hazlett, Ruth's was a burnished gold upon which the sun loved to linger. Quietly she moved about, saying little, never gay and seldom sad. She had none of the wild spirit which made Rebecca so bewitching, none of her willfulness; but always serene, always sweet, she was dearly loved by her more impetuous cousin.

No lover had little Ruth; but Rebecca had many among the Quaker youths, though none seemed to suit her wayward fancy; and poor Jacob Hancock, the most devoted of them all, sighed in vain for some token that she loved him. They had been playmates from childhood; and while with Jacob the childish partiality had become a passion, Rebecca thought of him only as the friend of her younger years, and seemed unaware of his love, though he showed it in every change of his manly countenance.

What might have been the effect of time and such a love as his it is impossible to say, but an aunt residing in Philadelphia wrote to her brother, requesting that one of her nieces might visit her, and he, thinking only of the prim, demure little maiden who a dozen years before had married a wealthy Quaker of that city, unhesitatingly gave his consent to her visit. Quiet little Ruth had said at once that she preferred to stay at home, and so Rebecca with her wonderful beauty left the homely cares of the farmhouse and anon was at the elegant home of her aunt. Very gay had Aunt Betsey become since her removal to the city—how gay, Friend Hazlett had no idea or he would have hesitated long before he allowed Rebecca to leave the fostering care of her mother.

Associating much with the world's people she had half unconsciously acquired many of their ways and habits; and of the many peculiarities which characterize the Friend, she retained only the quaint phraseology. Even this was ignored by Hannah, or Anna as she was generally called, a step daughter of hers whom it puzzled Rebecca much to understand. Without knowing why, she instinctively distrusted her. Selfishness appeared to be her most prominent characteristic, and all others were subordinate to this. Want of principle was hidden more deeply beneath a pleasant exterior, and its extent could only be guessed at. When her will was not crossed in any way, no one could be more agreeable than Miss Anna, and, as a consequence, she had many admirers. She was a brilliant conversationalist, a fine musician and possessed a good voice for singing, but in beauty she was far surpassed by her cousin as well as in all the qualities of the heart.

Rebecca showed a wonderful faculty for acquiring the manners which belong to a good society, and she wore with the air of a princess the rich clothes which her aunt insisted upon providing. It seemed as though she had been masquerading all these years in her simple Quaker dress, and that now was the magical twelve o'clock when she appeared in her true character. Not that Rebecca had thrown aside her individuality, but it showed to better advantage in her present surroundings. Her affectionate heart and quiet dignity were still retained, and these qualities were the first that attracted Anson Caldwell to her: she was so different from most of the belles of his acquaintance.

Rich, talented and handsome, and perhaps a little conceited, he had come to think of himself a target at which the shafts of Cupid were continually being launched, but never did he own himself wounded by the blind god until he saw Rebecca. To her, contrasted with her Quaker lovers, he seemed the embodiment of every manly virtue and possessed of every grace under the sun; and the affection of a lifetime lavished upon her by Jacob Hancock was vanquished by the love of one, perhaps less honest and true, but more pleasing to one like Rebecca.

Mr. Caldwell's attentions were too evident to escape the notice of Anna, who had no ill-will for her cousin, so long as she thwarted none of her plans; but Anson Caldwell had long before been secretly appropriated, for besides being handsome, he was rich, which she considered of far more importance. To see her cousin winning without an effort what she had wanted so long was most galling to one of her disposition, but she was powerless to do aught to prevent it until Rebecca's visit should end. And it ended as she had hoped it would: without a declaration of love from Anson, who, with some of his old distrust, neglected to say the words which would bind her to him. He only said at parting, "I shall see you soon. Will you welcome me?"

Her blushing face showed him how gladly she would do so, and soon she was speeding towards home filled with pleasant thoughts. Jolts, jars, new faces, moving scenes and she was again surrounded by kind friends, and looking at them all, she wondered how she could have been contented so long apart from them. Ruth was the same dear cousin, quiet as of yore, and Jacob, with his radiant face, appeared the personification of happiness, so pleased was he with the graciousness of Rebecca, who, on this night of her return, overflowed with gay spirits, which came bubbling up from her happy heart. She romped with the dog, and smoothed the sleek coat of puss, who was too lazy to show his approval except by winking and purring in the most comfortable manner.

Rebecca was up early the next morning, going about her old duties with her accustomed cheerfulness, and her mother was thankful to see that her visit had not spoiled her for useful occupation. While she sometimes longed for the cultivated society of the city, she never gave expression to the wish, and went on in this light-hearted way until Jacob overcame his bashfulness enough to ask her to share his home. Very kindly she told him she did not love him, so kindly that he did not give up hope but continued quiet attentions, aided to the utmost by Friend Hazlett, who thought him an excellent match for his daughter.

Spring had come and gone with its April rains and May flowers, and the rare days of June had again appeared; but Anson Caldwell came not, and Rebecca, weary with watching and waiting, became pale and dejected. The nights spent in tears brought no refreshment, and Dame Hazlett, with her warm mother's heart, sadly wondered what could be the matter with her usually sprightly Rebecca, who drank all of the herb drinks she prepared, and yet grew no better, though she abated not one jot of her usual labor.

"It never rains but it pours," became something more than an idle saying to Dame Hazlett, for about this time Ruth, always silent, became more subdued and sad, though, like Rebecca, she made no complaint. In great perplexity the mother tried to fathom the cause of their dejection, continuing to steep roots and herbs, prompted by the desire to do something, but knowing that they were worthless.

Jacob, too, was unhappy, for he began to see that his love was not prized by Rebecca, and when he came to the farmhouse, instead of talking with Friend Hazlett about farming and sheep raising, as usual, or about his mother's rheumatism with Dame Hazlett, he would sit silent and dejected.

One morning when the sultry days of July had come with their languor and depression, Rebecca stood churning at the dairy door. A large checked apron encompassed her form in its capacious folds, and as her white arms went up and down, her thoughts, unconsciously, influenced her movements. A quick, vigorous churning, and she was recalling the pleasant visit to her aunt's: the balls, parties, rides and walks. Her movements became more gentle as she thought of one whose presence had made her so happy, whose smile was dearer to her than all the wealth of the Indies. But where was he now, with his tender glances that spoke volumes? All those months had passed and yet he came not. Jacob still persisting in his attentions, Ruth looked pale, Father stern, Mother sad and—the churning ceased, her face bent over her hands and she was weeping. Slowly the tears trickled through her fingers as she silently wept, and she saw not the shadow cast upon the floor by her Quaker lover who had come upon her unawares. Seeing her thus, moved his loving heart, and going to her side he asked, tenderly, "What ails thee, Rebecca? Let me finish thy churning and thee go and lie down."

"Thank thee, Jacob, nothing ails me," answered Rebecca.

"Can I do nothing for thee? It grieves me sore to see thee so sorrowful," he said. "Is thy father unkind?"

"Yes, and 'tis all on thy account. Father and mother keep urging me to 'pass meeting' with thee, and though I have told thee that my heart is not thine, thee keeps coming here as though thee were my lover. Thee has always been a friend to me, Jacob, and why does thee worry me so now?"

"Worry thee? Worry thee?" exclaimed the young man, passionately; then controlling himself said, sadly, "I would in no wise constrain thee, Rebecca, but I thought thee would get love, but I'll worry thee no more."

Before, Rebecca had thought only of her own grief, but now, seeing his sorrow, she said, gently, "Thee is too good for me, Jacob. Let us forget that we are aught but the little children that used to play together."

"Perhaps thee can, but I cannot," said he, as though all life and hope had left him, and he was going out when Rebecca said, "Thee is not alone in thy grief. If thy heart is wounded, mine is broken," and the tears, which had only been checked for a while began to flow afresh.

Roused from his grief by her sorrow, he came back saying, remorsefully, "Forgive me, Rebecca, if I was selfish. Tell me thy trouble, and if there is aught I can do for thee, I will do it even if it break my heart. Does thee love another, and does thy father object to him?"

Months of secret grief were wearing away her life; and when Jacob asked so sympathizingly to know what troubled her, putting aside his own feelings the while, she told him all, and he listened, though each word seemed to pierce his heart, making it bleed anew.

He comforted her by saying all would yet be right, and gave her a hundred reasons which might have detained her lover; then the generous fellow left her to think of his own grief, which he had kept carefully hid from Rebecca, fearing to distress her. He leaned over the pasture bars and all the world seemed robed in black. The singing of birds fell upon his ear unheeded and the beautiful sunshine gave no light to him.

A light touch on his arm roused him from his reverie, and turning he saw Ruth with her dove-like eyes looking into his so sorrowfully.

"Don't fret, then, Jacob," she said. "It cannot be that Rebecca will throw away such love as thine."

"Thank thee, little Ruth, for thy sympathy, but I have nothing to hope for," and he looked kindly at the little figure at his side, whose heart seemed mirrored in her eyes. Something of the real truth dawned upon him as he looked and prevented the kiss which he was about to implant upon her brow. He said, instead, "Thee had better run in, Ruth; I'm afraid thee'll take cold," and as she obediently left him Jacob, looking at her retreating form, said to himself, *Why could it not have been Ruth? She loves me, and I love Rebecca.*

Ah, Jacob, you are not the first who has wondered why so much love is often lavished in vain and so often misplaced. There are men who placed their affections upon women whose beauty is their all, and who prize their love no more than a new bonnet; while others, by whom it would have been treasured as the dearest gift of earth, take their places at the fireside of another's home. The world mocks at the old maid's disappointment, but the angels weep o'er love misplaced. Many a man, fitted to become the head of a household, wanders alone because some time in the past a sweet voice sang in his ear, or hand clasped his own and, though she did not love him, no other could take her place in his affections.

While Rebecca was watching and waiting for one who came

not, that one was being deceived by the machinations of Anna, who easily worked upon his natural distrust, which even the truthfulness of Rebecca did not overcome.

Feigning not to understand his love for Rebecca, she told him of Jacob Hancock, whom she said had been Rebecca's lover since childhood; and growing yet bolder, one day, she declared the two were to be married the coming autumn. She told him, too, that they were engaged even before Rebecca's visit to the city; that she wished to keep it secret for some purpose, but that now there was no harm in telling it. It was strange that he should be so ready to believe all she told him; but 'tis often so, that men fall prey to their own distrust, and while seeking to avoid a far-off danger, fall into the snare under their feet.

If Anna expected Anson would offer her the love which she had tried to prove to him was worthless to Rebecca, she was most signally disappointed, for always distrustful, somewhat inclined to cynicism, he now completely deserted the drawing-room where he had once been an honored though infrequent guest. He was not one to wear his heart on his sleeve for doves to peck at; but he suffered nonetheless. His disappointment did not make him more tenderhearted as Jacob's did. He was cast in a sterner mould, and pride, unknown to Jacob, was almost as strong as his love, and this had been terribly wounded. He tried by every means in his power to forget her, but her bright, youthful face, so innocent looking, would sometimes rise up before his mind and cause him to almost doubt what Anna had told him. Then his distrust of all women would return, and he would mutter savagely, "Women are all deceitful, and if they look inno-cent it's because they have more dissimulation." Pardon him, ye who have kind sisters and a good mother. His parents died when he was a child, and his only sister was a fashionable woman with her heart crusted over by worldliness and pride.

He was a lawyer; for even in this city of Brotherly Love there are disputes to be settled, claims to be righted, that only the man of law can adjust, and he now paid unremitting attention to his clients, seeking by occupation to forget, though the task bade fair to be as interminable as Penelope's famous web.

One day, while seated in his office, the pert young clerk ushered in a young Friend. Without any unnecessary preliminaries he inquired, "Is thy name Anson Caldwell?"

"It is," returned the lawyer; "can I do anything for you?"

"Yes, I came to consult thee concerning some land in our town about which there is much dispute," replied the young man.

"Where does this land lie?" inquired the lawyer, who was taking notes of the conversation.

"In Orley, New Jersey."

"What name?" asked the lawyer, who the young Friend noticed appeared much interested since the name of the town was mentioned.

"Jacob Hancock," and the lawyer's hand trembled visibly as he noted it down. Could it be possible that fate had thrown in his way the one who had deprived him of Rebecca? He determined to make some inquiries; so after the consultation about the disputed land was ended, he said, as if incidentally:

"You are from Orley, I think you said. There was a young lady from Orley visiting this city last winter. Miss Hazlett was her name. Are you acquainted with her?"

"Yes," said Jacob. "We have been acquainted for years."

"I have heard," said Anson, "that she is about to be married."

"Thee has been misinformed. There are many who would

gladly pass meeting with Rebecca, but she favors none in our town," said Jacob, who was disposed to give him all the information the remark would warrant.

"I will go to Orley in a few days to see about that land," said the lawyer, as Jacob was putting on his broad-brim preparatory to leaving.

"It might be for thy interest to do so," returned Jacob; "but if thee should happen to see Rebecca, thee would oblige me by not mentioning my call here."

"I will remember," said the lawyer, and as the door closed he wondered much concerning his strange visitor: whether his visit was brought about to give him this information about Rebecca, or whether it was merely the result of accident. He had no thought of its being planned until requested to say nothing about it to Rebecca. However, he did not occupy his mind long with these conjectures, but something more tangible—his own happiness. Even the duplicity of Anna was forgotten in the anticipation of his visit.

Jacob had accidentally learned the name of Rebecca's lover, and, after much trouble, his address also, and then he resolved to discover, if possible, why he did not come, as he promised. Not to compromise Rebecca, he pretended his only object was to inquire about the land claims, though he experienced many twinges of conscience as he thought of this deceit.

It was only after long communings with himself that he could resolve to put beyond his reach what Hope, always the last to leave one's heart, whispered might yet be his. But perhaps this young Quaker had less of selfishness than most people, and the pale face of Rebecca haunted him, and, with an unselfishness few would understand, he was anxious to call back the roses to her cheeks, even at the price of his own happiness.

One First Day, when Friend Hazlett, his wife and Ruth were gone to the monthly meeting, Rebecca had remained at home, and was sitting under the shade of an old oak. She was holding a book in her hand, but it evidently possessed little attraction, for she seemed bound in thought, as she often was of late. So intently was she thinking that she heard no footsteps, until standing before her was one not often absent from her heart.

"Anson Caldwell!" she exclaimed, joyfully; then stopped, fearing she had betrayed too much.

"Yes, it is I. Are you glad to see me?" he asked, tenderly.

"I am not inhospitable, Friend Caldwell, and thee is very welcome," replied she, demurely.

"I hoped for a different greeting than this," he said, looking at her reproachfully. But Rebecca, finding she held the reins, was ungenerously disposed to retain them, and like a real woman, make him suffer before she forgave him; so she said simply:

"I hope I am not unmannerly, Friend Caldwell; but thee should not have expected so much, and then thee would not have been disappointed."

"But Rebecca, if you only knew how miserable I have been since I saw you, you would not tantalize me so."

"Thee does not look very thin, and thy step is quite vigorous," she said, mischievously, as she watched him pacing up and down the garden.

"I have looked forward to this visit, and now—"

"Thee should not have looked forward so long and perhaps thee would have been more welcome," said Rebecca, interrupting him.

"But, Rebecca, I was deceived by your cousin. She said you were to be married this fall to a young Quaker."

"Did Anna say that? How could she tell such an untruth? But how did thee learn thy mistake?" asked she.

"Do not ask me, Rebecca, but answer me what is of more consequence."

I am not good at describing love scenes, so I will leave this one to be imagined each for himself, aided by past experiences, quite sure that with such a help there is no danger of being misled.

When Dame Hazlett came home from meeting she was much surprised at seeing a stranger, and she looked with some dissatisfaction at Rebecca's blushing cheeks and the young man's glossy beaver* lying on the table. Why such apparently different objects should command her attention at the same time it would perhaps be difficult to explain, so I simply state the fact without attempting its elucidation.

The evening passed rather tediously, for various reasons. Mr. Caldwell could not fail to see that he was hardly welcome, Rebecca was worrying herself with useless conjectures about the manner in which Anson's proposal would be received by her father, Ruth's tender little heart was full of pity for Jacob, and Friend Hazlett and his wife, while they could not deny that he seemed an amiable young man, would much rather have contemplated his excellence at a distance. Mr. Caldwell's proposal for the hand of Rebecca met, as she had feared, with a decided "Nay" from the plain-spoken Quaker, who said she was going to marry Jacob.

"I think you are mistaken, Friend Hazlett, for Rebecca told me that she did not love him," answered the young man, respectfully.

"Oh, well," said the worthy Quaker, "girls never know their

Beaver hat (these were expensive).

own minds. I am sure Jacob loves Rebecca, and if he does he shall have her."

So Anson had nothing to do but wait patiently until Jacob came, who, when spoken to, refused the gift, though no one knows how he might have been tempted at that moment, but he said quietly:

"Friend Caldwell is a worthy young man. He loves Rebecca, and he is blessed with many of this world's goods."

Far be it from my thought to call Friend Hazlett mercenary, but for some reason he began to look more favorably upon young Caldwell, and think that after all he might as well give him Rebecca, since she loved him so well, so he gladdened their hearts by giving his consent to their marriage.

But Jacob, honest, generous-hearted Jacob, was not so easily forgiven. He had wounded the pride of the old Quaker, and it was long ere he was welcomed to their fireside.

⋇═◉◉═⋇

Just a year from the time they first met, Rebecca became Mrs. Caldwell, in the vain phraseology of the world's people. Three times had they risen in meeting (and announced their intention to wed before the elders), and then they were united according to the simple marriage rite of the Quakers. They returned to their elegant city home followed by a sigh and "God bless you" from Jacob, who had done so much towards making them happy.

Ruth often visited them, attracting many by her almost angelic face; but, unlike Rebecca, she found no one who could take the place of Jacob in her heart. Was it strange that Jacob should at last come to regard her with affection, and knowing her love, wish to gather its sunshine to illumine his lonely life?

A dainty little housewife she made, her simple home being much more to her liking than Rebecca's splendid mansion; and in after years, when Jacob contrasted his little Ruth with his stately sister-in-law, he wondered why he was so long in discovering her superior qualities; while Anson would as soon have discussed the rival merits of the buttercup and the rose as to have compared Ruth to Rebecca.

Anna accomplished her wish of marrying a rich man, though he was sixty, while she was only twenty-two; but looking into her fretful, careworn face, it would not be difficult to answer the question, "Is she happy?"

Mary R. Platt Hatch
(1848–1935)

Mary R. Platt Hatch, born in Stratford, New Hampshire, wrote novels such as *The Upland Mystery* (1887), *The Bank Tragedy* (1890), and *The Missing Man* (1893), as well as many short stories.

THE MILLER'S
THIRD SON

Helen Ward Banks

What the old fairy tale about the miller's third son had to do with Aunt Fanny's visit, nobody could have known. One of the sisters would get to travel abroad with the wealthy lady, and she planned to decide who it would be right away.

*L*ucy burst into the room like a hurricane. "Aunt Fanny's coming! Aunt Fanny's coming!" she cried.

Louise closed her Spanish grammar and Frances looked up from her storybook to face the exciting news.

"She telegraphed," went on Lucy. "She'll be here tonight and she'll stay a week. She's on her way to Panama!"

"Panama!" breathed Frances. "Doesn't it sound lovely! How I wish she'd take me!"

"I'd give anything to travel," agreed Louise. "Where is she going to sleep?"

"In my room," answered Lucy briskly. "I'm going in with the twins."

"I should think you'd give her your room, Fran," said Louise decidedly. "You're named after her, and your room's larger than Lucy's."

"She can have my room," hesitated Frances, "but I've got such lots of stuff to move, and the twins would muss up everything so."

"The twins don't meddle," declared Lucy. "But, anyhow, I don't mind changing. Louise, Mother wants you to go down and help her plan the meals a little."

Capable Louise put away her books. "Do tie up your hair ribbon, Lucy. Fran, if you're going down town get some new wash cloths. Aunt Fanny is so particular."

"All right," murmured Frances, deep once more in her book.

"Will you help me move, Fran?" asked Lucy. "It's sort of heavy alone. Will you mind?"

"I'll come in just a minute," promised Frances.

"Get Bridget to help you," dictated Louise on her way downstairs; "Fran's going down town."

"I'll get along," answered Lucy good-humoredly. "Bridget's busy."

She carried one load down the hall from her own room to the nursery and went back for another. From below sounded Louise's commanding voice:

"You children must keep out from underfoot."

"Come up here, twinnies, and we'll play a game," called Lucy.

Rosy the quick, and Posy, the slow, climbed the stairs eagerly. Lucy was such a good playfellow. They chattered and laughed and carried loads from the wrecked ship in Lucy's room to the desert island in the nursery.

"That's the last thing we need to rescue," declared Lucy, "but we'd better clean up the ship before it sinks. The rug is a raft. I'll throw it overboard, and you two get the carpet beater and go down on the grass and play you're hammering nails into the raft to make it strong. Hit hard! While you get that into shape, I'll scrub up the deck here."

Bridget's strong arm gave a few last strokes to the raft, and brought it back upstairs to lay on the clean, shining floor.

"I'm going down to put lunch on the table, Miss Lucy," she said as she left the room.

"All right," sighed Lucy, "I'm just through. Send up the twins, Bridget, to get washed."

As Lucy was finishing her task, Frances came into the room.

"Can I help you move, Lucy?"

"All moved, thank you, Fran. Rinse out one of the new wash cloths you got, won't you? and put it in Aunt Fanny's room."

"I'm just going down town now."

"What time do you think it is?" laughed Lucy.

"It can't be one o'clock!" exclaimed Frances, glancing at the clock.

"Come right down to lunch!" called Louise. "Lucy, do you know if Fran's home yet?"

"She's here," answered Lucy. "We're all coming."

Louise fastened a keen eye on Frances as the three girls went downstairs. "I don't believe you've stirred out of your chair!" she exclaimed. "And everybody else working strenuously!"

"She's going after lunch," explained Lucy, "and that will be all the better, for she can do the last errands."

"There'll be plenty," said Mother. "Aunt Fanny likes everything very nice, and she didn't give us much time to get ready."

"And she doesn't mind letting you know when she doesn't like things," added Louise.

Frances went down town after lunch, but she left her list at home. So she had to go back again for the things she had forgotten.

Mother helped Bridget season the soup. Louise set the table according to her most genteel notions, and Lucy saw to the twins' best frocks. When all was ready, Lucy took a daffodil from the bunch on the table and put it in a little vase on Aunt Fanny's dressing table. She looked with satisfaction around the fresh room until her eyes lighted on the washstand.

"Where's Aunt Fanny's wash cloth?" she demanded, bursting into Frances's room.

"Oh, I never bought any!" gasped Frances. "I'll go back."

"I'm all dressed. I'll go quicker," answered Lucy, and was off.

When Lucy came back, Aunt Fanny had arrived, and the family were having lunch in the living-room.

"Here's Lucy," said Mother.

Aunt Fanny looked at her disapprovingly. "I suppose an aunt isn't of enough importance for you to be on hand to welcome her," she said.

"I'm sorry, Aunt Fanny," said Lucy, looking to see if Frances would exonerate her. But Frances had gone for another teacup and did not hear.

Aunt Fanny rested from lunch hour till dinner time. She made herself entertaining at dinner with an account of a trip through Spain. Frances was so entranced that she forgot to eat, and Louise asked such intelligent questions that Aunt Fanny beamed on her approvingly. Lucy listened to it all with wide-open ears, but she had a twin on each side of her, and their wants kept her busy.

Lucy put the twins to bed after dinner. "Go to sleep like good girls, won't you?" she coaxed. "I want to go down and listen to Aunt Fanny talk."

"If you'll tell us just one story, we'll be good as anything," promised Rosy.

"Tell us 'The Miller's Son,' " begged Posy.

Lucy told the story through, until the two pairs of eyelids drooped.

"Isn't it funny," remarked Rosy sleepily, "that in stories it's always the youngest son who goes off to seek his fortune. Why is that?"

"It just happens," laughed Lucy, and kissed both twins and went downstairs, where Aunt Fanny and Louise were still talking about Spain, and Frances's eyes were glowing.

"I'm going to read the story of Spain all over again," Frances said. "It must be wonderful, Aunt Fanny, really to see the things you read about."

"I like to know the languages," said Louise. "I can do pretty well with French now, so I've been studying Spanish this winter."

"That ought to make you a good traveling companion," said Aunt Fanny. "Now, I'll tell you what I want to do. I'm going to hire a car tomorrow afternoon big enough to hold all of us, and we'll go over to Crampton Rock and have lunch, and come back the shore road. It'll be a nice ride. We'll get off at two sharp. Now I'm going to bed. Good night."

Louise went up with Aunt Fanny, and after she had settled her, came tumbling back into the living-room.

"Did you hear what Aunt Fanny said about a traveling companion?" she exclaimed. "O Mother, do you think it meant anything?"

"I suppose I may as well tell you," said Mother a little slowly, "that Aunt Fanny *does* mean to take one of you with her to Panama and South America. It will be only one, and she will make her own choice. That means two disappointed girls."

"Two?" questioned Louise. "Oh—Lucy! Well, I suppose Aunt Fanny'll take Fran because she's named for her, and that goes a long way."

"Oh, no!" protested Frances. "She'll take you, Louise, because you're such a good manager and speak languages and things. She's sure to take you."

"Well whoever it is," answered Louise happily, "you needn't be afraid, Mother, that we won't take it like heroes. We're not going to tear each other's eyes out."

"I'm sure of it," answered Mother. "Whoever goes, too, won't have all rose leaves, for Aunt Fanny is very exacting. She doesn't want to be kept waiting, and she wants things to go her way."

"I can manage most things. I'll take my chances with Aunt Fanny, won't you, Fran?" laughed Louise.

"I'd do almost anything to go to South America," breathed Frances, and vowed that she would without fail be early for breakfast.

But she wasn't. Neither was she ready when, at two minutes

before two the next afternoon, the big car stood at the door. Lucy was stowing away the big basket, Louise was helping Aunt Fanny and her mother, the twins were dancing on the curb. But there was no Frances.

"You get in, Aunt Fanny. You and Mother sit on the back seat," Louise dictated. "You'd better take Lucy between you. Fran can have one chair and Posy the other. I'll hold Rosy on my lap in front."

"I always ride in the front seat," said Aunt Fanny dryly.

"Do you think you'll be so comfortable there?" objected Louise. "I thought I could direct the driver."

"Very well," yielded Aunt Fanny suddenly.

They stowed themselves away according to Louise's orders. Aunt Fanny even allowed a cushion to be stuffed behind her back, where it was most uncomfortable. Then they waited for Frances.

"We're paying for this car while it stands still," said Aunt Fanny.

"I'll see if I can help her," said Lucy, and slipped out.

It was another ten minutes before Frances appeared. After she was seated, she found both her gloves were for one hand, and had to go back. Aunt Fanny opened her mouth to say something, but closed it again and said nothing.

It was a beautiful ride. Aunt Fanny seemed to enjoy her back seat, though she soon had the cushion under her feet. The luncheon on the rocks, too, was delicious. Aunt Fanny was very amenable; she obeyed Louise as meekly as did all the family, sat where she was told, and ate and drank what was given her.

After the repast, Frances went off by herself and sat with her arms clasped around her knee, looking out to sea. The twins pulled Mother off to hunt for shells. Louise wanted to show Aunt

Fanny the view from the bluff, but though Louise's reasons were good, Aunt Fanny suddenly rebelled, and Louise went alone.

Lucy, singing happily to herself, was giving the chauffeur something to eat and packing up the basket. Aunt Fanny, looking around for a seat, turned toward the most promising-looking rock. Lucy, after a swift glance, was there before her with a rug and the despised cushion. She waited with a little smile while Aunt Fanny adjusted herself, and then went back to the basket. When that was packed, she was after the twins, to set Mother free to talk to Aunt Fanny.

Aunt Fanny shared the rug with her sister-in-law. "That oldest daughter of yours is very executive," she said abruptly. "She could take charge of almost anything."

"Yes," agreed Mother. "Louise is a great help to me," and thought, *So it's going to be Louise.*

"She's a clever girl," repeated Aunt Fanny, "and so is my namesake. Frances will be a poet one of these days. It would be a pleasure to show her beautiful things."

Is it to be Frances, then? wondered Mother.

"What's Lucy's specialty?" demanded Aunt Fanny.

"Lucy's specialty? Why, I don't know—unless it is for filling chinks. Lucy is hands and feet for all the family."

There was silence for a few moments, and then Aunt Fanny began to laugh.

"There comes Louise. Now we shall all be packed home. If you want to know the truth, I made up this picnic to try out these girls of my brother's. I thought a short journey would show how fit they are for a longer one. I want to take one of them for their father's sake. I was very fond of him. But I'm pretty set in my habits, and I'm not going to spoil my own pleasure by taking along a thorn in the flesh. Last night I could scarcely decide between Louise and Frances. This afternoon—if you'll pardon my plain speaking—I don't want either of them. I may appreciate Louise's attentions when I am decrepit; just now I don't. She is most executive; you can't deny that her planning is good; but she's too obvious. I like my own way best. Then there's Frances. She is attractive and talented, but she's never on time. I can't miss trains waiting for her to go back for her toothbrush. I know now whom I want. I want that little quiet girl that's always just where a body wants her when she wants her. Lend me Lucy. I didn't think much of her last night, but I've been watching today. It's her room I'm sleeping in, isn't it?"

"Yes, it's Lucy's," said Mother.

Aunt Fanny went back home on the front seat, with no cushion behind her back. She was rather quiet through dinner. When they were back in the living-room again, she spoke in her usual abrupt fashion.

"On my visit here one of my nieces has shown me the most graceful hospitality in her power, for she has moved into other quarters and given up her own particular sanctum to me. I want to return that hospitality by taking her to South America with me. Will she come?"

All three girls looked at their Mother in dismay. She smiled back.

"That means Lucy," she said.

"Oh, no, Mother; not me," Lucy protested.

Louise pulled herself together. Had the disappointed ones not promised to be heroes? She went over to her little sister and put her arms around her.

"Good for little Lucy!" she exclaimed. "She deserves it. She's always giving, and we don't half appreciate it."

Frances came over, too, and kissed her. "I'm glad, Lucy. We'll miss you, but Aunt Fanny will enjoy having you with her."

"But it isn't fair when I'm the youngest," protested Lucy.

"It's like the miller's son!" cried Rosy. "It has to happen like that to the miller's third son."

"And I know why the nice things always happen to him," announced wise little Posy. "It's because he's always the goodest."

Helen Ward Banks

Helen Ward Banks, born in Brooklyn, New York, late in the nineteenth century, authored such books as *The Boynton Pluck* (1904), *The House of the Lions* (1924), and *The Story of Mexico* (1926), as well as many short stories.

THE PERFECT
BACKGROUND

Leota Hulse Black

Joan was the pretty one, the accomplished one; Jane was the plain one, the unselfish one, foredoomed to play second fiddle to her lovely sister.

Then came the big concert.

*F*rom the time Joan Marsh was a tiny miss of three, her love of the violin had been the joy and wonder of her parents' hearts. Her mother discovered it first. Watching the child at play, she was surprised and amused to see her carefully select two sticks, tuck one under her dimpled chin and draw the other across it, bow fashion.

"Look Muvver—dis is my vi'lin. Listen an' I'll play 'Baby's Boat's the Silver Moon.' Janey, you play the p'lano." And Jane, her plain little twin, obediently sat down at the tiny toy piano and hummed an accompaniment to Joan's solo.

As the years passed, Joan's ability gained for her widespread popularity. No one ever took into account the little sister who always accompanied her. Joan was the pretty twin—Joan the clever one—even the parents' first thought was for Joan and the musical career of which they dreamed. But while Joan's hours of practice were sketchy things woven into her happy-go-lucky days, Jane worked at the piano with a terrible concentration of purpose. The result was a beautiful, smooth background that was so subtly perfect that not even Joan realized that Jane adapted the accompaniment to Joan's bow.

When Joan was fifteen, Old Professor Bauer who had first molded her tiny fingers around the bow, said:

"It ees a shame, Mees Joan, to waste your time weeth me. Can you not go to the Conservatory for lessons?"

"I'd love to, Professor Bauer, but Papa has had financial reverses so it's impossible."

"Too bad—such marvelous talent—we *must* find a way."

A few days later Jane rushed excitedly in from school.

"Mamma, where's Joan? Listen, both of you, to this clipping—I met Professor Bauer on the street and he gave it to me!" And Jane read: " 'The Music Department of the City

Federation of Clubs will sponsor a Music Contest at the Civic Auditorium on November tenth. All young artists of high school age are eligible to compete. Prizes in Voice, Piano, and Stringed Instruments will be awarded. An added feature of interest is the scholarship offered by the Wreams Conservatory of Music, to the winner of first place over all. A special judge from the Conservatory will award this prize!' Isn't it *wonderful,* Mother? Joan will win, of course—her playing surpasses anything in the City. Joan, honey, what will you play? Let's get started at once! We'll practice hours and hours every day. We'll play it so perfectly that the judges won't be able to find a single flaw."

"Oh heavens, Jane, don't get so excited! I can play *anything* with a few days' practice—and it's three whole weeks off. I'm not going to *kill* myself to win that scholarship!"

"Yes, but *darling*—surely no sacrifice will be too great when so much is at stake. It's your *big chance.*"

"Well—I'll tell you this much—if I have to do a lot of extra practice, Jane has to help with my work and write my themes."

"Of course I'll be only too glad to do anything I can for you, Joan, if you'll only work hard on your contest piece. Honey, why don't you play Musin's 'Concert Mazurka'? It's such a brilliant number and you do the first movement beautifully now. In three weeks you'll play it perfectly."

But Joan's thoughts were not upon the Mazurka.

"Mother, if I play, I'll have to have a new frock—I simply *won't* appear in public again wearing that old blue thing!"

"Oh Joan—I was afraid you'd ask that very thing, and we really can't afford it. Jane must have a new coat—she really looks too shabby in her old one to go about with you."

Jane's eyes filled with quick tears.

"Oh Mother, let her have it—I don't need a new coat—I mean I'd so much rather Joan could have the new frock—truly I would."

"Well—of course if Jane feels that way about it, we'll see what can be done."

In the days of rehearsing that followed, Joan was often fault-finding.

"*Jane!* For *heaven's sake,* did you never hear of *tone-color* and *phrasing?* You grind that out like a hurdy-gurdy!"

"Oh, Joan—I'm *so* sorry—I guess I get to dreaming about the scholarship you're going to win and don't concentrate on what I'm doing. Isn't it a perfect *miracle* that it happened just at this time?"

"Oh, I suppose so—but let's hurry through this just once more. I want to play tennis."

"But Joan, aren't you going to practice any more today? The time is so short and you don't play the second movement with confidence—I have to sort of *push* you through."

"Now Sister Sorrowful, don't worry about *me*—I'll get it." And she was gone, leaving Jane sick with apprehension.

Two days before the contest Jane looked up from the piano. "Joan, 'course it won't make any difference, but I'm rather worried about what I'll wear—and I wondered if you'd care—if I wore your old blue dress. Not that it makes a *bit* of difference—no one will notice your accompanist."

"Why, Jane Marsh—whatever are you talking about? You didn't think for one moment that *you* were going to accompany me, did you? Miss Baxter from the Conservatory will accompany everyone—she's *wonderful!*"

"But Joan—you're so—so *used* to me—I'm afraid for you with anyone else—"

"My, how *modest* we are! You don't think you accompany better than a Conservatory instructor, do you?"

"Why no, of course not—it's all right—I don't mind if she only knows *what* to do."

"Well, don't worry—she knows her stuff."

The afternoon preceding the contest, Joan came home from rehearsal with Miss Baxter. Jane met her at the door.

"How did you get along, honey?"

"*Rotten*—I played *miserably*—but Miss Baxter said a poor final rehearsal was a good sign—she said I needn't worry. I'll be all right tonight."

"Oh, Joan, I was afraid it would be that way. Come on to the piano and I'll help you."

"No, I don't want to be tired tonight—I'm going to read."

⸺⊙⸺

Eight o'clock found the Civic Auditorium packed. Joan, looking like a lovely flower in the new frock, stood in the wings with little Jane like a faithful shadow by her side.

"Joan, honey, don't get nervous. You'll play beautifully, and think how proud Mamma and Papa and I will be of you!"

At last Joan's number was announced and she took her place by the Steinway. As she raised her bow for the opening bars, little Jane, in the wings, buried her face in her hands.

Oh dear God—make her play it right. Strengthen her when she gets to the second movement where she is so weak—

Joan was playing now with the poise and assurance of long habit. As the perfect tones fell upon the ears of the judges, their faces brightened with appreciation. Here at last was *talent*—but as Joan swung into the second movement there was a change—an uncertain fluttering of the bow—the accompanist paused—and the thought of failure swooped like a dark cloud over Joan's consciousness. Sheer panic seized her and she threw an imploring glance at Jane's tense pale face that peered at her from the wings in horrible fascination. And Jane, ever alert to Joan's needs, forgot everything except that need. Darting swiftly across the stage, she brushed the surprised Miss Baxter aside and slid under the keys of the Steinway. Without a moment's hesitancy she took up the threads of the accompaniment. Joan, in a flash, pushed off the hypnotic thought of failure and rallied. This was no longer a contest—all thought left her save the sweet unselfishness of the shy little sister who had not failed her in her great need, and she played as she had never played before. As the triumphant melody filled the Auditorium, new confidence mounted in her like the glow of the spotlight that played upon her serious young face.

The lone judge from the Conservatory watched Jane's hands in fascination. *Heavens,* he breathed, *how that girl can play—and it's not the superhuman playing of an individual momentarily surpassing herself— it's as steady and inevitable as the rising of the sun. She's a genius— a genius—*

On and on they played—Joan could feel the rhythm of them together. Her hands knew before her brain what Jane wanted of her and responded. She was utterly submissive to her will and Jane dutifully and gladly paved the way for her sister's brilliant execution—a duet that held in absolute harmony to the last bar.

As Joan held aloft her quivering bow on the last note, the applause broke. Jane had slipped quietly away. The applause was for Joan and it was right that it should be so.

When the judges' decision was announced, Joan walked onto

the stage with a humility entirely foreign to her nature, to receive the award of winner in the stringed instruments' class.

As the judge from the Conservatory who would award the scholarship appeared on the stage, a hush fell over the audience. Every eye was upon Joan. Her number had so far surpassed the efforts of the other contestants that without doubt the scholarship would be hers.

The judge paused a moment, then said: "I have been authorized by the Wreams Conservatory of Music, to award a scholarship to the individual appearing upon this program who shows the most marked ability and talent for future development. That is what I am about to do, and I have a surprise in store for you. Where is the little girl who saved the day for this talented young violinist?"

Joan fairly flew to the wings and led Jane, tearfully protestant, to the stage.

The judge turned—"My dear, it has been said that accompanists are born, not made. You have proved that statement here, tonight. You have also displayed marked poise, and an unselfish spirit that averted a near-tragedy. It is with pleasure that I award—"

"But—but you *mustn't*—why—why—it's *Joan's*—give it to her. I'm—I'm only the hands that form her background—"

Joan came swiftly to her side. "No dear, it's *yours*—you've deserved to be in the *foreground, always*—and this is *your* victory—yours alone."

Leota Hulse Black

Leota Hulse Black wrote some of the most memorable stories to appear in inspirational and family magazines during the first half of the the twentieth century.

BROTHER TOM'S
ROOM

Winifred Arnold

Nellie worried about her brother Tom, who was running around with a wild crowd. But she certainly didn't see what she could do about it.

Then she read that accusing article.

N ellie Bates, up in her pretty little room, knit her brows into a frown over her Sunday school paper. Nellie's room was the only pretty one in the house. Her father was poor, and Nellie had been his housekeeper ever since her mother's death, some years before.

There were only her father and her brother in the family, and they, so Nellie thought, being men, wouldn't care whether things were pretty or not. So Nellie had spent the little money she could get, and all her care and ingenuity (with which a girl can do so much), in making her own room as attractive as possible; and the results did her credit.

What difference did it make, she thought, *that the rest of the house was bare? Her father never knew whether the dingy sitting-room where he read his paper in the evening was cheery or not*—at least so reasoned Nellie—and she herself took her own friends right up to her own room.

As for Tom—well, Tom was never at home anyhow. He worked all day long, and the evenings he spent "with the fellows," and not in his dull little home; for Tom had been grow-ing rather "wild" of late, as lonely boys sometimes do.

Nellie, of course, felt as bad over this as any girl with a "wild" brother must, and she had tried, in a way, to help Tom back to the safe path. She had wept over him in private, had reproach-fully told him that he was a disgrace to her and his father, had lamented about him to her Sunday school teacher, and had even prayed about him a little. In fact, she would have told you that she had "done her best for poor Tom," and must now let him go his own way.

It was for just this reason that we find Miss Nellie frowning over her magazine. She had just finished reading an article on "Brothers and Sisters," and these words had held her attention:

Never dare to feel that you can let your brother go on in the downward path while you have left untried one possible way of holding him back, even a little one. Have you made his home as cheerful as it possibly can be? Is his room as attractive as your own? Have you sacrificed anything for him? Above all, have you prayed for him with all your heart and soul?

If these words had been personally addressed to Nellie Bates, they could not have appealed to her more strongly. Tom's room as attractive as her own? She blushed as she thought of the contrast. Had she ever really sacrificed anything for him? And, above all, had she ever really prayed? A hundred excuses for herself rose to her mind; but Nellie was an honest girl, and now that the veil of selfishness and indifference had been torn away by those words, none of the excuses she found were worth much. Certainly there was not one that could stand before the vision of Tom's room as it flashed across her mind. Even his bed was not yet made, she knew, though it was already afternoon. That surely must be done first! So down the hall she ran, and threw open Tom's door, blushing hotly at the scene before her—the unmade bed, the bare walls, the piles of yellow-covered novels on the table, the uncurtained windows, and the general dusty and cheerless aspect of everything.

At least, however, here was something definite to be done, so Nellie set to work with a will, sweeping and dusting and clearing up, till at last everything was neat and tidy, at any rate. And now she could give her attention to making the room look pretty. Here she was in her element, and soon she discovered, to her surprise, that there was really as much pleasure in making a room pretty for other people as for oneself.

Many a trip she made to her own room to borrow bits of its brightness for Tom; and the change effected by a dainty bureau cover, some books, a table spread, a bright cushion or two, and a few photographs was really marvelous. When it came to the walls, Nellie's task was more difficult, for she herself had only a few pictures, and those few were very dear to her heart. For a moment or two she wavered, but then she remembered that she really had sacrificed nothing as yet, and she hastened to choose from her little store the pictures that would suit Tom best.

As she came and went, she noticed in her own room the lovely calendar that her Sunday school teacher had given her for Christmas, and in Tom's, the bare space over the table, and for some reason her obstinate mind insisted on putting those two things together. They certainly did seem made for each other. Nellie stood still in front of her calendar, and argued the point. It certainly was beautiful—a lovely wreath of pink and white roses surrounding the Bible verse, "The love of Christ constraineth us," in shining gold letters. It seemed to Nellie as if she just could not give it up. Besides, it wasn't suitable for a boy, and Tom wouldn't appreciate it. But then she remembered the way he had hung over it, as she unwrapped it on Christmas morning, and even said wistfully, "Are you going to put it away in your own room, Nell?"

Perhaps, she argued, Miss Thomas would not like to have her put it in someone else's room. And then her honesty reasserted itself. She knew her teacher too well to believe that for a single moment. Well, anyway, she had made enough sacrifices for Tom. Hadn't she given him her precious pictures? But just then she looked up again at the calendar, and the golden verse shone its message down into her heart: "The love of Christ constraineth us."

Yes, that was the answer. She could do it for the love of Christ. And it was with a real smile on her face that she hung the pretty thing over Tom's table, cast one pleased glance around at her completed work, and then hurried downstairs.

You could hardly have found a more astonished boy in the whole city than Tom Bates as he threw open the door of his little room that evening. His first method of expression was that boy's safety valve, the whistle. Having thus relieved his feelings, he entered and walked around, examining and admiring. Finally he paused just in front of his table, and exclaimed under his breath, "It's Nellie's! What in the world made her do it?"

Was it only by chance that his eye fell just at that moment upon the rose-wreathed calendar with the shining message, "The love of Christ constraineth us"? A sudden mist came across the boy's eyes, and he turned away, noticing as he did so that on the table below, his books had been neatly arranged by the same sisterly hands.

It seemed so incongruous to have those torn, soiled, yellow novels so close to the dainty thing, that with a hasty movement he gathered them in his arm and threw them in a heap on his closet floor. Then, with a strange tenderness in his heart and a half-ashamed look, he opened one of his bureau drawers and drew out from the very bottom a half-worn Bible which his mother had given him long ago, and a picture of that mother, and placed them on the empty table. "I can put them away in the morning," he murmured, "but I sort of like to have them out tonight."

He forgot them, however, in the haste of his morning dressing, and a little thrill of gladness filled Nellie's heart as she read their mute message.

She would have been gladder yet had she known that Tom had cast a hurried glance into her room as he ran downstairs, and noticing how much barer than usual it looked, had started at once to make plans for showing his gratitude for her self-sacrifice.

The first thing, he decided, would be to buy some things for his own room, so as to give Nell's back. He could save enough money to buy a picture or two by giving up some of the things that he knew were harmful to him, and on consideration it seemed to him worth while.

Tom was only beginning to be wild as yet, and his wildness was caused mainly by the idea many boys have that it isn't manly to be good. It didn't seem very hard to refrain for a while, if only he had some other reason than because it was right.

However, it would take some time to save money enough for a picture, and grateful Tom wanted to do something at once. He thought over it all day, and finally came to the conclusion that he would ask Nellie if she still wanted the set of bookshelves that she had once spoken about. He had some boards that would serve very well to make them, and Tom was quite clever with tools.

When he suggested this to Nellie at suppertime, she was so delighted and enthusiastic that Tom decided he could stay at home one evening, so as to begin right away on his work.

The bookshelves, however, took more than one evening; and they turned out to be such a success that Tom undertook some for the sitting-room. Then Nellie urged him to make some for his own room.

"Yes," said Tom, laughing, "they'd look fine up there on my walls without a thing on them. Give a nice, literary air to the room, wouldn't they?"

"If I were a boy," said Nellie composedly, "and were earning money, I'd buy myself a good book once in a while. They don't cost so much, and they're a fine thing to have. Just think what a library Mr. Judson has, and he said he began with just two books."

Tom considered the subject, and again found it worth while to economize in his "larks with the fellows." Tom's library began, and with it Tom's reading.

Nellie's capacity for being surprised could hardly keep pace with the new developments, but her joy knew no bounds, and she redoubled her efforts, carrying her bits of brightness downstairs now, where Father sat, till he too cheered up and smiled during the evenings as he helped the children at their work.

In the meantime the Bible had never gone back to its seclusion in Tom's bureau drawer, and the calendar still breathed down its shining message from among the roses. Sometimes Nellie saw the Bible by her mother's picture lying open, but she never dreamed how much was going on in Tom's heart, till he came down one afternoon and said haltingly, "Goodbye, Nell; I'm going up to the minister's to see about joining the church."

Nellie jumped to her feet and flew to throw her arms around his neck. "Oh Tom, I'm so glad! I wanted so to speak to you about it, but I didn't dare."

"Oh, you spoke all right," answered Tom with a little smile. "You know actions do speak louder than words. And your calendar talked all the time."

Winifred Arnold

Winifred Arnold wrote for family and inspirational magazines during the first third of the twentieth century.

TONY'S TURN

Author Unknown

It took Louise fifteen long years to discover that her beloved Aunt Tony was more than a mother figure to her; she was more like a sister, like her other half.

The flu spoken of here was called the "Spanish Flu." It came in the waning hours of World War I and slew close to 40 million people. No one has ever found out what caused it. What we *do* know is that in history, only the Black Plague has been comparable in loss of life.

*T*here was a mile and a half of maple-bordered street between the high school and the battered old home place called Willow Brook just beyond the village. The bare maples were now misted with rosy hues, the sky was soft as the washed-in background of a water-color sketch, but for once Louise Carleton did not note that misty rose nor that misty blue. She walked the homeward street in a daze of pain. Only once before in all her life had she felt this same sensation of the happy, familiar sky suddenly falling, the happy, familiar earth suddenly gaping, and herself like a little helpless leaf blown about in the dark. How strange that so harmless a thing as her English notebook, merely a black loose-leaf notebook, could have set going an earthquake!

Outwardly Louise moved calmly enough. She was by nature quiet; you have to be when there are four big, competent, talk-ative brothers and sisters ahead of you. She paced steadily on, a slim little figure in a gray coat that flapped back from her blue dress with its round white collar and shiny black belt. She wore no hat; her ashy-gold hair with its spraying tendrils was drawn back to the nape of her neck and bound about with a narrow black ribbon. Her eyes were baby blue and wide, but there were black shadows beneath them now, and the sweet-pea pink had faded from her cheeks. Few would have guessed Louise was seventeen years old. Until that afternoon she had never realized it herself.

Strangely, as she walked, that other dreadful time kept mingling with her thoughts, that other time which was at once the saddest and the gladdest memory of her life. Like the crucial happenings in which she was at this moment living, those events of fifteen years ago had followed a long period of care-free joy. Just as Baby Lou had accepted her mother's arms and her father's whistlings and tossings, and the rompings and shoutings of the elder four, and her silver mug, and the sparrows flirting on the window sill, so had Louise, grown older, accepted the weather-beaten porches of old Willow Brook, the sheen of its shadowy wainscoting, the tracery of vines weaving to and fro against her moonlit window shades. How glad Louise had always been of the frank and kindly label, "a little dull," awarded her by her talented brothers and sisters, because it meant that she did not have to go off and be educated, but might stay at home always, with Tony.

Only one secret in all her life had Louise ever kept from Tony. And that secret being now ten years old, she had given it little thought—until only half an hour ago the terrible three in the principal's office had ruthlessly laid it bare! Obstinately, Louise kept protesting to herself, over and over, just as she had reiterated to those three: "But it's Tony's turn! Tony must have her turn!" But how could slow-tongued Louise have explained to three argumentative gray heads the meaning of words that had long ago become her secret slogan—*Tony must have her turn.* Louise could hardly have explained the meaning even to herself, so closely bound was this meaning with that memory of long ago.

Beneath the rosy maples Louise felt herself brought back to babyhood again—such a happy babyhood it must have been, all forgotten though it was! Then, one day, sharp terror descending on their home: starchy nurses all in white appearing in possession of the nursery; the doctor, not joking, but speaking sharp; something stalking just outside the door, some horrible, shapeless monster people spoke of in whispers. They called it the "flu." Dreadful pains in Baby Lou's elbows and knees, and a dreadful sickness in her stomach, and Mother not coming in at the door! The door shut between Mother's room and the nursery!

"Mother is sick, dearie." That strange nurse was speaking. "Try to keep quiet, so Mother will get well."

Fevered days went by; nights full of ugly dreams went by—but Mother never came. Daddy came once, gaunt and unshaven, in his long brown dressing gown. He lifted Baby Lou in weak arms; then that mean old nurse came and chased him back to bed. Dreadful things, Baby Lou felt, were happening just outside her closed door in the hall—stealthy rustlings; people going up and down the stairs in the middle of the night; somebody weeping as if her heart was broken—it must have been Madge, great big Madge.

Why didn't the rest come into her nursery? Why didn't Mother come? And Daddy never came either. *Everybody* was sick, that starchy nurse said. Then at last, one morning, Alec came, that big, big brother, fifteen years old. He looked very white and strange, but he was dressed in his dark-blue suit, and he said he was well again. He took Baby Lou up in his arms, and he said, "Oh Baby Lou, please stop crying for 'Mudder, Mudder,' all the time. Please stop, Baby Lou." And he bent and kissed the top of her head. "We just can't stand it, baby darling, to hear you cry for 'Mudder' any more!"

Just as suddenly as the evil had descended, just as suddenly something glad and wonderful began to happen. Baby Lou, alone and quiet in her crib, felt it all. In the silent, rustling house, there came a great ring at the front door. Alec rushed to open it. Utter silence for a full moment, then he shouted so that all the house rang, while the three others poured down the stairs, "A cablegram! Tony is coming back!"

Then up they all trooped to the nursery, and again Alec lifted Baby Lou in his arms, and he said, "Everything is going to be all right, Baby Lou. Tony is coming back! We are all going to the old house in the country. There's nobody there now, but Tony is coming back!"

Vaguely the baby wondered, as often enough Louise, when older, had wondered, *from where, from what, was Tony coming back?*

"Tony, Baby Lou," Alec explained, "is our aunt. Just the way you are Madge's little sister, and Florence's, so Tony is Mother's little sister. And Tony is coming back to take care of us all."

Just here the memory changed from the saddest of Louise's life to the gladdest. The house now buzzed with preparations. They were all going away to live in some new happy place where someone beautiful was to meet them. It would take Tony ten days to come back, and four days to get the old place ready for them. In two weeks they were to go, and then when they got to Willow Brook and Tony, so the other four explained over and over, then everything would be all right.

The journey was a blur in Louise's remembrance. She must have slept most of the way, waking to the snowy blast from the opening car door, as the five descended under Alec's tense directorship. He was carrying four suitcases. Madge was carrying Baby Lou. Six-year-old Blair was sleepy and whimpering. There were stars above and snow below. A big man in a fur coat was packing them into a sleigh, down on the straw. Whisk and jingle and off they went, with black branches flying by against the sky—branches the way they would look if Alec let you draw them with his fountain pen.

Then cries from all of them: "There! There! See! On the hill! Wake up, Blair! Wake up, Baby Lou! There's a light in every window! She's opening the front door! She's running down the steps!"

With a flurry of scattered snow, a last jingle of bells, they were all tumbling out at the porch. Everybody was swarming over a little dumpy figure with wide-open arms. She wasn't Mother, but she had Mother's voice. There was just that same undertone of laughing in it.

"Where is she?" the voice was saying. "Quick! Give me Baby Lou!"

It wasn't Mother, of course, for this person didn't seem much older than Alec; but surely these were Mother's arms. Baby Lou pressed her cheek to this new shoulder with a little sigh of uttermost relief, knowing herself forever safe in Tony's arms. And safe from all earthquakes, Louise had lived those fifteen years with Tony, at Willow Brook—safe, until half an hour ago!

Of the three people there in the office Louise did not know which one had most distressed her—portly, calm Mr. Hargrave, with a tongue that held all the school in subjection; keen Miss Austin, with eyes that bored into your brain; or the utterly unprecedented stranger. Mr. Plimpton had thick white hair, thick white eyebrows streaked as if with black ink, black eyes that burned, and a voice that burned, too. He held on his knee that guilty notebook. Two weeks ago Miss Austin had called for all the English notebooks unexpectedly, so that Louise's had to go in with the others; but when two weeks had passed without a word, she had begun to breathe more freely. Louise had never seen Mr. Plimpton before, but she had read of him in the local newspaper, and knew that he was spending a few weeks in a nearby town. She knew he was an artist. She had not known he was a friend of Miss Austin's.

Growing more and more apprehensive, more and more shaken by Mr. Plimpton's words, Louise had looked from his face to Miss Austin's, to Mr. Hargrave's, and found all three faces impervious to her excuses. Mr. Plimpton held the notebook all the time he talked. He seemed to know it by heart. He would dash at some page and hold it up in his long mobile hands. "You see this! And this! And this! And yet you won't listen to me! You won't do what I say!"

"I can't," Louise's faint, obstinate little voice had over and over repeated. "Tony must have her turn!"

They glared at her, but she only continued to shake that little ash-gold head of hers. "It's Tony's turn. Tony has never had her turn."

Mr. Plimpton threw up his hands in despair.

"Louise," said Miss Austin, "will you at least tell your aunt?"

"Oh, I can't!" moaned Louise.

"Then *I* will!"

And those three words were the reason Louise was slowly walking homeward, one bad half hour behind her and the guilty black notebook under her arm.

At the spot in the curving driveway where the tall barberry bushes, overgrown, pushed towards each other across the gravel, Louise always looked up. Just as she reached this spot, always the front door opened, and Tony appeared beneath the wan light. You could be as sure of Tony's appearing as you could be of the sunset, which, a little later, the two of them would gaze at from the west window of Tony's room. There stood Tony in the doorway as always: Tony, at thirty-eight, grown a little tired and shabby, like the aging house.

Louise waited until they were seated in the window, on the worn cushioned seat. She had laid the notebook between them until the moment came when she should have to open it. For the first time in fifteen years, it was actually hard to talk to Tony! Louise began almost as haltingly as she talked to everybody else.

"Tony, do you remember something that happened ten years ago, when I was seven?"

"A great many things happened ten years ago, or any years ago, for that matter," laughed Tony. "Which happening do you mean?"

"Don't you remember that morning, Tony? I couldn't ever forget it. I was sitting on the edge of the bridge, swinging my feet down under the handrail, and I had a white pad and some crayons. The pussy willows were coming out, and the willow trees were turning green, and the brook was so brown. I was drawing it all on my pad, and you came up behind, and I waited for you to speak, and I kept drawing away faster and faster, thinking you'd be pleased. Then I looked up at last, because you didn't speak, and Tony, you were as white as the sycamore, and I never was so frightened in my life! Tony, don't you remember that time, now?"

Tony was looking out the window. "Yes, I remember that time, now."

"And your voice was so queer. You said, 'Baby Lou, do you love me?' And of course I just hugged you as hard as I could; and then you said, 'If you love me, Baby Lou, will you give me your pad and your crayons and promise me never to draw again?' And of course I promised, Tony: I promised, but—"

Tony was still looking out of the window, her hands clasped

tight about her hunched knees. She did not turn as she spoke. "But you couldn't keep the promise?"

"Oh, Tony, I couldn't! I couldn't! I had to draw and paint everything! But I kept it a secret from you, from everybody! I knew it must have been wrong or you would never have begged me to stop. But I couldn't help it, Tony! It was stronger than I was, but always I tried to stop. Only, this spring it caught me worse than ever—why—oh, Tony, I wish it had never happened, but there it is, in my English notebook."

Tony shifted so that her back was toward Louise. She stretched out her right hand behind her, for the notebook. She opened it, and turned slowly, page after page. Then she turned around at last.

"Oh, Tony, Tony darling, you are as white as you were that morning down by the brook! I'm frightened!"

Tony's eyes laughed suddenly, eyes black-brown in her pale face. "I'm frightened myself, Lou!"

"Oh, no, no!" cried Louise. "Don't be frightened! They talked and talked and talked and talked, but I'm never going to do what they said, what Mr. Plimpton said."

"Plimpton? Gerald Plimpton? You've been talking to Gerald Plimpton?"

"He's an artist."

Tony answered sharply, "I'm familiar with artists' names, Louise."

Then she jumped up, took a few steps as if to shake herself awake, then sat down in her little rocker, facing Louise.

"Did Gerald Plimpton see this notebook?"

"Yes, Miss Austin sent it to him and asked him what he thought, and he came over and asked to talk to me; and they all three talked to me: Mr. Hargrave and Miss Austin and Mr.

Plimpton, all three there in the office. And, oh, Tony, I'm so miserable!"

"What did Gerald Plimpton say?"

"He said—he said—oh, such terrible things—that I must study, must go abroad with him and Mrs. Plimpton, just as if I were their daughter, all my expenses paid, to study in Paris! To learn to draw and paint all I want to always!"

"Oh, my Baby Lou, my Baby Lou!" Tony looked gray and gaunt as the sycamore tree.

"But, oh, Tony darling, I'm not going! I'm not going! You are to have your turn at last!"

"My turn, child?" asked Tony, amazed. "*My* turn? What do you mean?"

"I mean," cried Louise, speaking out at last: "you've never had your turn, your turn to have what you wanted. First, there were Grandfather and Grandmother; you gave your girlhood to nursing them. And then when they died and you seemed free and went off to Europe, you came back, Tony, to take care of all of us! And since then there's always been something happening for you to do, for us—for all of them having to be educated, and being so clever, and needing more and more money. Alec's only just started at being a doctor, and there was Madge's trousseau, and Florence studying to be a teacher; and we've had to go so awfully deep into principal" (Tony and Louise always spoke this word with trembling) "to start Blair in business. Always more and money going out, and the house getting shabby! And you, Tony, you've always done everything for all of us, and never had your own turn, to have anything you wanted, for yourself. And besides, the others—they don't mean to, of course, but they—" Louise checked herself sharply.

"Don't always think their old auntie as wise and clever and up-to-date as she might be?"

"Tony, they do love you, truly, but not—"

"Not the way you do? . . . . But you want to paint, don't you, Lou?"

"Oh, I never knew how much I wanted to until Mr. Plimpton talked. I'd kept it a secret for ten years, Tony. Can a person smother a thing like that inside of herself?"

Tony, that chuckling brown bun of a woman, appeared austere, far off, like an image of marble, with burning eyes. A new strange voice seemed to come from far away.

"I once knew somebody who *did* smother it inside of herself."

"Anybody I know, Tony?"

A sharp little laugh in answer. "I'm not sure either of us knows the other this afternoon. I've kept a secret, too. Louise, when I came back fifteen years ago, did you think it was just Paris I came back from?"

"I've always wondered if perhaps there was something else you gave up, but I've never guessed what it was."

"Louise, I might have shown you some things of mine—" Tony's hand caressed the closed notebook as if it had been alive—"but I burned every sketch, every picture. I've not dared to touch a brush or pencil in all these fifteen years. But, oh child, it sometimes seems as if I just *must* paint you as you look when you come through the barberry bushes on your way home from school!"

Louise gripped the edge of the window seat, herself dark against the sunset window sash, and leaned forward, gazing at Tony.

"Tony, you gave up painting—*painting!*—to take care of us! Then, then, more than ever you must have your turn!" Louise sprang up, caught the notebook from Tony's lap and flung it through the open hall door and down the stairs. She knelt and patted the cold, roughened hands. "Tony, this one of the five of us is going to give you your turn, at last!"

But Tony sat very still, searching Louise's face with those burning hungry eyes.

"Tony, was it to keep me with you that you made me promise to stop drawing, that morning ten years ago?"

Tony's gaze turned horror-stricken. "Oh, no, no! It wasn't that! Ten years ago—it was the first time I had had to dip into principal, and it frightened me. And the four of you seemed to all be needing an education at once. I didn't see how I could ever find the money to give you Paris and art, and if you couldn't have teaching, you might have to give up. I couldn't bear it for you, my Baby Lou, that you might have to smother that painting impulse inside yourself, as I have had to do."

Louise pressed her face down on Tony's hands. "Forget all that, Tony. I'm going to give you your turn. I told Mr. Plimpton I would never leave you."

Tony snatched away her hands, and laid them on Louise's shoulders. The color flooded back to her brown cheeks. Her voice was crisp.

"What on earth are you saying, child? *My* turn? What in the world do you mean? You told Mr. Plimpton you wouldn't go! Because of *me!* You call that giving me my turn?

"Oh, Baby Lou, at last you *shall* give me my turn! How could I ever have my turn except through your having yours, having it for me? Look at my hands, all bumpy now. They were supple and slender once. How can I ever have my turn to paint, except with your hands, my Baby Lou? How can I ever have my turn to see Paris, except through your eyes, my dear, my dear!

"The other four have gone their ways. They will never need their old auntie again. But you and I are different, you and I are part of each other. The others will live their own lives, fine, useful lives, I trust. But you, you have two lives to live, your own and mine. Unless you go with Mr. Plimpton, you can never give me my turn. Don't you know that you and I can never be separated, however far you journey? Whatever happens, always your head will be close to my shoulder, my love will be close about you, my Baby Lou, just as it was that snowy evening when you first came to me, fifteen years ago."

THE FAMILY
HINGE

Alice L. Whitson

*There was only so much flesh and blood a person
could take, and Ellen had more than reached that point.
She was sick and tired of being the "family hinge"
sister—and she let Father know just how she felt.*

On the broad veranda of the old Hunt homestead, in a gown of dainty white dimity, with the golden glow of a summer sunset falling softly about her, Ellen Hunt made a picture fair indeed to look upon.

Just for a moment she paused to look at the sunset, then swiftly descended the steps and made her way to a rustic table that stood beneath a towering tree in one corner of the yard. A frown darkened her usually pleasant face.

"Look at me," she mused aloud as she spread the snowy cloth and began arranging the napkins. "Here I am, like an old woman, setting a lunch table for others to enjoy."

Slowly she turned her gaze to the north side of the house, where an animated game of tennis was in progress—a game of four, in which her elder sister and brother with two friends were taking a hand. On the other side of the house, Tim and Tilda, the Hunt twins, with two small friends, were playing croquet.

A tear of self-pity rolled down the cheek of the girl as she went back to her work, and a sickening sensation enveloped her.

"I won't stand it any longer!" she declared, stamping her foot decisively; "I shall go out into the world and do something worth while! I'm tired of being the servant in this house—the hinge, as it were, on which this family swings."

"My! My!" interrupted a voice tenderly, "what's the matter with our mainstay?"

Ellen knew without looking up that the voice which had spoken belonged to her father, but for once it had lost its soothing effect, and turning, she faced him squarely.

"That's it, Father!" she exclaimed. "I am a mainstay in the family, nothing more and nothing less—just a necessary instrument to keep the home going; and I want you to know I'm dead tired of it."

For an instant Father Hunt looked at his daughter in astonishment. Never had he seen her in such an unpleasant frame of mind; but instead of reproving her, as she really expected him to do, he drew her into his arms, and lifting her face, kissed her affectionately.

"I'm afraid my little homemaker is weary with the drudgery of everyday life," he said thoughtfully, "and I suggest that she take a much-deserved rest."

Ellen opened her lips to speak, but her tongue seemed suddenly frozen to the roof of her mouth, and no words came forth.

"You've been such a splendid little woman," continued her father, "since Mother died, that we all have learned to depend on you more and more. Perhaps we've placed more burdens on you than we should. I so often thank God that such a daughter is mine—"

"But—but—Father," interrupted Ellen, "why should *I* be the family hinge? Why should the children and the older ones turn to me for everything?"

"Nothing mysterious about that," chuckled Father. "Your ever-willingness to serve and make the folks comfortable has led us all to turn to you."

"I can't understand it," Ellen declared soberly. "There is no just reason why I, the middle one of the family, should try to take the place of Mother dear. Kate and James are both older than I; from them I take orders and carry them out. It was Kate's plan to have a picnic lunch under the tree tonight, and what did she do about it? She merely said she would like to have it so, and I agreed to help Aunt Synda arrange it. Kate's part in the matter was to come home from the office with two charming young people, don her tennis clothes, and go out to the court, to be called only when the picnic lunch is ready."

"And the children," chimed in Father, "the twins, who are younger than you?"

"Oh, well," answered Ellen, "when they heard that Kate was having a picnic out under the trees, Tim asked if it would be much extra trouble to have the Moore children over, and—and—"

"And you agreed immediately that you'd see about it," finished Father.

Ellen nodded a confirming nod to her father's statement.

"I guess that's about it, Father," the girl said presently, in a more cheerful tone of voice. "I'm as much to blame for being the family hinge as the other children are to blame for swinging on me."

Just then Aunt Synda, the beloved old servant who had been in the family as far back as the eldest Hunt child could remember, came around the corner of the house with a huge pitcher of iced lemonade in her hands.

"I've got the ice cream ready, Miss Ellen," she said respectfully, as she placed the cooling drink on the table, "and I think you probably ought to call the children in for lunch, if they're going to finish eating before dark."

Ellen, acting on her advice, was soon the center of attraction, everybody calling on her at once for a helping of sandwiches or lemonade, visitors and home folks alike, praising the delicious lunch.

In spite of it all, Ellen went to bed that night with a heavy heart. She wasn't going to go through life with a whole family swinging on her for their personal comfort and pleasure. But the very next morning, when she entered the breakfast-room, she found the family waiting for her.

"Ellen," said her father softly, "I've been talking the matter over with your sisters and brothers; and we have decided that you are entitled to a rest from the family drudgery, and as an appreciation of our heartfelt gratitude we have all agreed to contribute a certain amount of wages to you for a nice long vacation. Fact is," he continued, "we're going to let you decide on the length of the visit, also the place you'd most like to go to."

A little exclamation of oh's and ah's followed this announcement, and Ellen, glancing from one to another, plainly showed her delight.

"I think—I think—" stammered the happy young girl—"that I should rather have a visit with my cousin Mollie King in New York City, than anywhere else in the world. But that might be too extravagant," she added, thoughtfully.

"Oh, no, it won't," chimed in brother James. "This is our way of showing you how much we appreciate the splendid way you've kept the home going, and we aren't going to be stingy: you shall have a visit with Mollie."

Three weeks later, Ellen Hunt found herself installed in the home of Mollie King, situated in the heart of the palatial residences that overlook the Hudson. Such a wonderful place it was, with its broad marble steps and winding stairways, its silken draperies and cut glass!

For a week things went along wonderfully well. Ellen could hardly believe it herself when she discovered she had been in this delightful fairyland for seven whole days. But the second week lagged a little, and on several occasions she found herself wondering how the folks back home were getting along without her. Not once in any of the many letters that she had received had anybody mentioned her returning; always the expression had been for her to stay away as long as she chose. They didn't even say they missed her. Somehow she wished they had said that, though between the lines she read a great deal.

Mollie had often visited in the Hunt home, and had always hoped to have the pleasure of returning some of the many courtesies that had been hers from the Hunt girls' hands, and Ellen's visit was her first opportunity. Morning, noon, and night she entertained her cousin in various ways, until Ellen begged to be allowed a day of rest.

With a whole day on her hands, Ellen resolved to enjoy herself by helping her aunt about the house.

"Oh, no, there's nothing you can do," Aunt Bessie said when Ellen offered her services.

"Isn't there a bit of mending I could do?" Ellen queried timidly.

"Mending?" repeated the woman. "I think not. You see, there are only three of us in the family. I have plenty of time to look after things. I think you'd find the park interesting this morning, Ellen."

Ellen made no more suggestions, but slipping back to her room for a sun hat, she made her way down the side stairs to the street.

The hot sun beaming down upon the white pavement caused Ellen to look for a sheltering tree, but no such luxury existed on the small plot of ground that comprised the Moore yard. Aimlessly she wandered down the street until she came to Morningside Park; there she halted, and after climbing a steep incline, sat down on a ragged boulder and let her mind wander at will.

Somehow the freshness of the park made her think of home,

and in spite of herself she wondered what they were doing. Suddenly her reverie was broken by a shadow on the grass, and glancing around, she looked into the face of a young girl of about her own age.

"I beg your pardon," the stranger stammered; "I—I thought you were asleep."

"No," said Ellen, "I wasn't asleep, but I had almost forgotten I was in this park."

"I can't fancy your forgetting that," said the stranger, "unless, of course, you're used to trees and flowers in your own yard. You see," she went on without giving Ellen time to answer, "I live down on the East Side, where trees and flowers have little space to grow, but I come up here once a week with my younger sisters because they need a bit of brightness and fresh air. I used to come more often than I do now," said the stranger thoughtfully, "but that was when Mother was living; since she died, the greater part of the homekeeping has fallen on my shoulders, and I don't have much time for idling."

"You—you—are sort of a family hinge, too," Ellen interrupted.

"A family hinge?" repeated the stranger. "What a lovely thought!"

"Lovely?" exclaimed Ellen. "Why, it sounds awful to me."

"How could such a beautiful thought sound awful? The very idea of being the hinge in a family—why, I think it's truly beauti- ful, and I shall always be grateful to you for that expression. It's like this," went on the stranger. "I'm the middle girl in a family of seven, three older and three younger than I. Being the middle one, as I have often declared myself to be, I have had the experi- ence of taking the leftovers of the older ones, and doing without to give to the younger ones; and when my mother died—well, it just seemed natural that the housework should fall on my shoulders; but I don't mind. We're hoping now that some day we shall be able to buy a little place out in the country, where we can have a real cow, and a few chickens, and a garden, and a real home where everything around it is just beautiful because of love for each other, and happiness."

On and on the girls chatted, until at the hour of parting they shook hands as firmly as if they had been friends for life. The next morning, in spite of her aunt's protestations and Mollie's plans for more merriment, Ellen packed her belongings and bought a ticket for home.

Two days later the Hunt family, sitting on the porch in the dusky twilight, heard the fast train stop at the flag station on their place for just an instant, and then move on.

"I don't suppose it could be Ellen," Father said softly, after a few moments of silence.

"I guess not," answered James. "Ellen's coming would mean too much happiness for us all."

"O Daddy, let's write for her to come home," chimed in Tilda. "I'm lonesome with her away."

"So am I, dear," Kate chimed in, "but we mustn't call her home. Poor little dear, she's been such a treasure to us all, she must have her stay unmolested."

"That's right," Father responded. "We must let the mainstay have a good rest."

Just then a slender young lady slipped through the side gate; tossing her suitcases to the ground, she threw herself into the arms of the whole family.

"My dear," broke in Father Hunt after the first excitement of Ellen's unexpected return had subsided, "we weren't looking for you back so soon. Are you quite sure you've had enough rest?"

Ellen glanced at the happy faces about her, then smiled at them all bravely.

"I'm quite convinced, Father," she said sweetly, "for while I was resting I accidentally discovered what a wonderful thing it is to—to be the family hinge."

Then before anybody could answer, she darted through the sweet-scented old hall in the direction of the kitchen, whence came the sound of Aunt Synda's voice singing.

Alice L. Whitson

Alice L. Whitson wrote for family and inspirational magazines during the first third of the twentieth century.

MERRY "LITTLE CHRISTMAS"

Agnes Sligh Turnbull

Sibling rivalry. All it takes is two children—and you have it. But what if one of them is beautiful, charismatic, multitalented, a born leader, and a scholar of the first rank, and one of them is none of the above? What does a mother do? And now that they're grown, she is filled with foreboding this Epiphany, this so-called "Little Christmas," for it appears that the family is crumbling around her.

What on earth can she do?

Not only is this one of the ten greatest Christmas stories ever written, it could very well be one of the ten greatest sisters stories as well.

*M*argaret Greaves gave a last wave from the front steps as Henry's taxi lurched off down the icy street, then, shivering, closed the door and moved dispiritedly toward the living room.

Christmas was over again, with all the so-called festive season, and she had never before felt quite so weary in body and mind, or so completely frustrated in heart.

This year, as always, she had looked forward to the great occasion with almost childish eagerness. Hank coming home from the university, Penny from college, Cecily and Bill, her husband, out from the city, the family together again, and, pervading all, that beautiful, delicate thrill of happiness which had been a part of Christmas in the past!

But it hadn't worked. It never did, now; only this year everything had been worse than usual.

Margaret sank down on the divan and looked about her. The room had the cheerless, untidy look which falls upon a house at the end of the holidays. *If this were only all!* she thought. If a good day's cleaning would set everything right, how simple it would be. But the trouble went much deeper.

Even so, she knew that the best immediate ease for the worries and disappointment of her heart was work. Penny's room upstairs was still in a whirlwind state after her departure yesterday, and Hank's not much better after his leaving two days before. At least this business trip of Henry's, while it left her lonely, would give her a chance to clean up.

She looked at the faded holly, the mistletoe, and the small tree. She would begin with them, for this was the day to take them down. It was Twelfth Night. It was also Epiphany, or "Little Christmas," as old Anya, who had lived with them when the children were small, had always called it.

Suddenly a soft, startled flush rose in Margaret's cheeks. She sat there, thinking, and then she spoke aloud.

"Little Christmas!" she repeated over and over. "Little Christmas, now, today, and mine if I want it!"

And she knew that she did want it! More than anything else in the world, she craved a second chance this year at keeping Christmas. Then, like an excited girl, she began to plan. First, she would make the living room clean and shining. She would take down the withered holly and substitute fresh greens; remove (with what a feeling of relief!) the absurd glass unicorns and golden balls that Cecily had arranged upon the mantel; she would even bring down from the attic the old creche, and the figures of the Shepherds and the Wise Men, which in the past had been the mantel decoration each Christmas.

Margaret remembered now the first time that Cecily had found fault with them. It was her first Christmas home from college.

"Mother, do we *have* to have all that old rubbish again on the mantel? It's all so frightfully old-fashioned. I'd love to try something original. Something *startling.*"

⊷═◉═⊷

As usual they had given in to Cecily, and the effect had been startling enough. It was the following year she begged to trim the tree herself.

"I've got the most marvelous idea, Mother! It seems awfully

childish to keep on hanging up the same old baubles. Do let me try out my idea. Please!"

Of course they had let her. It would have been hard to refuse her anything that Christmas. She had come home president of her class, with four A's on her report, and a special commendatory letter from the Dean. She was also to have the lead in the sophomore play, and had had a painting in the college art exhibit!

But that was Cecily—beautiful, brilliant, incredible. Beauty and brains, with artistic gifts added, had made her always the center of every scene.

When young Hank had been born, the fact that he was a boy had balanced the fact of his more or less ordinary features. And as he grew older he had held his own with sturdy masculine normality.

It was Penny, their third child, who had been the problem. Her hair was dark and straight, her eyes shy and gray, her features too strong to be pretty. In school her work was not even quite average. Somehow she was always falling behind. She couldn't make one of the biggest colleges, certainly not Cecily's, but she finally managed to enter a smaller one.

Margaret recalled again that first year that Cecily had taken over the trimming of the tree. For some reason she had not connected it before, but she realized now that it had been on that Christmas that Penny had been so *very* difficult. Henry had been annoyed to the point of sharpness, and Margaret herself had been mystified and hurt.

Now, suddenly, she wondered if it *could* have been on account of the tree? Penny had always been the one to bring down the ornaments from the attic and had always insisted upon climbing the ladder to fasten the star on top.

Margaret eyed the small fir upon the table, decked in skillfully devised paper rosettes, behind which all the tiny lights showed purple. It was, one had to admit, artistic and original, but it did not look like Christmas. Margaret went over to it now, almost wrathfully. She took off the rosettes and put them in the waste basket. She put away the lights, then lifted the tree, and threw it out the back door.

Once started upon her work, it was amazing how rapidly it went. She went to the attic for the boxes which contained the creche and figures. Then, slowly and tenderly, she arranged them as they always used to be.

She stood back and surveyed the room. It was beautiful! Tonight she would light the candles, and have a fire, and do all the things she always wanted to do at Christmas. Perhaps in the very doing of them she might find some sort of refreshment and wisdom to take up again tomorrow the cares that lay upon her heart.

She glanced toward the corner where the big tree had always stood. It was silly for her to want it there again tonight, but she did.

If she could but have it, clothed in its old ornaments, with the toys underneath which the children had always placed there, it would be like reliving those happy days when Christmas had been pure joy.

Margaret thought intently. Next door lived the Dyers. Their children were small and their tree was large. She did not delay, lest reason and decorum should overcome her. She caught up a coat and went next door. Little Mrs. Dyer was just dismantling the tree.

"Are you planning to do anything with it?" Margaret asked after the first amenities were passed.

"It's a problem, isn't it?" Mrs. Dyer said. "I think I'll just throw it out in the back yard for the present."

"Would you give it to me?" Margaret tried to be casual. "You see, I've a silly notion to try a little experiment in decorating—before another Christmas, you know—and our tree this year is too small to work on."

It didn't sound *too* fantastic as she had put it, Margaret hoped. Mrs. Dyer agreed with relief.

⟡

Margaret thought of her young neighbor as she went back home. She was the kind of girl she hoped Hank would marry some day. So bright and gay and modern, yet such a fine mother and homemaker. Would Hank choose wisely? Would he wait until he really knew what he wanted?

This girl he had taken out during the holidays was so pert, so sure of herself, so ultra-sophisticated. Her eyes looked hard and calculating and there was a brittle note in her laughter.

It worried Margaret terribly. Hank hadn't gone all out for a girl before. He had always "played the field," as the boys called it. Now what if the superficial glitter of this girl had really caught him? And she was all wrong for him, Margaret knew instinctively.

Above everything else, she had always prayed that her children might have happiness and life-long contentment with their loves, as she and Henry had had. At this point her heart seemed to turn over twice, as she thought of Cecily and Bill, for that, of course, was the most acute pain.

She was scarcely home before the oldest Dyer boy brought in the tree. She did not hurry. Indeed she loitered as she trimmed it, stopping often to hold the oldest baubles in her hand. The fruit, for instance—the red apple, the golden peach, the bright green pear. The children had particularly loved these for some reason. There was the little silver trumpet, too, and the pink wax rose, the blue bird, and the angel. These, also, had had special significance.

At last there was nothing left but the star that went on the very top. She thought of Penny, who had always begged to hang the star.

Penny, their strange, inscrutable daughter, who was flunking two subjects this first semester!

She just didn't seem to care. When she got home they had discussed it earnestly with her, but as usual could get nothing out of her. She had only mentioned casually that she had broken a swimming record. This, to Henry had been the last straw.

"A swimming record!" He had all but yelled it. "Do you think we're paying fifteen hundred dollars a year for you to go *swimming?* Now, this nonsense has to stop; you've got to get down to work."

Penny had said nothing, and gone up to her room. And now, what if she really flunked out of college? What was to be *done* about Penny?

She had always been dependable in other ways. Cecily often forgot things. It was Penny, silent and undemonstrative, who was always there when needed.

It was Penny's gift which had pleased her mother most of all this year—a tiny bottle of the rare flower perfume which Margaret loved. It must have eaten a big hole in Penny's allowance! It was plainly wrapped, with a small card bearing the words: "Merry Christmas to Mom from Penny."

Cecily's gift had been a bizarre green handbag which did not go with any single costume Margaret possessed. It was tied with yards of silver and gold ribbon, and the card read: "Oceans of love to the most wonderful mother in the world."

Margaret sighed. Before long she would know about Cecily and Bill. They had told her of what threatened, each in characteristic fashion.

"Mother, I can't believe it! It's simply *too* marvelous!" Cecily had begun when they were alone for a few minutes the day before Christmas.

Margaret was used to this introduction. It meant that some new success had come to Cecily.

"What is it, dear?" she asked eagerly.

"I've been offered the position of associate editor on the magazine!"

"Why, Cecily! Oh, that's wonderful! Darling, I'm so proud of you!"

"What's up now?" Penny had inquired, coming into the room.

Margaret had repeated the news and Penny, without comment, had passed on.

Cecily continued: "Nobody knows how I've wished for this job! How I'll love it! And I know I can make a go of it, only . . ."

"Only what?"

"Bill is being absolutely mulish about it."

"What do you mean?"

"Well, we had decided that I'd take time off this coming year to have a baby. With the new job, I can't. I think Bill ought to be reasonable. There's plenty of time." Cecily's lovely face had suddenly stiffened. A new note had come into her voice. "I might as well tell you that this may be serious between us. He's just about issued an ultimatum, and nobody can do that to me."

"But darling, surely you can compromise somehow." She

realized now, ashamed, that her immediate reaction had been that Cecily must not be thwarted in this, her crowning honor.

Cecily had turned away. "Maybe you can do something with him," she said, and all at once her voice sounded flat and tired. "You know he always listens to you."

Bill had followed her up to her room that night, where she was frantically wrapping the last packages. She had had such a hectic day, and even now the turkey stuffing had to be made before she slept. She loved Bill, and because he had no mother of his own, he had somehow taken her to his heart.

"We're in trouble, Mom, Cecily and I. It's bad."

"Oh, Bill, she told me. You *mustn't* let anything spoil your marriage. You must try to see each other's side of things."

"I needn't tell you how I love Cecily. You know that. But she's got to decide now what she wants."

"Bill, dear, she's young yet. She could take time off later. . . ."

"Some girls could, but not Cecily. I know her even better than you. In a few years this magazine thing will be a tremendous job. There will never be any time in Cecily's life for having children and making a home for them. As a matter of fact," he added slowly, "there may not even be much time for me, if she goes ahead."

"Bill, don't say that."

"I'm only facing facts. But one thing, Mom, you've got to believe. It's Cecily's happiness I'm thinking of, too, and not just my own. I've seen plenty of lonesome career women of forty-five."

"So have I."

"That's why I'm fighting with all I've got for both of us."

She had kissed him with her eyes full. "All I want is for you both to be happy. But try your best to understand each other. I'll tell Cecily the same. And let me know as soon as it's all settled."

⊷══◉═══⊷

Margaret gave a physical motion now of shaking the anxiety from her. No word had come from them yet. Whether the omen was good or ill, she did not know. She hurried through her solitary dinner, and then lighted the logs in the fireplace. Then she lit the candles, snapped on the button which illuminated the tree, and sat down, a sense of peace stealing over her.

This one night was all hers in which to make up for what she had missed, and gird herself for all that was to come. She suddenly knew that the one of her children who would most enjoy this with her would be Penny. Even though she would say little, she would like it.

"I broke a swimming record. . . ." The sentence flashed into her mind. Those were the words that Penny had injected casually the day they had talked with her about her work. And except for Henry's flare-up, they had passed the information by without comment, in their concern over her studies!

She had broken a record. What record? They hadn't even asked.

All at once Margaret sat very straight. That had meant a lot to Penny. She had been laying her triumph before them in her own way, and they had ignored it.

She saw it now with sudden insight: this was the very first triumph Penny had ever had. She had always loved to swim, but nobody had thought much about it. But now *she had broken a record!*

Margaret rose with instant decision, went to the telephone, and called Penny long-distance.

"Hello, dear." Margaret knew she sounded nervous.

"Hi, Mom. Anything wrong?"

"Not a thing. Penny, I want to know about that record you broke in swimming."

"You *what?*"

"Tell me all about it. Penny, please. What record was it?"

"Well," she could hear the faint note of pleasure that crept into Penny's voice, "you see the college here doesn't compete. We just have our own team. But of course we keep track of the records. And just before Christmas I busted the hundred yard freestyle American Women's Intercollegiate!" She hurried through the words, but her mother could feel her excitement.

"Penny! Why, that's simply tremendous! Weren't they thrilled at school?"

"Oh, they made sort of a fuss."

"Darling, I'm so proud of you I don't know what to do!"

There was a dead silence on the other end of the phone. Margaret went on.

"I wish you were here tonight. I'm all alone, you know, so I'm celebrating what Anya used to call Little Christmas. Remember? I'm having everything just the way we used to when you were children. The creche and the figures are on the mantel, and I borrowed the Dyers' tree and put all the old trimmings on it."

"Mom, you *did?*" Her words were quick, incredulous.

"Yes. Does it seem too crazy?"

"Is the bluebird on . . . and the rose?"

"Yes."

"And the *fruit?*"

"Everything."

"The peach was mine. I was always afraid Cecily would want

it, but she picked the apple. The pear was Hank's. You . . . you didn't bring the toys down too, I suppose?"

"Yes, I did. The doll and the bear and the dog. They always had to be there. This year things were not just right. I wonder whether you know that Cecily and Bill . . ."

"Cecily's a fool. If I had as nice a husband as Bill, I'd *want* to have his children."

"I'm sure you would, dear. I wish Cecily were more like you."

There was another breathless second of silence, and then came a strange, husky voice.

"Would . . . would you say that again?"

"I said," Margaret repeated distinctly, "that I wished Cecily were more like you."

"Mom . . ."

"Yes, dear."

"I'm awfully glad you called up."

"So am I."

"Are you going to call Hank?"

"I hadn't thought of it."

"I believe he'd like to hear about the tree. And Mom, tell Dad I'll make up the work. It won't be too much trouble. I . . . I sort of feel different now, somehow. Sort of . . . happy!"

"I'll tell him, darling. Lots of love. Goodbye."

Margaret sat at the desk, her eyes wet. So many things seemed clear now. She put in the call for Hank. She doubted whether he would be greatly interested, but it would be good to hear his voice. When she told him rather apologetically what she had done, Hank didn't laugh.

"Have you got the trumpet on the tree?" he asked.

"Absolutely."

"And the pear?"

"Yes."

"I remember how I always liked those best of anything. I had to fight Cecily for the trumpet, but I stuck it out."

"I brought the old toys down, too. You know, the favorites that you children always thought should enjoy Christmas with you."

"You did? Say, you're going sentimental in a big way, aren't you, Mom? I remember how Penny used to sneak them down and hide them behind the tree when we'd really outgrown them. Penny's a good kid."

"Yes, she certainly is," Margaret agreed, with a catch in her throat. She told him about the swimming record. Hank was excited.

"No! Honest? Broke the hundred-yard freestyle? Why, that's big-time stuff, Mom. She never said a word."

"Write and congratulate her, Hank."

"You bet I will. Why, that's really tops. You know Penny has a lot on the ball. Well, what else are you doing tonight, Mom, all by yourself?"

"Oh, just the things I didn't have time to do on the real Christmas. I like old-fashioned customs just—"she hesitated— "just as I like some old-fashioned qualities in girls."

"Yeah, I guess I do myself, when you come right down to it."

"They're likely to wear better in the long run, Hank."

"You can say *that* again!" There was a faint edge in his voice.

(*He's beginning to find that girl out,* Margaret thought. *He's going to be safe after all.*)

"Mom, I sort of like picturing the room the way it was when we were kids. Let's have it like that next year."

"We're going to. And now, good luck, dear. Goodbye."

⟶≡●≡⟵

Margaret went slowly back to the couch and sat down, a warm glow in her heart. Now for the evening. She had collected the selections she liked best of the seasonal literature. They were on the table beside her. They ranged from "The Night Before Christmas" to the Gospel according to St. Luke.

She smiled as she fingered the books. No matter if there were contrasts among her favorites, she would read them just the same. She would also play some carols.

"Mother and her everlasting carols!" Cecily used to say. "Don't you ever get tired of them?"

She put a fresh log on the fire and sat down again with a deep sigh of contentment. Even as she did so, there was a quick tap-tap on the knocker and then the opening of the front door. She knew at once that it must be Cecily and Bill. Cecily came into the room, her face white and set. Bill followed her, looking as though he hadn't slept for a week. Margaret knew what they had come to tell her. Now, tonight, this night!

But they were both looking around the room in amazement.

"Well, what on earth!" Cecily cried.

"This is Twelfth Night," Margaret said. "Little Christmas. I wasn't satisfied with our Christmas this year, so I'm celebrating it again. I'm going right ahead with my plans, even though you are here."

Bill was over at the mantel, looking at the creche and the figures.

Cecily was at the tree. Her mother couldn't see her face, but she saw her touching the various ornaments.

"Where's the apple?" she asked.

"Up there, higher, to the right."

"It and the angel were always mine," she said.

"What was that?" Bill asked.

"Nothing," said Cecily. Then she gave a quick exclamation. "My heavens, you even brought down the old toys!"

Bill was beside her now, peering under the shadow of the tree. Cecily picked up the doll, but suddenly put it down and turned away, as though she had been guilty of folly.

Margaret spoke firmly. "I am now about to play and sing some carols, and then read some Christmas selections. I ought to warn you."

Bill went over to the fireside chair and sank into it. His face under the table light was haggard and drawn. Cecily glanced quickly at him, then sat down on the couch. Her beautiful profile was still cold and bitterly set.

"I suppose we can take it," she said.

Margaret played and sang from memory, trying by a tremendous effort to think of the familiar words, and not allow herself to break down under the impact of the misery which hung over Cecily and Bill.

She moved from one old favorite to another, and at last she came to "Silent Night." As she sang, her heart all but broke in yearning over her children, sitting in the same room with her and yet so far away.

Bill was leaning forward now, his head in his hands; Cecily was sitting motionless, her eyes upon the tree. Once her mother saw her look at Bill and then glance quickly away.

Margaret rose and came back to her place. She tried to speak brightly.

"Now," she said, "I'm going to read my old favorites. You can still escape if you want to."

Neither spoke, so she began. She read "The Night Before

Christmas." When she finished, she looked musingly at the burning logs.

"When the children were small, Bill, we always let them help trim the tree the afternoon before Christmas. Then, after an early supper, they came down in their pajamas and bathrobes and sat on the rug before the fire while I read them this poem. Do you remember, Cecily?"

"Of course," she said in an odd voice.

Margaret picked up the next book. "Then, when they grew older, they still liked this Christmas Eve ritual, only we added bits from *A Christmas Carol*. They loved the Cratchits best of all."

As she read from the worn book with its familiar markings, she glanced up once or twice to look at the haggard young man and the stony-faced young woman. She found their eyes on each other, Bill's anguished and beseeching, his wife's—but she couldn't see into Cecily's.

Something of the humble happiness of the Cratchits seemed to be released from the pages, and to hover about the room.

"Do you remember how you children always worried about Tiny Tim's fate each year, even though you knew he wasn't going to die?"

"I remember," said Cecily.

Margaret's throat felt tight.

"And now," she said, "I'm going to read the sweetest story of them all."

She picked up the small black book beside her. Her voice was low, and she read slowly.

"And it came to pass in those days that there went out a decree from Caesar Augustus that all the world should be taxed."

As she went on, she felt the weight of her own emotion overcoming her. Margaret knew she would never finish the chapter.

"And she brought forth her first born son, and wrapped him in swaddling clothes and laid him in a manger; because there was no room for them in the inn."

Her voice caught. She closed the book and laid it back on the table. Silence filled the room. She was afraid to look up as the moments passed.

Then at last she sensed that Cecily had risen and gone over to Bill. Margaret raised her eyes then and saw her standing there, her cheeks wet with tears, her face bearing upon it the tender portent of the woman she would one day become.

"We've got to go, Mother. Bill's awfully tired. He ought to get some rest. It's been wonderful being here tonight. And, Mother, put the toys away carefully. You can't tell what may happen before another year!"

⊸⫘◉⫘⊶

When they had left, Margaret came back into the pine-scented, fire-warmed, candlelit room, her heart melting with joy! New wisdom and understanding had come to her along with hope and relief. On this, the anniversary of the holy night when the Wise Men had come to worship the baby in the manger, her own children had been given back to her, safe from the perils which threatened them.

They were all one now, as in the past, close and secure in the circle of love. If only Henry were here to rejoice with her, it would be complete.

She raised her head, thinking. She couldn't bear to have him shut out of the strange and wonderful happiness of this night. She could not telephone him, for this was the evening of the big banquet. But she could send him a wire!

A little smile played over her lips as she mentally framed it. She could picture Henry receiving it when he came back late to the hotel. He would be first startled, then, as he read, puzzled. At last he would tuck it into his inner pocket with that familiar, half quizzical, half adoring expression in his eyes. He would be thinking, "What's she been up to now?"

Margaret repeated the message three times before the operator got it.

"Merry Little Christmas, and all my love."

Agnes Sligh Turnbull
(1888–1958)

Agnes Sligh Turnbull, author of bestsellers such as *The Bishop's Mantle* (1947), *The Town of Glory* (1952), and *The Golden Journey* (1955), wrote of a world where values were crucial. She also wrote some of the most treasrued short stories we know.

VACATION DAYS

Dee Dunsing

*T*he twins were not alike—not at all alike. And never were those differences more apparent than during this gold-mining summer with Uncle Tip. And increasingly those differences got on their nerves.

Something had to happen. And did.

*W*ith a gesture of irritation and rebellion, Midge Carter straightened her aching back, said "Shucks!" with loud emphasis, and flung her gold-washing pan a good fifty feet into the sky-pointing pines.

Peggy, Midge's twin sister, only looked up silently from where she stood at the edge of the Colorado Little Fork, the water curling over her boot-shod feet. Then calmly she bent, scooped up a panful of dirt, and began to swish the water and mud out of it. When she had finished, she picked two or three tiny gold flecks from the bottom of the pan and stowed them in a small rawhide sack which her Uncle Tip had given her.

"I'm not going to quiet down either," Midge added, her black eyes snapping. "I'm going up there." She gestured toward the pine forest that sloped upward toward the towering brown peaks of the Saddle Range.

"Don't be silly," Peggy spoke at last. "You're wasting good energy."

"It's good energy, all right," Midge agreed hotly. "Too good for this job!"

"You're being infantile."

"Oh, am I?" challenged Midge. "Personally, I think you're being blind as a bat about everything. We were foolish to have popped out here on the strength of that newspaper article. 'Gold in paying quantities!' Humph! What we wash out of this creek wouldn't keep us in soap chips for a month."

"What if we did make a mistake?" spoke Peggy quietly. "We still need money, don't we? Anything we can make is better than nothing."

"But we can't finish school on it," fumed Midge. "One semester to go! And what will we make here, after weeks of back-breaking work—about thirty-two or thirty-three dollars apiece!"

Peggy strove to put a blonde lock in place with her wet muddy hands. "We came out here to pan gold," she said evenly, "and I'm going to pan it. Even if we don't make much, it's better than spending our summer vacation doing nothing."

"But how are you going to get through school that way?" spoke Midge impatiently. "What are you going to eat on, pay room rent with? Tell me that!"

"I don't know," Peg replied. "But I do know that however much I make will be that much to start on."

"Bosh!" Midge splashed across the stream and started toward close-looming Saddle Peak. "I'm striking out for something else. Tell Uncle Tip that I may be a bit late; but if I don't get home in time to help with supper, I'll do the dishes." She strode away toward the mountain, her strong young shoulders looking very square and determined.

"Where are you going?" Peggy called after her in a voice tinged with alarm.

"Don't know," was Midge's laconic reply.

"Come back, Midge! You're acting silly!"

There was no answer to that. From where she stood in the boiling stream, Peggy could see that Midge was digging her toes into the pine needles with extraordinary force, angrily pushing herself up the steep hill. *It was like her,* Peg thought, *to march off just now when they needed money so badly. The two remaining weeks would come and go like a tangy mountain breeze, and another financial shortage would block the way to their education. No matter if Klondiking on Uncle Tip's ranch had been disappointing, money was money, even a little of it. And tempers and rage were an extravagance which they couldn't afford.*

She became conscious that her own temper was rising, and that she too was wasting time. Being a very dutiful person she at once turned back to her work.

⊷══◉═⊷

Peggy and Uncle Tip were just finishing supper when Midge came home.

"Hi, everybody," she said briefly, as she went over to the basin to wash.

Peggy waited till her twin was seated at the table and buttering a piece of warm cornbread before she spoke what was on her mind.

"I didn't want to seem like a tattletale, or someone talking behind your back, Midge," she said soberly, "but now that you're here, I do want to tell Uncle Tip what happened today. I think we ought to have his opinion."

"Shoot," said Midge briefly, her black eyes gleaming a challenge in the yellow glow of the kerosene lamp.

"Well," Peggy began, "it's this way, Uncle Tip. Midge is discouraged because we're not making much out of Little Fork, and she batted off today up Saddle Mountain before she'd washed more than ten cents' worth of dust. I stuck at it and got over a dollar's worth. Now, don't you think she's being foolish?"

Uncle Tip's shrewd old eyes were quizzical under their shaggy white brows. "Don't know as I can say offhand." He turned to Midge. "What are you figurin' on gettin' up on Saddle Mountain?" he inquired kindly.

"There's always the chance of a big strike," Midge responded eagerly. "I know it's a long shot, but if I could find something, it would be worth while. The stray change we're washing out of Little Fork isn't enough to pay."

"Well, now, there's sense to that," agreed Uncle Tip.

"Not a lot," flared Peggy, irritated by his lenience toward Midge. "We'll only be here two more weeks, and it takes years of prospecting to find a lode. What we need now is a bird in the hand, not a whole covey in the bush."

Uncle Tip's old eyes seemed very soft and sympathetic, as if he wanted both the girls to be happy. "Midge ought to carry a mattock to grub around a mite with," he advised. "Otherwise, it seems to me she can't do any harm huntin' for a lode."

"No harm, but no good," flashed Peggy. "A girl's got to stick and drudge away at anything she tries. She can't get discouraged and give up."

"She shouldn't be stupid and stick at something hopeless," retorted Midge.

"Now, now," soothed Uncle Tip, "you girls quit pickin' on each other. You're both tired, and that's the cause of it. I've been wantin' to tell you a little story, and I guess maybe this is a good time to do it. Would you like to hear the story about the chicken and the snake?"

Peggy excused herself abruptly from the table. "I'm sorry, Uncle Tip," she explained tensely, "but I'm not in the mood for stories. Some other time, maybe."

⋅→═◉═←⋅

The afternoon sun made a golden halo out of Peggy's hair as she stooped tirelessly at her task beside the creek. Bend . . . scoop . . . swish . . . put the tiny glittering residue in her rawhide sack. It was the same process over and over. During the first few days she had nearly dropped from exhaustion; but now she was used to the grind, and could stand all day long beside the icy stream, slowly sorting out its precious freight.

With only two days left of their vacation now, she could boast a small amount of golden metal, but it was worth at least forty dollars, and to an impoverished student, forty dollars looms large.

She felt bad about Midge, but didn't quite know how to adjust matters. Her twin had persisted in hunting for a lode. Every morning Midge wandered off into the mountains with a sandwich in her pocket and a mattock in her hands; every night she came home scuffed and dirty and discouraged-looking. Now, at the end of the vacation, she had practically nothing to show for her days. Unless through some lucky chance she could get extra work in town, she would have to quit school.

Peggy had hoped that Uncle Tip would finally make Midge stop her foolishness. But he always evaded the issue.

As she was putting an extra large flake into her gold pouch, she heard an odd, distant sound. Because she was so busy and so upset by Midge's problem, she didn't pay much attention.

When she stooped to refill her pan, she heard the sound again. This time it was a faint ringing shout, undoubtedly of human origin. It might be—yes, it was!—Midge calling her twin's name!

Without an instant's hesitation Peggy dropped her gold pan, ran full tilt in the direction of the voice. "I'm coming, Midge!" she shouted as she sped along. "Coming!" Their little disagreement faded to nothing. Midge needed her now, and that was the important thing.

A short way up the slope she ran into dense timber which forced her to slow down; and farther still, wide arrays of gray windfall blocked her path. Running, climbing, leaping, she pushed her way through, calling to Midge as she went. Branch-claws caught at her sweater and breeches, and scratched her face unmercifully. She hardly noticed them. She was remembering when she and Midge were small girls, how Midge had often called for help like this. Midge, the daring, the adventurous one, who always climbed too high, or wooded too deep, or jumped too far and had to be helped out of trouble.

The voice kept calling, drew her toward a deep canyon-slash in the mountainside. She found herself staring up at steep walls, spotted with outcroppings of volcanic rock and tufted with giant ferns which had taken root in crack and gully.

"Midge!" she called loudly, not hearing the voice.

The answer came back immediately. "Here I am, Peg. Directly above you."

It was a full minute before Peggy could locate her twin. Midge's figure looked so tiny, clinging to a narrow ledge halfway up the canyon wall. The sight of it made Peggy's heart give a terrific jump.

"Hold on!" she called encouragingly. "I'll get you."

Through a gully-crack in the wall, she made her way up toward Midge, wondering desperately whether she herself could manage this climb. Climbing had always made her a bit giddy—even the old apple tree at home had seemed scary to look out of—and she knew that she ran the risk of toppling into the canyon herself.

"Take it careful, Peg. Plenty of time," Midge was calling to her, trying to appear as if all this were just a trifle, a mere matter of inconvenience. But Peg didn't miss the nervous, exhausted quaver of the trapped girl's voice.

At last she was parallel with Midge, but still a good twenty-five feet from her. On the cliff face, she could see the series of ledges that Midge had used in getting to her present position. She herself would have to follow that same series, give Midge a hand to hold, and steady her while she came back the same way.

"I'm coming!' she called gayly, as she took the first step onto the terrifying cliff face.

Peggy reached for a new handhold, tested it, went on. She was close now. With a quick glance about her, a glance that spurned the dizzy distance down to the canyon floor, she caught a glimpse of Midge's face. It was woefully white and beaded with tiny drips of perspiration.

One more step. Peggy tested her handholds more carefully than ever. This time they would have to bear not only her weight but Midge's. At last she leaned over and held out an arm.

"I say, James, can't you do a lady the courtesy of taking her hand?"

"Very—very good, miss." Midge leaned close against the wall, took her hand from its bit of projecting rock and gave it to Peg. "I'm going to have to put a lot of weight on it," she whispered.

"Go ahead," offered Peggy grimly.

There was a tense, shaky two or three minutes, while Midge, clinging tightly to Peggy's hand, pulled herself off the ledge and followed her sister back toward the gully. Every pebble or bit of dirt that shook loose reminded them, by its ominous clink in the canyon below, of what would happen if they lost their hold.

At last it was over. They were safe in the gully. Peggy leaned weakly against a boulder, and Midge sank down beside a clump of mountain oak and indulged in a fit of frightened tears.

⤙═◉═⤚

After a while they climbed silently down the gully and started for home. The sun had sunk below Saddle Peak, and the valleys were dark. As they waded across foaming Little Fork, they saw Uncle Tip setting a kerosene light in the window for them.

"He's worried, poor fellow!" murmured Peggy.

When they burst in the door, he was just putting on his jacket and cap to go and look for them. With a puzzled glance he stuffed his cap back into his pocket and scratched his head. "Now what have you girls been up to?" he asked.

While Midge was explaining, Peggy felt a sudden anger at her twin because of the useless, nerve-shredding ordeal they had just been through. "Midge certainly made a success of this vacation," she spoke sarcastically. "I'm amazed that she didn't break a leg or an arm to help out matters."

Midge stared at her with a surprised, dazed look. "Why, I—I almost forgot—"

"You forgot that we came out here to earn a little money?" Peggy suggested. "Yes, I know that quite as well as you."

"Now, now," cautioned Uncle Tip gently, "you two girls are just tired—"

"But I forgot," Midge insisted, a trifle wildly. "I forgot something awfully important." Her hand was searching in her pocket, and she brought out several bits of queer-looking rock. "This is the reason I got down on that ledge. I wanted to get some samples of this rock. What is this funny ore, Uncle Tip?"

Uncle Tip was taking his spectacles out of his pocket, putting them on, staring seriously at the bits of gray stone. He turned them over in his palm, and back again. "Midge," he said at last, "that is lead and silver and zinc, all mixed up. Was there much of it?"

"Lots, Uncle Tip! There were outcroppings of it all along the cliff," Midge explained excitedly. "I could see it from below—that's why I climbed up toward it."

"You've got something mighty valuable here," Uncle Tip said

solemnly. "Mighty valuable. I never saw such a rich concentration of this stuff."

Midge began to jump up and down. "A mine, Peg! I've found a mine! Hurray! We're rich!"

Peg felt excited and pleased, but at the same time she felt ashamed. Here she had been grumping about Midge's expeditions, and now Midge had found a valuable mine. She wished there were a mouse hole around. She was positive she could have crawled into it.

"Pshaw now, Peggy," said Uncle Tip, seeing her discomfiture, "you don't need to feel cheap on account of that old argument you two have been havin'. Why, you two are like that story I've been tryin' to tell about the chicken and the snake. Seems like I won't ever get it told; but anyway, it's about how they each one needed the other one to get along well. Now you stayed at home, calm and careful, while Midge went gallivantin' off to find herself a treasure. It's pure luck that she found it. But even when she did, she had to have you pick her off a ledge, or she mighta been there yet—a fortune in her pocket and no expectation of livin' long enough to enjoy it. See what I mean?"

He glanced at the two girls, at their respectful appraisals of each other.

"Well, I guess that ends the feud on Little Fork," he chuckled.

Dee Dunsing

Dee Dunsing wrote for family and inspirational magazines during the first half of the twentieth century.

THE
INSEPARABLES

Harriet Lummis Smith

Even though they weren't really sisters, they might as well have been: "We call them the inseparables, or else the Siamese twins. You never see one without the other."

And then a new girl came into town.

*I*t was while Anne Armitage and Betty Joyce were eating their ice cream that a girlish voice came distinctly to their ears. "We call them the inseparables, or else the Siamese twins. You never see one without the other."

Anne ate on stolidly, but Betty's cheeks flamed. "Do you suppose they mean us?" Betty asked her chum.

"Maybe. I don't know or care."

"Well, I do," announced Betty. "I think it's horrid."

Very deliberately Anne turned her head. Two girls sitting at a small table over against the wall were watching them curiously. Isabel Blake was a town girl. The other, pretty, animated, with dark mischievous eyes, was a stranger; but Anne guessed her name.

"It's that Ray Leverett whom Isabel's always talking about," she said. "Isabel's showing her the sights, including us."

The friendship between Anne and Betty was originally due to proximity. They lived in the same block; and years before, they had fallen into the habit of walking to and from school together. Though they were practically the same age, Anne seemed older; and from their first-grade days, Betty's mother had a way of entrusting Betty to Anne's guardianship. "Be careful when you cross the streets, won't you, Anne? Betty never looks." Even then, Anne had accepted the responsibility for Betty.

As time passed, Anne developed a feeling almost of proprietorship over Betty. She was conscious of something like annoyance when any of the other girls sought Betty's society.

"What did Phyllis Parker want of you?" she demanded after Phyllis had called Betty to her locker one day and kept her there till the bell rang.

"She was telling me about Amelia's accident."

"Why all that air of secrecy?" Anne demanded. "Everybody knows about Amelia."

"She was just talking about it," explained Betty. "She didn't say it was a secret."

"I should hope not," Anne answered contemptuously.

And when next Betty encountered Phyllis, her impulse was to look away. Anything was better than having Anne annoyed.

On this particular afternoon as the two girls finished their ice cream, Isabel Blake spoke just behind them: "Hello, there!"

"Oh, hello!" Anne turned with marked deliberation. Betty did not speak, but smiled nervously.

"This is my friend, Ray Leverett," Isabel said. "You've both heard me talk about her. And Ray, these two are Anne Armitage and Betty Joyce."

"Otherwise known as the Siamese twins," Ray said. Her rather pert gaze met Anne's steely eyes, then focused itself on Betty, who was blushing.

"Well," Betty stammered, "I suppose folks do call us that."

"You must be great friends. Now, Isabel and I get along wonderfully because we see each other only about once in two years."

As Betty laughed politely, Isabel said, "We're going to the library to see that stamp exhibition. Don't you girls want to come along?"

"We're going tomorrow," Anne replied.

Betty looked at her appealingly, as if hoping she would soften the bluntness of her refusal; but Anne said no more, and Betty murmured, "Yes, we've arranged to go tomorrow. Thank you very much."

"What's the point in all the gratitude?" Anne asked as the others went on. "The exhibition's free."

"Yes, but it was nice of them to ask us to go along."

"Was it? Well, I'm glad it wasn't necessary for us to accept. I know I should detest that Leverett girl. Did you ever see anybody who had such an air of being perfectly satisfied with herself?"

While Anne was relieving her mind, Ray was expressing herself with equal emphasis. "And you call those two Siamese twins. Why, they're about as much alike as a nice Angora pussy-cat and a prickly porcupine."

Isabel laughed. "Of course they're not alike. We call them that because they're always together."

"Good reason why. That big bossy one has her claws in the little timid one and won't let her go. I believe she—Betty's her name, isn't it—wanted to come with us today. The grouch wouldn't give her a chance to speak."

"Oh, that's Anne's way," Isabel said. "She always takes it for granted that she can decide for Betty."

⟶⟾◉◉⟾⟵

Isabel had planned to ask some friends to luncheon on Friday, and that evening she went over the list with Ray. "You've met Abbie and Marguerite. Phyllis is the one I told you about, with the lovely voice. The two Anderson girls live in a nice rambling place in the country."

Isabel checked off the names on her fingers. "That's five, and you and I make seven. Eight is the nicest number for our dining room, so I can ask one more."

"How about Betty Joyce?" suggested Ray.

"Well, we couldn't invite Betty without Anne, and that—"

"Why not?" Ray cut in.

It took Isabel a moment to understand the question. "You mean, invite Betty and leave Anne out?"

"Why not?"

"Well, I never thought of such a thing. You see they're always together."

"It's time that nice little Betty was getting a break," Ray declared. "Something should be done about that combination."

"I'm not sure Betty would come without Anne."

"Give her a chance anyway," prodded Ray.

Fifteen minutes later the Joyces' telephone rang and Betty accepted the invitation with characteristic pleasure. But Isabel said to Ray, "She says she'll be so glad to see you again; but of course she doesn't know that I didn't ask Anne. When she finds out she may call up and make some excuse for not coming."

"Well, we'll see," Ray smiled.

As a matter of fact, the possibility that Anne had not been included in the invitation didn't even enter Betty's head. When she saw Anne next morning, she asked at once, "What are you going to wear to Isabel's?"

"To Isabel's? What do you mean?" Anne looked puzzled.

"Why, to the luncheon Friday."

"You mean—" Anne was beginning, and then caught herself up. "I haven't been invited to any luncheon," she said icily.

"Oh, Anne—but of course you will be."

"I don't know why. If Isabel Blake doesn't like me any better than I like her, I don't know why she should invite me." Anne waited for that to take effect, then added coldly, "I suppose you'll go anyway."

"Why, I've accepted." Bewilderment was in Betty's tone.

"Go, of course. I'll manage to amuse myself." Anne's frigid manner did not suggest her secret panic. That Betty should wish to attend a party to which she—Anne—had not been invited was so unexpected that she could hardly believe it.

For a day or two the relations between the friends were noticeably strained. Anne was hurt by Betty's failure to resent the fact that she had not been included in Isabel's invitation.

"If it were an evening party, it would be different," Betty insisted. "But naturally she can't have many for luncheon."

"What surprises me is your sudden popularity with Isabel Blake. I didn't know you considered her a special friend."

"I don't, of course," Betty said, "but I have always liked her."

"Well, I dislike her about as much as any girl I know."

The incredible thing, from Anne's point of view, was that nothing she could say lessened Betty's pleased anticipation of the forthcoming luncheon. More than once the appalling thought flashed through Anne's mind that perhaps Betty was glad to go somewhere by herself in order to prove that she and Anne were not really inseparable.

Anne had finally succeeded in making Betty uncomfortable so that on Friday she went to the luncheon with a sense of guilt, as if she were showing herself disloyal. But the girls were so friendly, and Ray in particular made such an effort to be entertaining, that Betty enjoyed the afternoon hugely. When she reached home, she promptly broached a plan that had occurred to her an hour or two earlier.

"Couldn't I ask Isabel and Ray to go to the lake with us tomorrow? Ray would just love it."

As Mr. and Mrs. Joyce were willing, Betty called Isabel on the phone and gave the invitation. The two girls accepted enthusiastically. But with two guests secured, Betty's manner became anxious.

"Now I'd better call Anne," she said. "I'll sit in front with you two, and Anne can sit in the back with Ray and Isabel."

Mrs. Joyce shook her head. "It's too long a drive for us to sit three in the front seat. Besides, I'm not sure that Anne would be an agreeable addition to the party. I'm afraid she doesn't like Isabel."

"But, Mother, if I invite those other girls and don't ask Anne, she won't like it a bit."

"You can ask Anne some other time," Mrs. Joyce said with decision. "You two are great friends, of course, but that doesn't mean you are not to be allowed any other friends."

⤙⟴⟴⤚

The next morning Anne waited expectantly for Betty to make her appearance. About ten o'clock she left the house and walked slowly down the street. Betty was not on the porch; and swallowing her pride, Anne climbed the steps and rang the bell. She was startled when from the window of the next house someone said, "The Joyces are all away."

"All away?" she repeated dazedly.

"They went to Loon Lake for the day. They took Isabel Blake along and that girl who is visiting her."

"I see. Thank you very much." Anne walked away with her head in the air. But, though she retained her outward self-control, she was sick with anger and humiliation. That was the end of her friendship with Betty, she told herself. Of course Betty would come around the next morning pretending that nothing was wrong; but she would soon learn her mistake.

Anne passed a dreadful day. Her frenzy of jealousy made her physically ill. Her head ached. The sight of food nauseated her.

And, as from her point of view Betty was to blame for her discomfort, her indignation grew by leaps and bounds. She told herself over and over that she would never forgive her.

By seven o'clock that evening Anne was feeling so ill that she decided to go to bed. She was just starting upstairs when her mother called, "Come to the phone, Anne. Mrs. Blake wants to speak to you."

Mrs. Blake sounded frightened. "Anne, do you know when the Joyces planned to return home?"

"I don't know anything about it," Anne said sullenly.

"We expected the girls for dinner, and they have an engagement for the evening. I thought probably you might have heard Betty say—"

"No," repeated Anne, "I don't know anything about it." But the sullenness had gone from her voice; and as she hung up the receiver, her hand was shaking. She went up to her room but did not go to bed. Instead, she sat where she could see when the lights came on in Betty's home. She sat there till ten o'clock, and the house was still dark. Then the doorbell rang.

Anne came running downstairs just as her mother opened the door. It was Phyllis Parker outside. "I came over," she began, "to see if Anne had heard—"

"Heard what?" Anne cried shrilly. "Oh, Phyllis, heard *what?*"

"Somebody living near Loon Lake has telephoned," Phyllis said. "There's been an accident. A car went through the side of the bridge over Wolf River below the falls. The side of the bridge is all smashed. They can't see the car, but they're sure it's under water. And the Joyces haven't come home. It's too terrible."

Anne swayed where she stood, and Phyllis ran to her. "We all love Betty," she sobbed, "but, of course, you were her dearest friend, and it's worse for you than any of us. As soon as I heard, I came over." And then, as Anne stood rigid and silent, she added anxiously, "Perhaps you'd rather I'd go now."

"No," Anne said, speaking with difficulty. "Please stay."

⇥═◉═⇤

There were many sleepless homes in town that night. The failure of the Joyces to return, coupled with the fact that some car had plunged into the deep waters of Wolf River, left little doubt as to the fate of the family. Anne, lying wakeful as the hours passed, opened up her heart to Phyllis. She did not spare herself. She confessed her jealousy, her selfishness, and denounced herself so savagely that sometimes Phyllis protested, "Oh, no, Anne. You're too hard on yourself."

Late in the night Anne fell into a sleep of exhaustion, but Phyllis lay tense and wakeful at her side. And as dawn was breaking, she slipped out of bed and stole to the window, breathing gratefully the fresh morning air. And this was how Phyllis happened to see an old-fashioned carryall drawn by two plodding horses come down the street and stop at the Joyces' door. As she rubbed her eyes, hardly able to believe their testimony, three familiar figures alighted and moved in a dejected line toward the house. Phyllis uttered a cry.

The next moment she had Anne by the shoulder and was shaking her. "Wake up, Anne! It's not true what we thought. They're all here, safe and sound!"

As a matter of fact, the Joyces were home safe, though they had left the car in Wolf River. During the next few days they told the story countless times to interested listeners. On the way home from the lake they had stopped to pick bittersweet, and

Mr. Joyce parked the car by the side of the road on a rather steep incline. Apparently the brakes did not work as they should. He was some distance away when the car began to move. He ran toward it, but the car moved faster than he. With increasing speed it sped down the hill, smashed through the side of the wooden bridge, and disappeared under the rushing waters of Wolf River.

They were forty miles from home and on a lonely road. It was late in the afternoon. They set out bravely in the direction of home, hoping that a car would overtake them or that they would reach some dwelling where they could get aid. It was midnight when they reached a farmhouse that was occupied and succeeded in waking the sleeping inhabitants.

The farmer had no telephone and no car. Very reluctantly, in spite of Mr. Joyce's generous offer, the farmer at last brought out a dilapidated carryall, hitched up two stout farm horses, and with his five passengers started in the direction of town.

Anne was the first person to whom Betty told her exciting story. When she had finished, she took a long breath as though more was coming. "I can't tell you what good sports Ray and Isabel were. Isabel was so lame she could hardly hobble, but she was so plucky. I shall always love both of those girls," she ended, and looked at Anne almost defiantly.

It was Anne's turn. "I must tell you about Phyllis Parker. When she heard about that car in the river, she came right over and stayed all night with me. I won't forget it," Anne exclaimed, suddenly breaking down, "if I live to be a hundred."

"Listen, Anne," Betty cried, "we've made a mistake. Just being friends with one girl doesn't mean you can't have other friends, too."

"Of course it doesn't," Anne choked out. "And sometimes it's a good thing for inseparables to be separated."

Harriet Lummis Smith

Harriet Lummis Smith, born in Auburndale, Massachusetts, was a prolific writer of inspirational and values-based stories early in the twentieth century. The author of *Other People's Business,* she also wrote three books in the Peggy Raymond series and the four later books in the *Pollyanna* series (1924–1929). Smith died in 1947.

HOMECOMING

Joseph Leininger Wheeler

PROLOGUE

*A*lumni weekend at the Academy was always a big event—if not for the dormitory students, at least for the returning alumni. On this balmy spring afternoon, ten members of the high school class of 1967 gathered together to make plans for their thirty-fifth reunion. Steve, long ago their class president, now took roll call:

"Jonathan?"

"Here."

"Lucy?"

"I'm here."

"Bridgett?"

"You bet!"

"Philip?"

"Last I knew."

[Laughter, as the response was so . . . Philip-ish.]

"Betty?"

"Present, sir."

"Joan?"

"She said she'd be five minutes late."

"When hasn't she been?" muttered Lucy with a grin.

"Richard?"

"Check!"

"Marilyn?"

"She's with Joan," volunteered Betty. . . . "Oh, I heard a door shut. . . . There they are!"

"Present! Present!" sang the long-ago roommates.

"Let's see, that leaves only Henry."

"Nobody leaves Henry," groused one of the two class clowns. "All present and accounted for, your lowness . . . sir!"

⋆⊷⊜⊶⋆

All six feet and three inches of Steve stood up. Panning the group, he studied each classmate in silence for a second or two before moving on, the sequence broken only by Philip: "You know, Steve, Lenscrafters has a sale on now for extra-strong glasses for the visually impaired."

"And the Mayo Clinic," added Henry, "just yesterday announced that a new shipment of . . . uh . . ."

"Brain transplants?" suggested Lucy.

"Right you are, old dear."

"Now don't you old-dear me, you doddering fossil!" glared his long-ago classmate.

"Now, now, children—behave!" admonished Marilyn, vainly trying to be severe.

Ignoring his hecklers, Steve continued his mental inventory. Finally he announced, "Yes, we're all here—"

"But not all there," broke in Henry.

"Speak for yourself!" ordered Philip.

"He is, he *is*!" muttered Henry, to the accompaniment of generous applause.

Somewhat red of face, Steve rhetorically stated, "I *do* believe I was speaking. . . ."

"His short-term memory is still there; that's a comfort," volunteered Henry.

Steve glared, and peacemaker Marilyn stepped in, again trying to keep things from really getting out of hand. "Boys? . . . Oh, *boys?*"

That did it, and a sheepish grin lit up Steve's face. "We're still the same, aren't we? Even after thirty-four years—"

"Don't press your luck, Methuselah," butted in Philip. "Haven't seen you appraised on *Antiques Roadshow* yet."

This time it was several minutes before order could be restored and Steve could regain the floor. Before resuming, he spiked several loose cannons by this threat: "Next big-mouth that interrupts me will chair the rest of this meeting. That's a cross-my-heart-and-hope-to-die promise."

Absolute silence followed, for well they knew that Steve would keep that promise.

Capitalizing on this rare mood of seriousness, Steve said, "Yes, like it or not, the years are flying by, and some of us, at least—" he cast a wary eye at Henry and Philip—"are getting older. Take note, fellow members of the Class of '67. One year from now those of us who can still stand up unassisted will be back here for our thirty-fifth. We've been asked to coordinate the weekend's activities."

And so they finally got down to work.

ACT ONE

The cypresses on the bluff cast long afternoon shadows, and the evening fog was coming in before the program was finally nailed down and they could break for dinner.

Two hours later, they were back. Back for the most important decision of all.

A third of a century before, the class had turned to Bridgett when an extremely tough decision needed to be made. These days she was superintendent of one of California's largest school districts, and earning a salary well into six figures—but to her classmates she was still the studious and thoughtful Bridgett of long ago.

Still that Bridgett, yes, but now so much more: the Bridgett of the newspapers, magazines, radio, and television. The Bridgett the great world out there took so seriously, and referred to as "the renowned Dr. Rutherford."

She could be, on occasion, as hard as nails, as conciliatory as a judge up for reelection, as astute as Solomon, as soft as a mother's kiss. Tonight she was all of these—and more, and she spoke simply and from the heart.

Before proceeding, she bowed her head and prayed these words.

"Dear Lord, be with us this evening as we make a decision so important to our class. Grant us, for this occasion, divine wisdom."

Then she raised her head, silently looked around the room at her visibly aging classmates, reached for some handwritten notes, and began.

"Dear friends—dearest friends life has brought me—so supremely important do I view tonight's decision that I took the time (more time than you'd believe possible) to write out my thoughts rather than merely winging it. I wished to neither pad nor shortchange by so much as one paragraph, sentence, or phrase.

"Earlier today, as we kidded each other just as we did in the long ago, the thought came to me: *Nothing has changed.* When we are together, we unconsciously shed the responsibilities, the positions, the dignities life has brought us, and we are young again. Seeing each other, not as we are today, but as we once were . . . thirty-four years ago.

"That was this afternoon. This is tonight. For tonight's decision, we'll need to access—not just what we knew way back then, but everything we've learned since."

Her classmates sat spellbound, and no one dared to disrupt her earnest words with the usual banter.

"Early this morning I took a long walk on the beach. The fog so thick I could almost feel it. Far away I heard again the muffled sound of the foghorn, that foghorn I've heard so many times in my dreams, but never actually seen.

"Took off my shoes and socks, hid them under some driftwood, and braced myself for that familiar shock—that moment when an icy wave both caresses and jolts. That sensation like no other: when the receding wave seeks to sweep me out to sea. Far out I hear the thunder of the seventh wave—a big one—coming in. And in the viscous fog, I can hear but not see the raucous sound of the gulls. And, at my feet, the eternally searching sandpipers.

"You know how I feel, for each of you has walked these sands, each of you has blotted out the rest of the world on that familiar yet ever-changing beach. In the past, sometimes we rushed out to meet that first wave, filled with so much joy our feet barely touched the sand. Remember what first love was like? The magic? The glow in our faces born of the conviction that no one in all the world had ever loved as we?

"On the other hand, remember the times when it seemed we'd never get to that first wave? When our dreams were all crumbling and nothing, it seemed, would ever go right for us again?

"This morning, all these thoughts were born of the surging surf. Oh, it was bittersweet, this merging of the breakers of long ago and the breakers of today! I realized, for the very first time, that my life-strength had already peaked and was remorselessly ebbing, and that one day a wave like those of this morning could claim me for its own.

"So I couldn't help wondering: *Lord, how many more times will I be privileged to return to this shore? Am I doing the best I possibly can with this life You've lent me? Am I making a real difference? When it's all over, and my spirit is swept back to You, will I rate a 'Well done, My good and faithful servant'?*"

Bridgett paused a moment to regain her composure. The silence was so absolute it hardly seemed anyone was breathing. Each set of eyes transmitted the same message: *Go ahead; you're telling my story too. Just what is it you want us to do?*

Now she answered that unspoken question. "Our class has been luckier than most; we've lost only three. But death is remorseless: sooner or later he gets us—*each* of us. Each fifth-year reunion will see fewer of us left. As for those of us who yet remain, fewer and fewer of us will be strong enough to get here, to walk once more on the sands of our youth.

"That's why—" and now her words rang out like the clarion call of a medieval trumpet—"we can delay no longer! Why it's now or never that we honor the mentor who has meant the most to us in life, has made the greatest impact."

Philip now spoke in a subdued, almost diffident voice that didn't even sound like him. "A mentor—period, or a mentor here on this campus?"

"Here."

"Oh."

Bridgett continued, but her voice altered to a softer tone. "I suggest that we take a ninety-minute break. Remember, we don't have to hurry, as we don't say good-bye until tomorrow after breakfast at Capitola. Go anywhere where you can be alone—even the beach. Take notes. Ask yourself questions such as, 'Who of all the teachers and administrators I knew here on campus means the most to me—*now*? And why is that so?'

"Remember that it will not necessarily be the ones we raved about back then. Early popularity more often than not melts in the light of cold reality. Perspective is denied to the young—it's only after life has battered us that we can see the past clearly. That we can back off from what once loomed too close to us and see it in its true colors.

"Quite possibly, you may discover that the crucial life-changing resulted from one interaction with someone rather than a progression of them. So, in your search, look at the days that, had they never been, would have made your life so much different."

Bridgett had thought of everything—even the tablets and pens she now handed out.

"Now go! . . . See you at—let's see—" she looked down at her watch—"how about rounding it off at 8:30?"

ACT TWO

The atmosphere of the room they returned to was totally changed. Instead of bright fluorescent lights, there was a crackling fire in the fireplace, and half a dozen kerosene lamps that Bridgett had rounded up cast a soft glow on each entering face. The windows opened just far enough so that the booming surf could be clearly heard.

After all were seated, Bridgett, not standing now, but from her armchair next to the fire, greeted them with these words: "Since we are time-traveling tonight, Steve and I felt kerosene lamps would be more reflective of that past."

[Mutters of agreement and delight.]

"First of all, would you mind sharing with us some of your thoughts? Specific candidates will be discussed later. But for now, so we can develop a frame of reference, let's each share the journey—succinctly—of the last hour and a half. In no particular order."

After a short silence, Joan broke the ice, eliciting laughter by her first words: "Since I've been known to you as one who is invariably late to everything, I've decided to shock you by being first!

"As . . . uh . . . some of you know, nursing is my profession. Being a floor nurse doesn't provide much time for reflection. And nursing supervisors have even less time. Tonight's quiet time troubled me deeply. Perhaps because I'd never before realized how few have been my life's reflective moments. . . . It may very well be—" and here her voice broke—"that had I taken more time out from the rat race and noise . . . I'd have made fewer mistakes marriage-wise." Marilyn scooted her chair closer to Joan and put an arm around her.

"So what deep insights came to me tonight? . . . Oh, I don't know how deep you'll consider them, but, for what they're worth, here they are:

"As, in my mind's eye, I returned back to this campus in the early sixties, I again had to deal with the baggage of insecurities I brought with me. A number of you are aware that my dad left my mom when I was eight. I realized tonight that my life has never been the same since he slammed the door on Mom—and me, that never-to-be-forgotten night. I've never felt totally secure . . . since. My entire life has been a search for termites in the floor beneath me. Even in floors built on concrete!

"And when I came to this campus, these insecurities were at their peak. If it hadn't been for—" here she stopped in confusion, plugging her mouth with her hand, and sputtered to a halt. "Guess that's for later. I'm done for now."

⟶━◉◉━⟵

Just as they had been inseparable in the old days, so it was now. Marilyn spoke next. "Joan's heartfelt words moved me—oh, so very much!" she began. "Couldn't help thinking of that ever-so-shy girl Dean Spoor foisted off on me my sophomore year. Thought I'd *never* get a full sentence out of her!"

"And then you couldn't shut me up," quipped Joan.

"Well, perhaps, once in a while," laughed Marilyn. "So what were my thoughts? Bridgett, you started something. Joan and I walked down to the beach together but didn't say a word. We sat down and leaned back against a sand dune, out of the cold wind. I, too, thought about the swiftly moving years but hadn't Bridgett's eloquence to describe it. I took a mental snapshot of that gangly girl from Modesto who got out of her folks' Ford that balmy early fall day—so long ago! I felt so insecure. First time I'd ever been away from home for more than a few days. And I didn't have the slightest idea of what I wanted to do with my life."

"Except for boys. You knew—"

"Hush your mouth, Roomie! . . . So I floundered my way into campus life, desperately searching for a life raft . . . more on that later."

⊷▬◉◐⬞

To the surprise of everyone, Jonathan spoke next. Surprise, because in his school days he had invariably been the quiet one. Actually, quiet was an understatement; *mute* would be a more apt term. He rarely studied, and when a teacher asked him a question about the day's assignment, almost never did he have an answer. Amazingly, he had perfect attendance. *Why?* His classmates hadn't a clue.

After he left the Monterey Peninsula, Vietnam did something to him. Awakened him. He came back home with a chest full of medals. After the war, he reenlisted and went through officer training school. Now he held the rank of lieutenant general and was the commander of a large army base in Southern California.

But for his classmates, it was a new experience to hear him speak. His voice was still quiet, but now his earlier insecurities appeared to have left him, and power and conviction resonated in his voice.

Smiling, he began by saying, "You're probably a bit surprised to hear me speak—"

The irrepressible Henry broke in. " 'Surprised' isn't the word, Jonathan—*amazed* would be closer to the mark."

Jonathan continued. "Yes, I'd guess that back then I knew you better than you knew me. I'm assuming you considered me to be about as close to a zero as a human being could come. And you'd have been right. I doubt if any of you knew my background. I was never told who my biological parents were. In fact nobody appeared interested in me. I was bounced from home to home as a ward of the state—*none* of the people who ran those facilities were interested in adopting me. Lost count of the number of schools I attended—it was all a blur. Until I came here. Somebody in the state office felt a private school might wake me up—so I was sent here. I didn't wake up here either. . . . Let me qualify that—I *did* wake up, but I didn't let anyone know I had. Too bullheaded. And stupid. At graduation, my diploma was unsigned. Didn't get a signed one until after I completed my course work while I was in Nam.

"But back to this campus. You all know I was a loner. No one wanted to room with me, so the Dean let me room alone. In fact, I never made but one friend here, and that friend wasn't even a student. That friend changed my life. I'll reveal his name later."

⇥≡◉≡⇤

It was a long time before anyone dared to speak. *Four years on campus—and not one of them had even tried to be his friend! That he was here in this randomly chosen committee was no thanks to any of them!*

Finally, Richard stepped in when the silence had reached the embarrassing stage. Richard, who'd been a nobody in the old days and was now one of the Bay Area's most eminent neurosurgeons.

"Jonathan is a tough act to follow," he declared, "and there are no words in my vocabulary that could possibly take me off the hook for failing to be that friend. I failed many times here on campus—but this may very well be the greatest failure of all." Turning to his classmate, he said, "Jonathan, *I'm sorry.*"

Jonathan smiled and said, "Remember, it takes two to make a friendship. I failed to do my part too. So let's forget it."

But it could not be forgotten, and Jonathan sensed that his words had triggered an inner earthquake, causing everyone in the room to reevaluate everything that had happened to them since they first arrived on campus.

Richard now continued. "I came here, a home-schooled missionary kid, as out of sync with you as it was possible to be. Socially, I was a disaster—I was scared to death of girls. In sports, if anything, it was even worse. And since I didn't come here until my junior year, and most of you started here as freshmen, your friendships were already made, and it was hard for a latecomer to break in.

"Eventually, I began to bridge the cultural gap that separated us, but never did I enter the elite crowd that ran things. In retrospect, that proved to be a good thing. As I look back and study each classmate individually—present company excepted!—" he grinned—"I'm not at all sure it's a good thing to have it all too early. Because I was a geek, I studied hard. Even harder when I got to college, and then med school. It was a long, grueling process. At times I thought I'd never get through those interminable residencies.

"Before I graduated, much of my earlier self-confidence had returned. Some of you became personal friends, and with the passing of the years have become ever dearer to me. But even that might not have happened had it not been for—"

"And you'll open the envelope later," announced Philip.
"You said it, ol' buddy!"

⋦═◉═⋗

Betty spoke next. The campus dream girl all those years ago, she
was still attractive—but no longer beautiful. There were lines in
her face that etched a story of sorrow to those who cared to look
closely. Now, facing this tribunal of her peers, her courage almost
failed.

Her voice shaking, she said, "Richard's story brings back *such*
memories! I remember one day when Lucy and I were sitting on
a bench and he walked up to us. Remember, Richard?"

His face turning twelve shades of scarlet, Richard could only
retort, *"Remember?* How could I ever *forget?* It was one of the
most embarrassing days of my life! To walk up to the two pretti-
est girls in school and say, 'Would one of you go to the banquet
with me?' "

[Gut-wrenching laughter.]

When it finally calmed down, Betty surprised everyone by
saying, "But Richard was right: thanks to my looks, figure, and
money, I was an insider of that group he longed to enter. Popularity came to me too soon. I went on to make all the wrong
decisions with all the wrong people."

And now she turned to Richard, her voice ragged with emotion. "You know, Richard, if I had it to do all over again, and
had swallowed my pride and accepted your invitation—perhaps
my life might have turned out differently. . . . You all know
what a mess I've made of my life. Dropped out of college.
Three failed marriages. Never succeeded in any career. Now
I'm married again to another very successful man. And . . . uh

. . . why I'm sharing this, I don't know." Betty began to cry. "I—I don't know if this one will last either. All my possessions came to me as gifts rather than from my own work. You know," she said, turning again to Richard, "you and Ella have been so happy over the years. You're both such committed Christians, and your children have all turned out so well! Mine . . ." and tears streamed down her cheeks again. "Oh, you all know how mine have turned out. I'd give everything I have in the world if only I could start all over again the day Dad brought me here."

⊷⟚⟛⊷

Again there was absolute silence. Who would dare to follow Betty's impassioned outburst? For a while it looked as if none of them would. Finally, irrepressible Philip said: "In the interest of getting through our agenda before dawn, I'm offering my services as class martyr."

"Isn't that a new role for you, Phil?" questioned Henry, ever so innocently.

Ignoring his tormentor, Philip continued. "As you can plainly see, my martyrdom continueth. 'Whom the Lord loveth, He chasteneth.' " Then seeing Henry's mouth opening for another salvo, he immobilized him by uncharacteristically turning serious.

His usually jocular manner was totally absent as he said, "Betty, it took guts to share all that heartbreak with us. I knew things had been tough with you, but not *that* tough! . . . Sort of tears me up inside. To—to hear the campus dream girl admit that the rest of her life has been hell—well, it's causing me to reevaluate a lot of things. Jonathan's story shakes me up too.

"Since this evening appears to have evolved into sort of a

show-and-tell, guess I might as well follow suit. As you know, I've never taken life too seriously."

"You can say that again," muttered Henry.

"As you know, I've never taken life too seriously. *There!*" he said, turning to Henry, "I've said it again, so keep quiet. Your turn's coming."

"That's what I'm afraid of," acknowledged that unquenchable jokester.

Philip picked up where he left off. "And that rather flip attitude toward life didn't change after graduation. College was a bore, so I dropped out. Since then I've tried about every kind of job you can think of. My longest job lasted fifteen months. The job world bored me too. Marriage-wise, my track record's no better than Betty's; marriage bored me too. So did church. Looking back through the years, tonight I realize I haven't had the commitment of a rabbit. To tell you the truth, I don't even like myself very much. My cockiness was always the mask I wore in order to fool the world into thinking I didn't care about deep things. But I did. I just didn't have the willpower to stick to anything. Should have listened, years ago, to . . ."

"More on that later?" suggested Marilyn.

"Yep."

⊷══◉═◉═⊷

Steve spoke next. "Only hours ago I entered this room feeling somewhat smug."

"Still 'El Presidente'?" offered Henry.

Flushing, Steve answered, "Yes, Henry. Stupid me, mistakenly assuming that that long-ago election still meant something. I've learned tonight that it didn't. That I was so dense I failed to realize I never knew you at all! Worse yet, I never even knew myself.

"And that is inexcusable for a . . . uh . . . minister to admit."

"Worse than that—a conference president!" contributed Henry.

"Yes, worse than that. For, after graduation, I went on to study religion. *Study* it—only now do I realize the significance of that seemingly innocuous word. Even earned a doctorate in divinity. Was I ever proud of that! . . . *Was*. Until as late as noon today.

"You know I come from a long line of ministers. So there was never a question about my career. That's what it has been—I can see it now—just a career. A way to make a living. A way in which to achieve importance. And the pulpit became just the means to an end—administration. Oh, how I hungered for that! All my priorities were misdirected. I . . . uh . . . now realize I've never known what it really means to be a minister. Goodness knows, some teachers tried to tell me—"

"You mean, more on that later?" asked Joan.

"Yes."

⤞❍⤝

Lucy said, "Guess it's my turn. I've been squirming in my seat ever since Betty and Richard shared their stories. Richard, I too remember that day. How Betty and I laughed after you left. Laughed as we told the girls about it in the dorm. And laughed for years afterwards. But somehow it doesn't seem so funny to me now. Not when I compare my subsequent life with yours. Like Betty, I thought beauty was everything: a free ticket to all of life's goodies. Way back in that former life, you all spoiled me rotten—or rather, I permitted, even encouraged, you to do so.

Dropped out of college during the second semester. It was harder work than I was used to.

"I married to escape that real world out there. Someone promised to 'take care of me.' He did—for fourteen years. Then, when my looks began fading, and I was pregnant with our third child, he unceremoniously left me one bleak October evening. Haven't seen him since. No child support either. I felt my entire world had caved in. What were we to do? The only option I had was to eat humble pie and return home. I say 'humble pie' because for years I had more or less thumbed my nose at my folks and the values by which they lived. I didn't even know if they'd take me back. But they did: John (eleven), Karen (four), and me eight months pregnant, with no money and no career skills. Collectively, we must have terrified them! Bless their hearts, hiding their dismay, they welcomed us home. It strained their budget tremendously, but we lived there with them for almost eight years. During that time baby Sarah was born and I enrolled in an adult degree program. Graduated with a B.S. in business five years later—and two years after that, my small business had grown to the point where we could make it on our own.

"God came back into our lives during the years we spent with my folks. Now the kids are all grown, and graduated from college—I didn't let them repeat my mistake. I'm ever so proud of them, and I'm convinced that failing at parenthood is just about the greatest failure there is! As you know, I've never remarried. Since the kids left the nest, I've felt the loneliness more and more. But I just haven't trusted my judgment, for I made such a stupid decision the first time.

"And to save someone from completing my story—yes, there *was* someone who warned me long ago."

⟶━●━⟵

At last, no one was left but Henry. As that fact registered, every face but his began smiling. But the widest grin was worn by Philip. Henry let them stew in their suspense a while before he began to speak.

"Guess I'm cornered at last. Always have hated to speak in public, but it appears there's no other alternative. You may not believe it, but this evening has been hard on class clowns. Like Phil, all my life I've hidden my real feelings behind a mask. Since I'd always been able to make people laugh easily, I just kept doing so. Went to college, graduating with an illustrious C-minus average, thus fulfilling my folks' high expectations for me."

Phil covered his mouth with his hand in a vain attempt to keep from snickering.

Henry just stared at his friend as though he were a species of bug he'd not yet identified, solemnly remarking, "Unlike myself, there are some hopeless boys who never grow up," and went on.

"Bummed around the country for a while, trying my hand at all kinds of things. It has taken me quite a while to grow up, but—" here he looked resignedly at Phil and shook his head—"not as long as some."

[More laughter.]

"If there was one thing I could do as easy as making people laugh, it was making money. Made it hand over fist. Came back to the Monterey Coast and settled down. Married, as you know, my old sweetheart, Liz. We had two children, now grown. Got *very* busy making money. Too busy, in fact, to spend much time with Liz, my kids, or God. When I was declared the highest-grossing land developer on the Monterey Peninsula, I became absolutely insufferable.

"Li . . . uh . . . when Liz had stood it as long as she could, she stopped me one evening as I was leaving for a night out with the boys, and this is pretty much what she said: 'I'm *through*, Henry. You're not the person I thought I was marrying. Mistakenly, I assumed that someday you'd . . . uh . . . grow up and become a man. Apparently I was wrong. In order to climb to the top of the heap you haven't cared who you hurt, or what methods you used to get there. I—I' "—and here Henry had to blow his nose—" 'I no longer respect you. Neither do your children. So I have no choice but to leave you, for what I say and think mean absolutely nothing to you.' At the door, she paused, turned, and said, 'God help me, Henry, but in spite of it all, I still care about you. I don't think I love you any more, for love cannot survive the loss of respect. But I'll continue to pray for you, morning and evening, and hope God will someday answer those prayers.' "

After a long pause, Henry continued, "As some of you know, Liz never returned. But neither has she divorced me, declaring that God has not released her from her wedding vows." Now Henry broke down completely. His entire body shook as though afflicted with malarial chills. Stubbornly he attempted to hold back the tears. Those attempts eventually failed.

His classmates just sat there in shock.

After a time, Bridgett stood up and said in a strained voice, "What do you say to a twenty-minute break?"

ACT THREE

Twenty minutes later they were all back, and the fire was restoked. Bridgett stood up once again, cleared her throat twice, and said, "Now for the conclusion of the matter: choosing the person who made the greatest difference in our lives while we were here. It may be easy, or it may be tough—we'll just have to see. Lucy has agreed to be secretary. If there are no objections, I'll take you in the same order you spoke before. And since it's growing late, let's each get to the point as quickly as we can. I'll be last."

⊶═◉═⊷

"Joan?"

"Well, I guess I was the first to leave you hanging, wasn't I. I've already told you how insecure I was when I came here. But mere words can't possibly capture the depth and breadth of my bog of depression. I came here convinced that I wasn't worthy of friendship, much less love. The future spread out across the sky as one vast cloud of unrelieved darkness. I shuddered as I walked into room 203 for the first time, for it felt so cold. The fog had already come in, so the sky was dark. Mother was on a tight schedule—seems like she always *had* been—and had not even come up to the room. Just unloaded my stuff, pressed a twenty-dollar bill into my hand, kissed me good-bye, and left. So there I was alone in that cold room.

"A rather soft knock on the door startled me. Standing there was Dean Spoor. Smiling, she asked, 'Joan, do you mind if I come in?'

"I stuttered, 'N-no.'

"So she did. I had enough wits about me to ask if she'd like to sit down. She did so. Then she startled me with words I've never forgotten: 'Joan, you have no idea how I've looked forward to this moment.'

"I could only stare at her in disbelief.

"She went on: 'Yes, ever since we briefly spoke together in my office last spring—it seems your mother was in a hurry that day—I've been hoping you'd come and be one of my girls!' That staggered me. She wanted *me* to be one of her girls? She must have confused me with some other girl! Some other girl who was worthy of being loved. But no, it was me.

"How she'd learned so much about me I never found out, but before she walked into my room that day, she *knew* me inside and out. Now, through well thought-out questions, she learned even more. And I had no idea she could read me like the proverbial book, and learn so quickly what I needed most, but she could. After chatting with me for what must have been half an hour on one of the busiest days of her year, she jarred me with a request: 'Joan, dear, I'm in a little bit of a bind; do you think you'd be willing to help me?' *Help* her? I'd have given her everything I owned, if she'd asked for it! But no, all she wanted was for me to step into a sudden vacancy and become one of her dorm monitors. Of course I gladly accepted, just to be near her. Later I learned she'd set me up."

"You were anything but the first in that respect," observed Lucy.

"Yes, set me up. She knew that no girl in her dorm was arriving with lower self-esteem than me; that no girl needed responsibility more than me. I displaced one of her veterans in the process, but the veteran knew Dean Spoor would find her another position she'd like just as well, and she did. And the student gave up her job happily, as a favor to the Dean she adored. She did it too because the Dean, in a few well-chosen words, made her so empathize with me that she half loved me already.

"Each year that passed made me love Dean Spoor more, for she so genuinely loved me! She loved all her girls with a love I could not at that time fathom. *Especially* why she loved me! And when the world closed in on me, her sixth sense told her so, and I'd again hear that soft knock. Again I'd hear her say, 'Would you mind telling me about it, dear?' I always did. At the end, she'd offer wise counsel that was so logical I wondered why I couldn't have seen it myself. Then she'd ask if I didn't mind her praying about it. After my nod, she'd take my hand in hers and pray ever so earnestly that God would help me through. Then she'd take me into her arms, kiss my forehead, and say, 'I love you, Joanie.'" At that, Joan broke down completely.

Eventually, Joan regained her composure and was able to continue: "By the time I graduated, she had brought me a long way. Not far enough, clearly, for I've made so many mistakes since. But in almost every such instance, I went against counsel she'd given me earlier. Through the years, in the college of hard knocks, I've become stronger. But if my life has meant anything at all to those I love and care for, I owe it all to that woman!"

"Dean Spoor, one vote," noted Lucy.

⊷⊷◉⊷⊷

"Marilyn?"

"As if there could be any other choice! Before, I didn't share much with you. Permit me to amplify a bit."

"Take whatever time you need," responded Bridgett.

"Before I had so much as set eyes on Joan, Dean Spoor had me loving her as though I'd known her all my life. Even prepared me for her extreme shyness."

"Hard to believe now, huh?" said Joan, chuckling.

"Yes, it is, dear roomie. . . . Back then, I too was insecure, but being loved at home, my floors had no termites in them. I just didn't have the slightest idea what I wanted to do with my life. It didn't take the Dean long to learn my story, just as she'd learned Joanie's. But the psychology she used on Joanie wouldn't work on me, for I'd always had all the responsibility I could handle. My problem was that there were so many things I wanted to do, and felt capable of doing, that I hadn't the slightest idea of how to achieve focus. And one-on-one wouldn't work with me: it had to be on the sly when I didn't expect it."

"So she set you up with stories," declared Joan, as though there could be no question about it.

"Right! Where she found all those stories for evening worship, I'll never know, but they were always good ones. Not moralistic, for she preferred stories that carried their own freight. And, I don't know how she did it, but it was almost eerie. When I needed a certain story most, she'd read it next worship! Seemed that woman could read my mind!"

[Concurring laughter from Joan, Lucy, Betty, and Bridgett.]

"It was spring of our senior year, and as I still hadn't decided on what I wanted to do with my life, I grew increasingly restless—"

"And hard to live with," supplied Joan.

"When I got to the point where I didn't think I could stand another day of uncertainty, the Dean read 'Monty Price's Nightingale' for worship. Afterwards I stormed into her office and almost screeched, 'You set me up!'

"Smiling, she played the innocent, raising her eyebrows and asking, 'How?'

"'Because you knew I needed that story!'

"She didn't deny it, but merely answered, 'Well, didn't you?'

"'That's not the point!' I shouted. 'It's that you deliberately planned it just to get to me!'

"She laughed and said, 'Well, if I did, it evidently got to the right destination.'

"That got me, and I laughed too. For Zane Grey's great true story had to do with an Arizona cowboy whose entire life was dominated by a force (whether this force was good or evil we never learn). What we do discover is that this force was so all-consuming that nothing could stand in its way. Monty called this inner siren his 'nightingale.' It would sing louder and louder to him each day until finally the moment would come when its call could no longer be resisted. He'd pack his few belongings, saddle his horse, and ride off to his rendezvous. But finally Monty's nightingale was challenged by an equally powerful force: his love for a little girl. Just as Monty was once again riding off in answer to his siren, he saw a plume of smoke on the horizon. If that wind should change course—but that possibility was too terrible to even consider! But the wind *did* change course, and headed straight for the ranch where Monty suspected the little girl had been left alone that morning. At last! A counter-force powerful enough to hold its own against his nightingale. What should he do? The story reveals what. So now, Dean Spoor asked me, 'Marilyn, dear, what is *your* nightingale?'

"'I don't know.'

"'Then you perhaps have two whose calls are equally strong?'

"'How did you *know?*'

"'I just suspected it. But you do, don't you.'

"'Yes. And I also suspect you know their names.'

"'Perhaps. Might they be music and writing?'

"'Yes.'

"'In a showdown like Monty's, which do you think would win?'

"'You know the answer to that too, don't you!'

"'I *think* I may. It's writing, isn't it?'

"'How do you *do* it?'

"She just smiled and waited. We talked until three o'clock the next morning. At the end, she took my hand in hers and said words I've never forgotten: 'Marilyn, you are choosing one of the most difficult careers there is. Almost nobody can make a full-time living at it. A tiny few manage to pull it off. It will be tough, it will be lonely, you will constantly struggle financially (not knowing where your next dollar will come from). Again and again you will berate yourself for choosing that career.'

"'Why do you keep saying *will*?'

"'Well, you *will*, won't you?'

"'Of course; it just bothers the dickens out of me that you knew.'

"Again she smiled that tender smile of hers and added, 'But, in the end, after all the travail, all the struggle, all the tears, you will look up and say, "I'd do it all over again if I had the choice."'"

Marilyn paused and said, "How she *knew* all those years ago just what my choices would be, my eventual preference, the odds against me, my course of action, and the results . . . is still beyond me."

"Second vote for Dean Spoor," intoned Lucy.

⊷⊶◉⊷⊶

"Jonathan?"

"Well, first of all," began Jonathan, "I have a request. How do I get a copy of your latest book, Marilyn?"

"By asking me," was the demure answer.

"Consider yourself asked then. . . . Now for the business at hand. I must confess, classmates, that I came here today convinced I'd suffered more on this campus than the rest of you put together. It has been humbling—and healing—to discover my error. Collectively and individually, you have given me a great gift: peace with my past. Peace, and empathy, with each of you.

"I've already reminded you how much of a loner I was on this campus. With students and faculty alike. The principal who came here my senior year, Murdock, quite frankly, I couldn't stand. He early on pigeonholed me as a loser, a blank, and he never changed his mind. Quite simply, he just wrote me off and forgot I existed. I've tried to blot his name out of my conscious memory.

"A number of the staff took their cue from him; for he tolerated no dissent. If you disagreed with him and he found out, you were lucky to last out the year. But one teacher dared to do just that. My English teacher. Even though I bull-headedly refused to turn in any work or answer any of his questions, he kept his cool and greeted me each day with a smile. He'd say, 'Always great to have you in class, Jonathan'—and mean it. I couldn't get over it. Finally I realized that I could lie to him in every way but one. My eyes gave me away every time: revealed to him the startling fact that I wasn't brain-dead after all.

"One day in March of my senior year, he asked me to stay after class a minute. I figured it would be the same ol' same ol', but it wasn't. As close as I can remember, this is what he said: 'Jonathan, our time together is almost at an end. I just wanted you to know I've enjoyed every day of our association together—and my records tell me that you haven't missed a class in four years. The only student with perfect attendance!'

"I could only sputter out an undernourished, 'Thank you, sir.'

"Then he put his hand on my shoulder and said, 'Somewhere

along the way I somehow let you down, more the shame on me! If I hadn't, you'd have communicated with more than your eyes. But I'm convinced, Jonathan, that there is greatness inside you. Someday—days, weeks, months, or perhaps even years from now—you'll awaken to life, to your calling. When that day comes, the world will marvel. You will become a great power for good. And to this end I shall pray each day. So just remember, Jonathan, as you leave this campus, that at least one person here will be thinking of you each and every day that passes.' Here a shadow crossed his face: 'If not here, wherever it is that I'll be,' he qualified.

"Learned later that Mr. Murdock, strongly suspecting that Mr. Baldwin wasn't in full agreement with his policies, had decided not to renew his contract. Fortunately, the board decided not to renew Mr. Murdock's contract first, so Mr. Baldwin stayed."

"Mr. Baldwin, one vote," said Lucy.

⊷≡◉≡⊶

"Richard."

"How anyone in his right mind—" then, looking at Henry's opening mouth, he hastened to bark out, *"scratch that!*—could follow Jonathan is beyond me. But I'll try.

"It was toward the end of my first year when Dean Reynolds called me in."

"I don't believe it!" groused Philip.

"Called me in, told me to sit down, and then gave me his patented silent lookover."

"During which you aged years," proclaimed Henry.

"Yes indeed! Finally he asked me a rather strange question. 'Richard, what are you doing here?'

"Sputtering, I answered, rather inanely, 'I don't really know; I was just told you wanted to talk with me.'"

"Good answer!" chortled Philip.

"'No,' Reynolds said, 'you misunderstood me. I meant, what are you doing here at this school?'

"Still puzzled as to what he was angling at, I answered, 'Trying to earn my high school diploma.'

"'Is that all?'

"'No, I guess I'm also deciding on a career.'

"'Is that all?'

"'N-no. I guess I'm also preparing for life.'

"'Do you find it hard on campus, being a missionary kid?'

"'Very much, sir!'

"'In what way?'

"I told him, at length.

"He was silent for some thirty seconds, then startled me with, 'What would your minister father think if he heard the dirty language you use when speaking with your friends?'

"Now I really sputtered, wondering how he knew. I didn't have the ghost of an idea how to answer. So he continued:

"'You know, Dick, when a missionary kid talks dirty in order to be accepted by the group, it doesn't work; it only makes him an object of ridicule. Do you have to descend that low in order to be well-liked?'

"'N-no. I hope not, sir.'

"Then he smiled. 'Richard, you have great potential, and are one of the most talented young men in my dorm. You could accomplish most anything you set out to do. But only if you don't forget your roots, only if you don't sell out your integrity for cheap popularity, only if you don't sell out your God. . . . Am I making any kind of sense?'

"'Yes, sir. I'll try, sir.'

"'Good! You can go now.

"'And Richard?'

"'Yes, sir.'

"'Drop by often. Let me know how things are going.'

"I did. And from that moment I date the rest of my life."

"Dean Reynolds, one vote," said Lucy.

⊷══☉══⊷

"Betty."

Something had happened to the onetime dream girl since she spoke earlier. Her shoulders were straighter, she stood taller, and a new light of resolution blazed in her eyes. In fact, it was hard to believe this was the same woman. With a faraway look in her eyes, she said, after first checking her notes:

"As I remember, it was late in my junior year that I heard that soft knock on the door. Knew in an instant whose knock it was, so I sang out, 'Come right in, Dean!'

"She did, her eyes lit up with merriment. After she sat down, we small-talked for some time as we'd done a number of times before. But this time I sensed there was a deeper motive for her visit. Finally, leaning back in her chair, she looked at me pensively and said, 'Betty, you're so lovely you almost take my breath away.'

"In my pride, I took this observation as a deserved compliment—especially as I'd been the recipient of similar tributes from so many others. So I answered, 'Thank you, Miss Spoor.'

"Almost imperceptibly her smile changed; I could tell my answer had not pleased her. Then she asked a question that jolted me. 'Betty dear, what have you accomplished in almost three years besides growing more beautiful?'

"This time I didn't know what to say, so I replied rather sheepishly, 'Not much.'

"She followed that up with, 'And what, dear, do you plan on doing with the rest of your life?'

"Thoroughly on the defensive by now, I could only say, 'I don't know.' And I didn't. All I wanted to do was to keep on having good times, keep buying expensive clothing, avoid work and stress, and soak up adulation like a sponge. But of course I couldn't say that to *her*—she'd have thought even less of me!

"Miss Spoor pondered my answer a moment, then continued. 'But would you really *like* to know?'

"Again I answered truthfully, and I'm afraid more than a little sarcastically, 'Not really.'

"This time I could tell instantly that I had wounded her—*deeply,* and I wished there was some easy way I could take back those two words. But I was too self-centered to try to redeem myself in her eyes.

"She rose to leave, and had almost reached the door when her steps slowed. Something had altered her resolution to leave me to stew in my own egocentricity. Her mood had completely changed since she first came in. Gone was the earlier joy. In fact, her face was the saddest I ever—" Betty choked. "Oh! If you only knew how many times I've replayed that look of sorrow in her dear face! It has haunted me day and night ever since!

"And these were her parting words: 'Betty dear, it's clear that my words don't mean much to you, so don't worry; I won't bother you any more. But before we bring this subject to closure I must tell you this.' Her voice had a little catch in it. 'I know that wasn't your better self speaking. Today you are still my cherished sleeping beauty, taking credit for looks and curves you had almost nothing to do with. But someday that beauty will leave you, and the only beauty that remains will be within you. It'll come, mark my words, that day—sooner than you believe possible.

"'Why do I call you *Sleeping Beauty*? Not because of your outside beauty, but because deep inside you I know there is gentleness, caring, a desire to make a difference in this world, a willingness to be of service, a selflessness. But that beauty inside you has been caged by that selfish jailer you have catered to for so long. Someday—oh, how I hope I'm wrong, but I suspect it is far ahead in the future—you will awaken at last, having lost the loveliness that today has the world at your feet. You will soul-search, you will look into the years ahead of you, and it will be perhaps the saddest day of your life. That day you will realize for the first time how many years you've wasted of God's greatest gift to you—time. *Then*, my very dear Betty, you will fire that jailer and release your long imprisoned inner beauty. From that moment on, you'll begin the rest of your life, the only part of it not destroyed by selfishness and pride.' Then she hugged me, kissed me gently on my cheek, told me she loved me, and walked out of my room. Today, it struck me that she didn't ask if she could pray with me. I know now it's because she knew I wasn't ready for it. She never brought up the subject again."

Betty paused for control, then cried out in a voice racked with pain: "Those words were spoken to me *thirty-five long years ago!* And only tonight have I awakened. But oh, how grateful I am that she proved right in another respect: that long-caged sleeping beauty inside me has now broken free. The rest of my life, from this moment on, *will* be different. . . ." Then, in poignant words that would haunt her classmates until they died, she wailed, "Oh

Lord! Forgive, forgive your foolish child," and her head dropped into her hands.

After a long, long silence, Lucy, in barely a whisper, said, "Miss Spoor, three votes."

⊷═◎═⊶

"Philip."

"Following Betty another time will just about do me in," declared Philip. "So please bear with me as I try to transition from Betty's heartbreak to my story. . . .

"For me it's no contest as well. *Has* to be Dean Reynolds. You talk about Dean Spoor knowing you better than you knew yourself; well, I'll swear Dean Reynolds had X-ray vision."

"Hear! Hear!" interrupted Richard.

"Couldn't get away with a thing with that man. He'd call you into his office, stare at you through those cross-examining eyes of his, and, terrified, you'd wonder, *Which of my misdeeds has he found out about now?*

"In your case, he had plenty to choose from," volunteered Henry.

"Seems to me Dean Reynolds enjoyed your company every bit as much as he did mine," reminded Philip. "Well, I'd sit there for what seemed hours, but in reality must have been only seconds or minutes, as he scrutinized me in dead silence. Then he'd lean back, never taking his eyes off me, and say, 'Well, Phil, what do you have to say for yourself?'"

"And you'd blurt out your whole life story," said Henry, not as a question but as fact.

"Pretty much. He'd throw you off guard because you wondered, *What do I have to say about WHICH INCIDENT?*

Was it putting blocks under Chrome Dome's patrol car so the wheels would merely spin in the air when he'd try to chase us? Was it ringing the great bell, the one rung only for vespers and deaths, at midnight?"

"How did you escape getting caught for that one?" asked Henry. "There were three locked doors between outside and that bell rope."

"There were always those willing to lend a hand if the cause was a worthy one," answered Philip, with a cherubic smile.

"Was it flipping pads of butter onto the cafeteria ceiling? Was it throwing water balloons at well-dressed passersby? Was it throwing marbles down the hallway during dorm study halls whenever things got too boring? Was it hauling Percy Huffinger's Volkswagen to the top floor of the dorm?"

In a slow reminiscing voice, Henry said, "I remember that it took a lot of work to get that little beastie up to the top floor. We waited until faculty meeting so Reynolds would be out of the way. You know, as I remember it, we were so ticked at Percy's always finking about us to the Dean that we had Jim Bob prepare an extra treat for him."

"Wasn't he the wizard who could do virtually *anything* with an engine?" questioned Jonathan.

"The very same," replied Henry. "He fixed Percy's Volks so it only had one speed: lunge forward and stop, lunge forward and stop, lunge forward and stop. Percy had a heavy date that night with a pretty new girl and planned to impress her. He did. Phil had thoughtfully siphoned so much gas out of the car that Percy ran out of gas halfway to town. Percy's date walked all the way back to school in one direction and Percy walked several miles to a gas station in the other direction. Tsk, tsk, Phil."

[Laughter.]

Phil resumed his catalogue of contributions to campus life: "Was it turning on the fire siren in the middle of the night?"

"I always wondered about that one," mused Jonathan. "I happen to know that siren chain was way down in the boiler house, with locks on the outside fence door, the building door, and the inner cage door. Keys for those would be daunting enough, but how did you get back into the dorm before they caught you? The campus was swarming with faculty as soon as they found out it was a hoax."

"Oh, *that*," laughed Philip. "I wired a bucket to the siren chain, inserted the end of a hose into the bucket, then turned the water on *real slow*. I was back in the dorm before the bucket got heavy enough to turn on the siren. Simple as that.

"Actually, I *did* have a close call with that one. You remember that assistant dean we had with us for a while? Hughes was his name. Well, the very next morning, he saw me in the foyer getting my mail and thundered out, 'Phil, I bet *you're* the one who turned the siren on last night!' I just grinned back and said, 'Of course I did, Dean,' and he never believed me. Of course Hughes was not too smart, couple dominoes short of a box. Left us in the middle of the year—something about his health," said Philip solicitously.

"Well, getting back to Reynolds, was it the various middle-of-the-night contributions in the hall bathroom: peanut butter and honey smeared on the toilet seats, or the bucket of water that would automatically empty itself on whoever stumbled into the bathroom in the middle of the night? Was it short-sheeting whoever had the nerve to leave campus for the weekend or go on a music tour? Or hiding their sheets in the hollow part of their sinks? Was it getting the boys together to haul Ron over to the flagpole by the girls' dorm and tie him to it, leaving him there with nothing on but his shorts?"

"It was cold that night too, as I remember it," said Henry. "I believe that Reynolds finally rescued the poor fellow. But not before he'd brought a lot of excitement into the dull lives of the girls. Spoor phoned Reynolds and told him to come and retrieve his flagpole sitter so her girls could get back to their books."

[Laughter.]

"Was it throwing cherry bombs into the shower just before breakfast? Was it one of our big weekends when everyone was dressed up in suits, and the copper tubes in the toilets were reconfigured so that instead of refilling the tank when the flush handle was pulled, they'd drench the poor guys at half-mast? Was it positioning alarm clocks set to ring at two-minute intervals in the organ pipes when Murdock was speaking? A lot of the fellows kindly sacrificed their clocks for this noble cause, bless them! None of us ever dared attempt to reclaim those alarm clocks. Murdock would have killed us. A dozen perfectly good alarm clocks lost forever. Come to think of it, I don't believe Murdock took his full half hour that day. A pity," sighed Philip. "Small things, like these. I never knew which one Reynolds was talking about."

About this time, all self-control ceased as everyone laughed until they hurt, and Henry mumbled, "And I thought *I* was bad!"

When order was finally restored, Philip plaintively observed, "Well, as you probably guessed, Reynolds would catch me almost every time."

"Couldn't have been that difficult for him," quipped Steve, "for most any disaster on campus, in all likelihood, originated with either you or Henry—so he only had to call in two to round up all the culprits."

"I resemble that remark!" wisecracked Henry.

"Yet," continued Philip, "it was impossible not to like the guy. Because underneath his stern demeanor his eyes never failed to twinkle the teensiest bit. Betcha anything he was a handful himself when he was young. . . . Then he'd assign me some more free labor."

"In that respect, you and Henry must have saved the school thousands of dollars," guessed Marilyn, struggling to keep a straight face.

"Well, I could go on . . . ."

"Please don't!" urged Henry.

Between chuckles, Lucy noted, "Dean Reynolds, two votes."

⊶⧉⊷

"Steve."

"Surely you're not asking *me* to follow an act like that!" grumbled Steve, still laughing. "Oh well, here goes.

"Actually, I could just as easily have cast my vote to Reynolds' side of the ledger, but there was another person who cared enough about me to tell me what I had no interest in hearing. Believe it or not, it was Miss Spoor.

"You remember how we'd often put on programs in area churches? Some of us would speak, others would perform music. Well, one night, after such a program, we headed back to school. Miss Spoor (our sponsor) and I had the entire back seat of the bus to ourselves. Once we were well on the road, Spoor complimented me on my devotional, and I swelled up like a toad: *By cracky, I WAS good tonight!* I told myself. She eyed me for a moment, then asked me a question that had evidently bothered her for some time:

"'Still planning to study for the ministry, Steve?'

"I answered, 'Yes, of course!'

"'Why "Of course?" ' she shot back.

"That threw me, for I didn't have a good answer. Finally I came up with an answer I thought would squelch her: 'Because I come from a long line of ministers,' I bragged.

"Didn't impress her at all. She merely said, 'So? You owe me a better answer than that.'

"But I didn't have a better answer than that, so I just sat there fidgeting, wishing she'd leave me alone.

"Seeing she wasn't getting anywhere with me, she looked at me as though she'd just handed a five-dollar bill to a teller and got back only fifty cents in change for it.

"She was silent for what seemed like forever before she said, in the most serious tone I ever heard her use with anyone, 'Don't do it, Steve. Unless you're convicted with every atom of your being that God is calling you to the ministry of caring for the needs of His sheep, it would be sacrilege for you to choose that calling.'

"But, as you know, I ignored her advice. Many's the time her words have come back to me as I tossed and turned during sleepless nights. Tonight, however, after all the long years of misplaced priorities, I am belatedly responding to her counsel. If my wife, Judy, will agree—and I'm confident she will—I plan to resign my administrative job and ask for the toughest, or smallest, pastorate in the conference. I'd like to start all over again—I owe Miss Spoor no less."

"Four votes for Miss Spoor," announced Lucy.

⊷⊶⊙⊱⊷

Then Lucy put down her pen, referred to her notes, and began. "Dean Spoor had a great impact on my life too, and I almost chose her as my number-one candidate. But one person had an even greater impact on my life than she did. Mr. Baldwin. Early in my freshman year, Mr. Baldwin asked me to be his reader."

"That man certainly knew how to pick 'em," declared Henry admiringly. "Had English and I not been mortal enemies I would have gone on and majored in it just so I could hire pretty readers like Lucy."

Lucy's face turned red at the laughter that followed.

"It wasn't just what Mr. Baldwin said or did in the classroom that impressed me, although I adored his classes. He always made them so interesting! And, like Spoor, he was always reading us stories. Not being in love with grammar, I much preferred stories.

"Do any of you remember the days when Murdock began his campaign against hair dye?"

A chorus of agreement arose from the female contingent.

"Well, shortly after I dyed my hair blonde, Murdock's secretary called me in and told me I was being called on the carpet in front of the *entire faculty*. Needless to say, I was scared to death! I died a thousand deaths in the week leading up to that fateful evening.

"It finally came. Murdock's secretary ushered me in, and then, horror of horrors! led me to a seat at the front of the room. Murdock then proceeded to paint me in scarlet colors as the vilest student imaginable. A more malevolent man I've never known! I couldn't bear to look at the faculty—felt they must hate me too. I began to cry.

"Suddenly Mr. Baldwin's hand went up.

"'Yes?' responded Murdock, curtly.

"Mr. Baldwin then said, matter of factly, 'My wife dyes *her* hair blonde, so I don't see anything to get excited about.'

"A titter of laughter swept the room, and if looks could have killed, Mr. Baldwin would have caught fire before my very eyes. Oh, I could have run across the room and hugged him!

"Oh! And there was another time—I must have been Murdock's great cross. It was in the days of Murdock's crusade to lower dress lengths. [Laughter.] It was a gala event, with student association leaders from all over California meeting on our campus. Everyone came dressed to the nines. And I was escorted in by my then-steady—"

"Did you grant him two weeks, or was it three?" asked Henry.

"Shush, Henry! . . . Well, it didn't take long for my nemesis to discover his favorite prey. He walked over to me with that sadistic glint in his eyes I was so familiar with—oh! he was *so* smug and self-righteous! Right in front of all these student leaders I was so anxious to impress, he said (loudly, I might add), 'Lucy, you've defied me again—your skirt is *way* above your knees!' Believe me, it wasn't 'way above'; it was barely above!"

"Pardoning the pun," injected Henry.

"Then Murdock swelled up like a strutting turkey and commanded, 'Go to your room! And don't you dare come back until you're decently clothed!'

"I'd never been more mortified in my life! Nor as angry. Stupidly, I struck back. In a voice every bit as loud as Murdock's, I said, 'Why don't you pick on Betty? Her skirt's shorter than mine.'"

"The funny thing is that it *was*," chimed in Betty.

"And then I said, 'Is it because her dad's chairman of the board?'

"That did it. His eyes glaring, and literally shaking in almost a blind rage, he shouted, 'Go to the dorm *now*—and don't you dare come back! I'll deal with you later!'

"I left, of course, knowing full well that this was it: I'd be on my way home pronto.

"About an hour later the monitor called me, telling me that a visitor was waiting for me in the lobby. When I got downstairs, there stood Mr. Baldwin. After we seated ourselves in the parlor, he calmly observed, 'That was quite a show you put on tonight.'

"'You were *there?*' I asked.

"'Ringside seat.'

"'Oh! But he made me so angry! I—I just hate—'

"Baldwin stopped me, and that twinkle that always got me came on in his eyes. 'Lucy, if you don't back off quickly, I'll lose my favorite reader. In fact, unless I miss my guess, Murdock is so furious that you'll be on your way home by this time tomorrow. . . . But what bothers me even more is the intensity of your hatred.'

"'But, but—' I began.

"He continued, 'Hear me out, please. As long as your hatred of Murdock continues to consume you, he will own you. You won't be free until you forgive him. Worse yet, God Himself won't be able to forgive you for anything until you forgive first. Scripture tells us so.'

"'But Murdock will never forgive me in a thousand years!'

"The twinkle grew brighter, only it was now more than a tad conspiratorial.

"'Even if you groveled?'

"Oh, how I laughed. I knew Baldwin's shrewd advice would work, for Murdock could live two weeks on one good groveling."

"Well, it worked for pretty girls, but us fellows could have groveled a month and got nowhere with His Highness," grumbled Henry.

"Early next morning," said Lucy, "I made my appearance in Murdock's lion's den, groveled, and contritely asked his forgiveness."

"And stayed in school," added Betty.

"And stayed in school," corroborated Lucy. "And I'll say it for myself: two votes for Baldwin."

⋯━◉══◉━⋯

"Henry."

"All right! My turn at last! Since it's almost midnight, I'll try to be quick. I almost chose Reynolds, as he and I share so many fond memories—but Phil stole all my thunder. So I've chosen Papa T. J. Funny no one ever called him by his last name—Lieber.

"What a difference from Murdock that principal was! What particularly impressed me (with my sievelike brain) was his phenomenal memory. I remember the first time we met—already he knew all about me, including names of my parents, where we lived, schools I had attended, etc. And he never forgot any of them, even when our paths crossed years later.

"Over time, he and I had almost as many heart-to-heart chats as Reynolds and I. I was one of his crosses—but not his *only* cross—" he said, clearing his throat and looking meaningfully at Philip. "A number of times I had been on the brink of expulsion, but each time somehow escaped. On this particular day at the end of our junior year, however, I sensed that the Big E had finally come. As to the incident in question, I was even ashamed of it myself—it was that bad.

"Well, Papa T. J. just looked at me sorrowfully and asked rhetorically, 'Henry, what shall we do with you?'

"Flippantly (to better cover up my inner anguish, for I knew he had no choice this time but to expel me), I answered, 'Probably give me the boot.'

"I could tell it was my attitude far more than my words that hurt him.

"Then, in a pain-filled voice, he asked, 'Is that what you want, Henry?'

"This was such a different response from what I expected that I did the last thing I ever expected to do in his office: I began blubbering, 'No, no, no! I don't want to leave! I—I—*love* this place! Oh, please don't kick me out—pleeease!'

"After a silence I thought would never end, in a kind voice he said, 'Do you know how many times we've already forgiven you for acts much less serious than this one?'

"'No.'

"'Neither do I, for I don't keep score of such things. But if we *do* forgive you one more time, what assurances do we have that it won't happen again?'

"I couldn't answer. In fact, I was so relieved I could only bawl like a stupid baby.

"That was enough for him. He rose, put his arm on my shoulder, and asked if I minded if we prayed about it. I nodded. Then he prayed the most moving prayer on my behalf I've ever heard. Then I prayed the jerkiest, most incoherent, prayer of my life.

"We stood up. Then he said, 'Henry, I believe you. I trust you. I'm convinced that this time you won't let me down. And, in future years, I know I shall be proud of you.' "

Then, once again, Henry broke down before his classmates. After recovering, he stood to his feet and said, "Almost thirty-five years have passed since that memorable day—and I have never yet lived up to his prophecy. But I will now! If Betty and Steve can do it, I can too. As of this moment, I'm inviting God back into my life. . . . Tomorrow—" he looked at his watch—"make that *today*, I'm rushing off to the town where Liz now lives, where I'll be making some promises. Promises I'm determined to keep. Same for each of my children, so help me God!"

Struggling for control, Lucy said, "One vote for Papa T. J. . . . and at least half a vote for dear Liz."

⤙⊙⊙⤚

Now at last Bridgett stood up. Her face, like the others, was stained by tears. For a while she appeared incapable of speech. Finally she said, "Forgive me, but I feel I've been run over by a semi. I've never experienced such an emotional roller coaster in my entire life. And a number of times this thought has returned to me: *In none of the schools in my district could this evening have happened, for God is no longer welcome in our public schools.* No, this sort of evening could only happen in a Christian school! How grateful I am that I was privileged to attend this one!"

[Murmurs of agreement.]

"But now it's time for me to cast the last vote. For me it happened in my sophomore year, girls' night on the beach. The surf was high and the fog was thick. I'd been walking barefoot for some time, my thoughts reeling. Felt like I was in a whirlpool and in danger of being sucked down into the maelstrom of no return. Nothing was going right. Dad and Mom were talking divorce. My boyfriend had just broken up with me. I was so depressed, I was failing most of my classes. My world, it seemed, was coming to an end. I didn't feel I could ever return to campus; in fact I was so desperate I struggled against the insidious temptation to walk out into the surf and then swim out to where the inexorable riptide would carry me out to sea.

"Suddenly I heard soft footsteps behind me. It was Miss Spoor. I stopped. She didn't say a word, just moved up to me with her arms opened wide. I stepped into them. We found a dune and I emptied my broken heart to her. Once I realized it must be long past midnight and asked, 'What will the girls say when we don't return?' She merely smiled and said, 'Don't worry, dear, the assistant dean is covering for me tonight.' So we stayed there until well past dawn. She held me in her arms all that seemingly endless night. As the sun began to come up, I gave my heart to God and peace came to me at last.

"That summer and the following one I stayed on to help her in the dorm and with recruiting. I practically lived in her apartment. Without her I'm virtually certain I wouldn't be with you tonight. My life would have gone nowhere—if indeed I'd still be alive. Whatever—" and here her voice began to break—"I've been able to accomplish, I owe it all . . . to *her*."

Then, after a long emotion-filled silence, she continued. "Earlier this evening, as I tried to define my relationship with her, I looked in the library's *Random House Unabridged* for words such as *mentor*, *mother*, and *sister*. *Mother* didn't work, for she never tried to usurp my biological mother's role. *Mentor* was closer. But *sister* was closest. Listen to the tenth definition under the word *sister* and see if you don't agree it meshes with tonight's stories:

"Sister:

"*Nautical. To strengthen (a broken or weakened member) by securing an auxiliary piece alongside it.*"

[Applause that went on and on.]

EPILOGUE

"Lucy, would you mind tabulating the votes for us?"

"All right. I'll read them in reverse order:

"Papa T. J.—one vote.

"Mr. Baldwin—two votes.

"Dean Reynolds—two votes.

"Dean Spoor—five votes."

[Prolonged applause.]

"So who should invite her to our thirty-fifth alumni weekend?" asked Bridgett, then sat down, her job done.

Steve stood up, but not the Steve they had known before. He no longer took his leadership as a given but was both humble and open to counsel. He asked, "So what is your will?"

Jonathan stood to his feet. Not the almost invisible Jonathan of long ago, but the tall, straight military commander of today. All eyes turned to him. And these were his words:

"This night represents my own homecoming. For the first time in my life, I feel a part of you. One person made this experience possible. What do you say to our empowering Bridgett with this mandate? Taking the news to Miss Spoor (wherever she now lives) that she is warmly invited—indeed *expected*—to grace our thirty-fifth with her presence. All the expenses on us. And no excuses tolerated for possible nonappearance."

[Applause.]

"You know, although unquestionably Dean Spoor deserves the honor we have voted her, I personally don't feel comfortable in completely leaving Papa T. J., Baldwin, and Reynolds out. I happen to know that all three are still alive and well. If I have your blessing, would you be willing for me to write each one a letter detailing what we've said about them tonight?"

[Murmurs of agreement.]

"And I'd like to send each of them roses in our names," added Betty.

"Pass the kitty, then," added Philip.

Jonathan continued, "My mind keeps coming back to Bridgett's sister metaphor. How incredibly apt: 'to strengthen a broken or weakened member'—you know, we were *all* broken, we were *all* weakened."

He paused a moment to collect his thoughts, then, turning to Henry, he gravely asked, "Henry, I understand that you live in a seaside villa on Carmel's Seventeen Mile Drive with an incredible view. Would the Class of '67 be welcome there Alumni weekend?"

A new Henry now rose to his feet, saying, "I would be deeply honored." And the old Henry threatened, "And the one of you who fails to show up . . . we'll turn over to Papa T. J.!"

⊷⊶⊶⊷

HOW THIS STORY CAME TO BE

After several false starts, the Lord answered my prayers and gave me this plot. I could not have written it earlier. But then I was invited to share the thirty-fifth reunion of a parochial high school class I'd served as faculty sponsor many years ago. I was privileged to spend most of a day and an evening with them. That experience proved to be the catalyst for this story.

Also woven into the story were alumni weekends at various schools and colleges I've been associated with, especially the life stories I heard there. Mixed in too are hundreds of life stories I heard during the years I directed an adult degree program.

Some readers may be surprised to learn that precious little of this story is fiction. Although I tinkered with the names somewhat, all the four finalists are known to me, keeping in mind that, to a certain extent, each is a prototype (a composite of qualities and characteristics). Readers may be even more surprised to discover that every last one of the escapades attributed to Philip and Henry actually occurred on campuses where I studied or taught. Some of them, in fact, come perilously close to home.

The campus setting is deliberately left indistinct so that the story can be shared in Christian schools everywhere, where doubtless many will recognize in these characters mentors who have changed their lives for the better, just as these did for the alums in our story.

One of the serendipities of turning the writing of a story over to God is that you never learn until the very end what will happen. In the case of this story, I was amazed at how real the fourteen (fifteen, with Mr. Murdock) characters became by the end of the story. At the beginning, I never dreamed that three of the ten students would make life-changing decisions by the end of the story. But God did.

❧

A veteran of many alumni weekends, I have developed a philosophy about them. You newly minted graduates, let me take you time-traveling twenty, thirty, forty years into your future. What will you see? What will you discover? Over time, which of your relationships will have meant the most?

What you will find is an Alice in Wonderland situation where everything has been turned over or reversed. It is often the geeks, the plain ones, the nerds, those who never saw the inside of a clique, who now carry the world on their capable shoulders. They tend to be the best-looking and youngest-looking members of the class. As for the early-bloomers, the campus kingpins, what about them? Alas! More often than not, since adulation came so easy and so early, they ceased to grow. Some of them are like gridiron heroes whose growth stopped with the championship ring. They live in a time warp of what once was and never will be again. Since they have rarely struggled, they have never become, never grown. Of all the classmates you see, they may be the saddest.

You will also discover that everything picks up where it left off. It's like the years between have never been. The aging face and body mean nothing; it's what's inside that counts. Thus aging belles are belles still, in spite of what the mirror reveals. The class clowns are the class clowns still, funnier if anything than they were before. But, paradoxically, perhaps because they are subconsciously bitter at still being typecast, some are subject to sudden 180-degree mood swings.

In a way, it's like each member of the class is a velveteen rabbit, dearer each year as one by one the numbers decrease and fewer show up. Your true "soul sisters" will grow ever more precious as the light of time reveals what matters most.

To your peers of tomorrow, your successes in the great arena of the world will mean little unless they are accompanied by humility, genuineness, and *agape* caring. It's what is inside of you that they will notice when you too are old and attend the next alumni reunion.

*Joe Wheeler fan? Like curling up with a good story?
Try these other Joe Wheeler books that will give you
that "warm all over" feeling.*

HEART TO HEART STORIES OF LOVE

Remember old-fashioned romance? The hauntingly beautiful, gradual unfolding of the petals of love, leading up to the ultimate full flowering of marriage and a lifetime together? From the story of the young army lieutenant returning from World War II to meet his female pen pal at Grand Central Station in the hope that their friendship will develop into romance, to the tale of a young woman who finds love in the romantic history of her grandmother, this collection satisfies the longing for stories of genuine, beautiful, lasting love.

Heart to Heart Stories of Love will warm your heart with young love, rekindled flames, and promises kept.
0-8423-1833-X

HEART TO HEART STORIES OF FRIENDSHIP

A touching collection of timeless tales that will uplift your soul. For anyone who has ever experienced or longed for the true joy of friendship, these engaging stories are sure to inspire laughter, tears, and tender remembrances. Share them with a friend or loved one.
0-8423-0586-6

HEART TO HEART STORIES FOR DADS

This collection of classic tales is sure to tug at your heart and take up permanent residence in your memories. These stories about fathers, beloved teachers, mentors, pastors, and other father figures are suitable for reading aloud to the family or for enjoying alone for a cozy evening's entertainment.
0-8423-3634-6

HEART TO HEART STORIES FOR MOMS

This heartwarming collection includes stories about the selfless love of mothers, stepmothers, surrogate mothers, and mentors. Moms in all stages of life will cherish stories that parallel their own, those demonstrating the bond between child, mother, and grandmother. A collection to cherish for years to come.
0-8423-3603-6

CHRISTMAS IN MY HEART
Volume VIII

These stories will turn hearts to what Christmas—and life itself—is all about. Powerful and inspirational, each story is beautifully illustrated with classic engravings and woodcuts, making the collection a wonderful gift for family members and friends. Reading these stories will quickly become a part of any family's Christmas tradition.
0-8423-3645-1

CHRISTMAS IN MY HEART
Volume IX

From the tale of the orphan boy who loses a beloved puppy but finds a loving home for Christmas, to the narrative of an entire town that gives an impoverished family an unexpectedly joyful Christmas, these heartwarming stories will touch your soul with the true spirit of the season. Featured authors include O. Henry, Grace Livingston Hill, Margaret Sangster, Jr., and others.

Christmas is a time for families to take time to sit together, perhaps around a crackling blaze in the fireplace, and reminisce about Christmases of the past. Enjoy the classic stories found in this book and understand why thousands of families have made the Christmas in My Heart series part of their traditions.
0-8423-5189-2

CHRISTMAS IN MY HEART
Volume X

Christmas in My Heart, vol. 10 will bring a tear to your eye and warmth to your heart as you read the story of a lonely little girl who helps a heartbroken mother learn to love again, or the tale of a cynical old shopkeeper who discovers the true meaning of Christmas through the gift of a crippled man. Authors include Pearl S. Buck, Harry Kroll, Margaret Sangster, Jr., and others.
0-8423-5380-1